# THE GOOD BODY

# BILL GASTON
# THE GOOD BODY

**A NOVEL**

ReganBooks
*An Imprint of HarperCollinsPublishers*

A hardcover edition of this book was published in Canada in 2000 by Cormorant Books Inc. and Stoddart Publishing Co. Limited.

THE GOOD BODY. Copyright © 2000 by Bill Gaston. All rights reserved. Printed in the United States of America. No part of this book may be used or reproduced in any manner whatsoever without written permission except in the case of brief quotations embodied in critical articles and reviews. For information address HarperCollins Publishers Inc., 10 East 53rd Street, New York, NY 10022.

HarperCollins books may be purchased for educational, business, or sales promotional use. For information, please write: Special Markets Department, HarperCollins Publishers Inc., 10 East 53rd Street, New York, NY 10022.

First ReganBooks edition published 2001.

---

Library of Congress Cataloging-in-Publication Data

Gaston, Bill, 1953–
    The good body : a novel / Bill Gaston.
        p.   cm.
    ISBN 0-06-039411-0
    1. Multiple sclerosis—Patients—Fiction.   2. Hockey players—Retirement—Fiction. 3. Fathers and sons—Fiction.   4. New Brunswick—Fiction.   I. Title.

PR9199.3.G373 G66 2001
813'.54—dc21                                                        00-045885

---

01   02   03   04   05   NK/RRD   10   9   8   7   6   5   4   3   2   1

*For R. A. Gaston*
*"Gaspipe"*
*1924-1999*
*Basketball Player*

# THE GOOD BODY

I

... on a sheet of clear ice, each man
can skate his name, cleanly as by hand
—Milton Acorn

... it is this delight, not yet known,
that takes you through the seasons.
—Rita Donovan, *Daisy Circus*

"I'm not the type of person who likes
to have a lot of operations."
—David Adams Richards, *Road to the Stilt House*

Doing seventy, pointing north, window wide open and elbow on the edge. The falling night rushed and pounded the left ear like loud flux, like chaos itself. Here we go, what's next.

Good to blow out the cloying perfume reek — yesterday he'd hung a second pine freshener from the rearview, and this morning in the car's enclosed heat he'd snapped its string and tossed it, wincing in the smell. It was like someone had spilled Mr. Clean in the seats. He'd left the old one up and dangling. Drained of scent and almost grey, a cardboard antique, it was a talisman that had come with the car, with him a decade now. Longer than any one person.

The old tree cut-out twirled in the car's night wind. Bonaduce looked higher into the rearview itself, the dark Maine interstate rushing away in the wrong direction, back to his old life. His gut flipped at the notion of steering with this sight alone.

North out of Bangor, five hours to go, there began a whacking on his roof so he pulled over to check things. The autumn cool felt okay on his neck. Stars were out and glaring in this clean air but he had no time for them. Funny how on trips you relax less the closer you get. He stuffed the flapping tarp under a suitcase corner and tightened the bungee cord, thinking he probably should have crammed more of this stuff in the back seat. But he loved using this roof rack, the gypsy load up there straining full, giving him a feeling in his body he could not name. Something like, home was where the car was. Something like, he was free and life was lucky. Loose Bonaduce.

When next he floored it to pass a car, the tightened cord howled in the wind. He passed another car and there it was, a shrieking steadiness, loud right over his head. The next time he passed he opened the window, reached up and grabbed the cord, but his grab only changed the tone, upping it an octave. He decided then to hear it not as noise but as a note, and smiled at the possibilities of this, the kind of smile rare to him since he'd heard his news and made his decision.

Playing the bungee cord meant he had to stay at speed, at least eighty for a clean tone. The road slicing the middle of Maine was fine and straight, but when he found himself falling into a downhill curve it took some teeth-clenched cool to keep the speed and the music going. It also cost him two tickets. These he tossed the second the cop was out of sight, for they were American tickets, and he was leaving for good. Between tickets he learned, by pinch, the cord's nearly three octaves. Its lowest notes were lost in the engine's drone, while its highest shriekers buzzed and thrilled his fingers in a way almost ticklingly sexual. By the time he crossed the border, and got his first Canadian ticket, which he kept, he'd roughed out "American Woman" and "Blue Christmas." He wondered if Jason would like, or even know, either song. He was well into the stupid arena-pleaser, "La Macarena" (he hoped Jason didn't like this one), when up came the lights of the small city he had decided would be home again.

Fredericton, there it was. He could admit he was nervous. The good butterflies. Only amateurs aren't nervous.

When to call Jason, when to announce himself? And would he call Leah at all?

But here he was, Bonaduce back in town, after twenty years. Middle of the night, guitar on the roof, skates in the back, maybe two months' grace in the wallet. In the head, a doctor's news jockeyed for space with his plan.

At passing speed, squinting into the next few months, he hit the city limits, playing on his howling bungee an improvised, humble, speculative tune.


He woke. It was a Monday morning. He knew where he was, even the motel's name.

He did his stretches in front of the window, hanging on to the air conditioner. Okay. So what was all this worry about school? He'd done it before and always got himself over the hump. Ten, fifteen years had passed, so what. He had the way with words. Half Irish, half Italian — if that didn't make a poet, what did? If it took a while to get the pen looping and the tongue flapping, he could fall back on profs' mercy. Sir, I haven't thought seriously about literature or any of this in, let's see. Haven't really read a serious book in, let me think now.

Sir, it'll take a while to get the brain in game shape.

Start on push-ups today. He dropped to the brown shag, deciding to begin with two reps of thirty, add five more each day. Good it was a Monday. Monday was when you began something. And fall. A fall Monday was when you started school, or training camp, where — one of his favourite things — you put on the new uniform and looked down your chest at the unfamiliar colours of your new second skin. You read the upside-down emblem, which in the old days was embossed with heavy luminous thread: Express, Americans, Indians.


The secretary looked decent. Thirty, lanky, henna in the hair, baggy sweater, string of clunky wooden beads. She threw him a little smile while she dealt with two younger types ahead of him. He smiled back, meeting her eye over these kids keeping two adults from doing business. If he was a "mature" student, then by extension these two in front would be immature. Maybe she'd laugh at that.

Profs buzzed through, heads down in sheets of fresh xerox, rolling their eyes at some nuisance or other. It was going to be strange here, no question. A few looked younger than him. He hoped he wouldn't have to call them "sir." Jesus, could he physically, actually do that? "Doctor" would be even worse. Doctor Paragraph, heal me. There goes Doctor Comma, off to lunch with Doctor Diphthong.

Better if he got women. For some reason the power struggle had different rules with women. Too often during his part-time undergrad stints the manprofs had seemed less than comfortable with the basic look of him, the scarface and Bonaduce bulk, maybe the perceived readiness of his muscles, who knows. In any case, they had been driven by some urge to give him grades lower than deserved, to meet him not in the alley but with a chickenshit mark in the mail. His essays were decent enough. That one course, the Modern British, a seminar affair with about ten of them around a table — he'd been at the weights all summer and wore a T-shirt the first day and the reedy prof had had furtive eyes for his chest and whatnots and at the end of it all he'd received the shittiest mark of his life.

"Bobby Bonaduce?" The secretary looked up from the file folder that no doubt held record of that very mark.

"Robert."

He had decided to be "Robert" here. He must have signed his forms out of autograph habit. In grad-school world the "Bobby" would not help his already shaky credibility. He wasn't exactly a goon at a tea party, but he wasn't not that either. Forty-year-old named "Bobby." Neck thicker than any other two around here.

"I'm definitely 'Robert.'"

"Well" — she handed him a course list — "I'm definitely 'Lorna.' Since you're so late — we're a week and a half into classes—"

"Guess I'll have to buy a couple essays off somebody." He gave her a deadpan she didn't see.

"—since you're so late you have to get the professors' permission, so you'd better choose fast and go and—"

"Can you tell me which of these are women?"

"Sorry?"

"There's just initials here." He rattled the course list at her. Only when he saw the look on her face did he realize how the question must have sounded. Maybe she thought that he thought he was sexy or something and wanted women profs for that reason. Or that she had in front of her some stiff old throwback who wouldn't be taught by a woman. Jesus, Lorna was looking at him hard. Maybe it was only that his morning five o'clock shadow was upon them both, and the scars were coming out bright white, and she had no clue about him, whatsoever.

He woke up surprised at any number of things.

At the window's view he did his stretches, which sometimes did and sometimes didn't affect the stupidity in his right foot, and considered the town below. The cathedral had recently gotten a new copper roof. The newest part was still shiny, while the older part was already turning black, on its weird way to that green.

Yesterday's drive through town had sparked so much memory, things he hadn't thought about for years. The butcher shop where Leah had insisted they buy their meat. The church where the wedding was, all those quiet Moncton relatives of hers he didn't know and met only the once. That tavern, now a pizza chain, where the owner had set up a used electroshock machine on the bar, some customers laughing, others wary of it.

Up the hill, a glimpse of the hospital where Jason was born had put Bonaduce right back in that yellow room. Light from that window falling on that tiny squinty face. *My god it's a little old wrinkleman.* He'd watched it all, a fairly daring thing for the dad to do in those days, though apparently it was strange not to do it now. Impromptu, the doctor asked if he wanted to cut the cord. Scissors were handed over and he'd stood hesitating long enough for the doctor to ask if he was shy of blood. He shook his head, unable to voice questions to do with the cord there, its pulsing, its unearthly colour — because, because whose was it? Leah's or Jason's? Who would it hurt, the cutting? When the doctor reached for the scissors Bonaduce went ahead and did it, it was tough like steak sinew. The blood came rich and thick, and neither mother nor son seemed bothered.

Down the hill from the hospital was the corner gas station where on Christmas Eve they'd bought a tree, Bonaduce home from a road trip for the only Christmas the three of them would spend together. Gripping the crook of the lowest branch, he'd dragged it home over the sidewalk snow, a perfect winter night, the heavy quiet. Leah carried Jason, who peered out from his ball of soft blankets, wide awake, watching it all. Two new parents agreeing that from the staring look in his eyes you could tell he was listening even harder, he was hearing more than seeing.

Twenty years later, driving in traffic, Bonaduce could see that look of his baby boy listening.

He hadn't meant to drive by her old place, but there it was, the tiny upstairs apartment, her window you could see from the street. All those early times there, her awful little bed, not much sleeping to do anyway, they couldn't get enough of each other. And that time — Bonaduce smiled, speeding up — her apartment door was unlocked and he'd walked in and surprised her at the kitchen table eating that unbelievable stuff right out of the can. Which had explained the mints she sometimes munched at the start of a date. A few months later that sober evening at the same table, her pregnancy news, his monotone proposal. Hustling out then after hugs and laughter and her tears, late for the team bus, shaking his head at life and breathing hard, fleeing this building, now painted a flaccid green, used to be white.

The station wagon was chugging a little, ominous. It missed the highway, it didn't like this city stop-and-start. For a last taste of nostalgia he kept going, up to the arena, and the boxy old thing made him feel his first job again. He'd been twenty, Jason's age.

The pride. Paid to play. Paid to *play*. People buying tickets to watch. He'd gone straight out and bought the Datsun 240Z, grinning into debt. He was making a living that would only get better, the NHL only a year away, for sure. For now, the Fredericton Express. He'd had trouble keeping down the grin as he checked out the dressing room, shook hands with the guys, found his stall with his jersey hanging in it. For days he sang about it in his head, singing his jersey number to the tune of the Bee Gees' "Stayin' Alive." *Ha. Ha. Ha. Ha.* Number *five*, number *five*.

Stretching at the window, he scanned Fredericton's rooftops. She lived on Grey Street now. Where was Grey Street? Jason's addresses had been different from hers the last couple of years, good; he'd left the nest, no mamma's boy. Did he live in a party house, wading through pizza boxes, cracking rude jokes with the boys, or did he have solo, studious digs? There was so much to find out about Jason, so much of it so basic. The ever-kindling guilt of the wayward Bonaduce.

He packed the car, checked out, found a cheaper hotel, unpacked again. Cheaper was better so long as the bed was hard. After a lunch of cheese, crackers and two apples, he drove down Waterloo Row to park by the river. Nice fall day. He recalled fall here to be a good one, breezy clear blue days, just the kind that helped the fresh start.

He got out of the car, looked at the river, took a breath. He'd done it. Fredericton. Here he was.

He had his jogging stuff on; he dipped down into groin and ham stretches before the run. It was stupid to be afraid of bumping into either of them, it wasn't that small a town. Though it hadn't grown much. A few more red-brick buildings downtown, a few fewer elms. Of course the river hadn't changed at all. Twenty years ago he'd parked here in the same spot, doing what he was doing now — getting ready to jog but also watching, smelling, this moving mass. Feeling the weight of it, the dark authority of a big river, the hugeness of its intrusion and, as it swept by, the impersonal departure. No hello or goodbye. Rivers were essentially foreign. Almost eerie. Bonaduce had always thought of rivers as the place people drowned.

Watching the water leaving town, he found the names coming unbidden: Rochester, Kalamazoo, Tulsa, Las Vegas, Utica. Fredericton again. Some by trade, some by choice, in two decades the places he had called home.

Staying down in a toe-touch, he tightened his shoes. Blood filled his head, he wasn't in shape. But some months ago in Utica his right hand had bungled this job of tying a shoe. Today the hand was a magician again, fingers so fast you could hardly follow them.

He erased the phony poetry thought about a river once taking him away and now bringing him back.

Jog. *Jog.* Onomatopoeia, a litword he remembered. Buzz, whack, yodel, they sound how they mean. *Jog.* Jog the legs, the spine, the body into a pleasant stupor, hardbreathing. Jog the brain into a memory he should have had but didn't, Jason with him here, jogging this forest path, puffing along behind, unbearable sound of your child's pleading breath. *Hey, Jase, you, lookin', forward, to, puttin' on, the skates?* No answer but the boy's noncommittal grunt, the boy in pain, hung over from a night out with his buddies, and a non-jogger to boot, in youth scornful of these maintenance measures. But jogging anyway, knowing the truth of the father's example. *Son the, mortal coil needs care, the bone-rig needs, tending for the, long haul.* Parking lot in sight, the dad does the corny thing, letting his puffing boy catch up and pass him at the finish.

. . .

Pen and blank sheet of paper on the tiny formica table. Large McDonald's coffee. Printed at the top of the sheet:

TO DO:

He felt cold and crusty under his clothes from the run. And ridiculously winded — two days of solid driving, the body falls way out of tune. But full feeling in the feet. Running, he'd felt almost bloody graceful. Doctors are best at arrogance.

Sad to end up in a food court. He'd cruised the town hungry, passing little pasta parlours and coffee bars, for some reason not stopping. Why not just accept it as a comfort that you feel at home in a food court? In this mall, with this coffee, you were anywhere on the continent. To get a bit cosmic with it — or "postmodern"? He had to get to the bottom of "postmodern" — he was everywhere on the continent at once. McDonald's had done this, and Ted Turner had done this too, hiring his unidentifiably clean Yankee voices. These Fredericton mall kids wearing Nike hats — shoe company conquers the planet's feet and now does the head. It was like something out of *Batman* — Sameness Drops diabolically added to the water supply.

1. skates sharpened

Aside from these Freddie kids looking less dangerous than American kids, scowls a little less earned maybe, and almost no kids of colour, the people of Fredericton looked just as stunned as they did in Springfield or Kalamazoo.

Impossible not to look stunned in a mall. Automatically tired, skin pale under fluorescent sky. Suggestion of mouth agape. A dumb hunt. You could imagine a scene a million years ago wherein some Cro-Magnon entrepreneur stocked a forest clearing with tethered hare, mudpools of carp, mounds of fruit, a few big-ticket U-Kill antelope, and let the Neanderthals in to "hunt," provided they had the shiny rocks to exchange. This the birth of the Mall Age. Of the Vicarious Era, marked by rapidly devolving human muscle. Which led to sports fans, to people paying others to play their hard-body games for them, thus giving Bonaduce a job, and so what was he complaining about.

2. place to live

A question of balance here. If he went for the one-bedroom over the bachelor, he'd need a part-time job. If he got the meanest shared flop he could find, he could maybe make it on the assistantship they'd promised him today. He could get a thousand for the car if anyone believed him that it came from south of the Rust Belt. But carless he'd have to rent closer to campus, higher rent, vicious cycle. And how could you go carless? How, when midnight came and your foot started tapping, could you not have your car out there waiting with its roof rack and headlights and map of the big picture ...

Maybe he should sell the car as a gesture to roots here.

There was still the chance, a small chance, of the cheque. The Utica courts might come through. How could Wharton get away with it? How could a guy declare bankruptcy, fold a team and renege on the payroll, even as his car dealership stayed open and looked healthy as hell, rows of shiny Japanese cars and Day-Glo pennants flapping in the breeze? So what if during the period in question Bonaduce hadn't been quite up to playing. A contract was a contract. Eight thousand dollars — almost twelve Canadian — would be just fine. Fournier was still with his girlfriend in Utica and he'd promised to keep Bonaduce posted.

Rent, books, food, money money money. He'd never had a secure thing but here he was at forty thinking week-to-week. Hand-to-mouth Bonaduce. But a thought: while Canadian schools couldn't give athletic scholarships, there were rumoured "subsidies" for the best players. So maybe he'd get some under-the-table. He'd go see the coach, stick out his hand and announce his intentions. Bob Bonaduce, I'm back in school, I'm thinking of playing for you. Or, "trying out." Best be humble, polite. There was no question of not making it. The floppiness had almost left, the motor was fine thank you. At his age he had a good year or two left at this level, no sweat.

3. Get coach's name, call coach

Though once he announced himself to the coach, the cat was out of the bag. A less-than-cool way for Jason to find out about any of this.

4. Call Jason

Writing this, he caught himself feeling almost comically nervous. Jesus. So what else?

5. Buy books

He'd scanned the reading lists. Regardless of what courses he took, the number of books he was to have read over the summer was enormous in itself, and the number he was to read between now and Christmas was similarly impossible.

He studied number 5. What about not buying any books at all, see how that went. He crossed out number 5.

Jason's letter had done it. The letter had come during one of those days, the kind which tell you from the start you're having a turn under luck's big magnifying glass: traffic lights would either all turn green for you, or all turn red; you could win the lottery, walk on water, or be singled out in a mall and executed by a maniac. Anything *would* happen today.

First — he was just going out the door, to the doctor for test results — a call came from Fournier about Wharton folding the team and skipping out. Season over, no pay, no job. Then — he was back from the doctor, just in the door, feeling hollow and cold and shaking his head in recognition of what a lifespan is — Jason's letter clattered through the mail slot, hitting his knee, making him jump. Jason, whose letters came maybe every two years, one letter for every three of his. Bonaduce would've written more but hadn't wanted to force the relationship more than his unanswered letters did already.

He picked up Jason's letter, looked at it, waggled it for weight, announced to its return address, "Hey, Jason. Dad's got multiple sclerosis."

He was being dramatic of course, in the throes of fresh news, not belief. He read his son's letter, barely skimming the surface of its content, seeing more the texture of his boy's typing, feeling its effort and intent, amazed that his boy could think, decide, punctuate. A recent big decision, said the letter, was to quit his last year of junior in favour of university, playing there. More and more guys, Jason explained, had been jumping into pro from college.

And Bonaduce, seconds later, phoning the University of New Brunswick for registration forms. It was one of those things you couldn't put much thought to. He knew it was utterly corny every whichway. Tiny Tim territory. In no direction could you escape the corn of it. While Bobby Bonaduce could still skate, he was going north to enrol in school and play on the same team as his long-abandoned son.

God bless him, every one.

He unhooked the roof-rack bungees and lugged his stuff inside. The guy named Rod had disappeared upstairs but the big girl, Margaret, helped. Things were finally taking a good turn — after six ugly days he'd found himself a place. Town full of students, what did he expect. But here he was, and you couldn't argue a hundred-forty a month. Over on the north side, or wrong side, of the river, and a few miles out of town, the old house was paint-thirsty and gap-shingled, and right on the highway. He'd be sharing its one bathroom with three girls and two guys. His room was so small that, in his head, he was thinking quotation marks around "room." He suspected his housemates were making a secret buck off the landlord by renting out what was perhaps an old sewing room — but you couldn't argue one-forty a month. Heat included. No closet, but furnished. Or, "furnished." He could find a board to put under the mattress. You could *panhandle* one-forty a month.

"We each keep our own food like, separate," Margaret was saying as he slid a suitcase under his bed. "But I mean, sometimes we make meals together. Not that much. Weekends. You could keep your food, I don't know, in like, a box or something."

Margaret probably thought a bit about food. She was fairly tall but up around the one-seventy, one-eighty mark it looked like. But nice, smirking and gum-chewing like a guy. She was leaning on his door frame and he could smell her minty breath. When certain people are nice you feel bad noticing their body.

"Marg? I like your earrings." She had what must be ten of them, mostly small hoops, in her right ear.

"Of course you do." Smiling, chewing her gum, her sarcasm including her as much as him, and nothing but pleasant.

"Whatcha got, about ten in there?"

"About. I could make us some tea?"

"Great. GREAT." A roaring *whoosh* from the highway made him repeat himself. It wasn't rush hour yet.

"Herbal? Black? Gunpowder?"

"Herbal, great." He was tempted to go Gunpowder to see what he got, maybe some in-crowd concoction. Booze or drugs even, you never knew. Not hard to tell from Margaret or the decor what sorts his roomies were. Probably casual smokers. A little tokahontas never hurt anyone, he might even join them. Each room had a couple of arty candles. The rooms themselves were painted in the clash-colours of past tenants. Not overly clean. Without looking for them you could see cobwebs in ceiling corners, and the smell of incense armwrestling mildew. Rod and Margaret had been asking one-fifty but dropped it ten when they saw his car and he said sure to her question, "Some of us are like, students too, and could we maybe get a ride in when you go?"

Margaret shouted from the living room that the tea was ready. Absurdly, first he checked his hirsute self in the mirror strung up on a hook on his wall. It would be too utterly bizarre to dig out his razor and shave. But he patted his hair down.

They sat blowing politely into their teacups. Margaret had closed a window, but they still needed to talk loud to overcrow the *whooshing*s, especially the semis, whose shadows also pounded into the room, preceding the *whoosh* by a split second. In the silences Margaret seemed a little nervous, and Bonaduce's stomach hollowed as he recalled the formula: three girls, two guys ... Now three guys, even-steven. Newly alert, he looked up at Margaret just as she looked up at him too. He looked blinking back into his tea. Well, Jesus, don't be an asshole. Forty, broke, roughish face. No catch himself. Anyone studenting at his age had obviously foundered on one of life's more basic reefs.

"Actually at night I love it. My room's like, right above yours. Puts me to sleep."

"Sorry? It?"

She jerked her head toward the window. "Truck-noise."

"Ah." Bonaduce exhaled. "Well I keep a little fish bonker beside my bed for the same purpose." Bonaduce made as if to whack himself two hard ones on the bean and Margaret laughed.

"No, they're spaced apart at night. You can hear one coming, a low like, sort of something way in the distance. I pretend I'm sleeping on the beach in Maui and it's like, this wave coming, and it comes roaring in just like a breaker, *whoooOOOSSSHHhhhh* ... So where'd you like get the scars? Rod said you were either an axe murderer or a hockey player."

The room had a pastel, thickened feel from the layers and layers of paint, the latest one pale lemon. Floating dust added a dreaminess. Margaret chewed her gum with confidence, eyeing him with an off-kilter but intelligent glint.

He rasped like Brando, "Rod was right. See, I never did get the hang of skating." He waggled demonic brows at her. She smiled, no more afraid of any of this than he was. She'd be fun, she'd be okay. He could play guitar and sing in front of her, no problem.

"So Marg. What sort of student are you?"

"Not good, if that's what you mean."

"What are you taking?"

"Archaeology, only they don't really have a program here."

"Ah."

"I'm thinking of packing it in."

"No way."

"Well, yes."

"Marg? There's this saying. And as your elder, you have to listen and obey."

"I have always obeyed you."

"Marg? 'You sign your name, you play the game.'"

"Okay, sure," she said, not considering the Bonaduce maxim for more than a second. "And so like, what if the game's the shits?"

"Doesn't matter. Quitting feels shittier. It's true."

Unconvinced, or maybe she'd stopped listening, she pointed out the window to the stand of trees across the highway, near the river.

"Look. A pileated woodpecker. *Wow* they're big. I think it is one."

He tried to picture Marg in the academic world and couldn't quite. It wasn't just the way she talked. It was her humanness. He imagined her walking the halls head down, ashamed, insulted. Perhaps there were some human profs there too, but this morning he hadn't met them.

. . .

He'd sought out his preferred profs and got in to see two. First, Doctor Gail Smith and her "Canadian Writers of the British Diaspora." He liked CanLit.

Bonaduce had long ago become wary of that brand of person who strategically doesn't say much, leaving you to stammer in the articulate pressure of their gaze. Some reporters tried that. But reporters you just played dumb with.

Her door was wide open. He knocked anyway and she watched him do this. She was maybe five years his junior. He stated his business. After a silent stare of ten seconds or so, sizing him up, she turned to her computer screen to ask, "Why do you want to take my seminar?" She hadn't exactly emphasized the "you" in her question, nor was its tone quite "What is two plus two?" but nonetheless it threw Bonaduce for a loop. First he answered her silence with some of his own. No way a joke or knowing smile (she still wasn't looking at him) or chummy reference to their shared age would deflect the question. There were correct answers, and there were honest answers, and as usual the honest ones were ridiculous: Because I need to take something. Because you're a woman. Because, though the doctors are wrong, I might not have much ice-time left and I want to play hockey with my son.

"Because I wanted to find out, you know, more about it."

"It ...?" Staring harder into her computer and starting to type.

"Canadian writing. And—"

The typing stopped. The room froze with intelligence.

"—and, you know, the, the British diaspora."

"*Dee*aspora?"

"Well, tom*ay*to, tom*ah*to. But, sure, *die*aspora." He knew that she knew that asking him the word's meaning would only be cruel.

Typing and reading her screen, speaking in a monotone that suggested jowls-to-come, Professor Smith used whatever portion of her brain it took to say, "Lowry this week. *Volcano*. Brian Moore next." She pronounced Brian *Bree*an. "Lorna has the reading list."

He held up his xerox sheet and smiled. "I already have ..." She was so busy not noticing him that he didn't finish.

Maybe if he had shaved.

Professor Daniel Kirk, his course called "New Traditions in the Carnivalesque," was perhaps fifty. He leapt to his feet, he stuck out his hand, he was all bootlick and smile, saying, "Dan Kirk! Read your application! Used to go to the Express games!" but Bonaduce knew he'd be calling him "Professor." He was the kind of eager, buttclenched male animal who would smile and meet your eye while checking out everything about you, alert to danger. His office felt like a lair of radical pettiness.

Bonaduce felt himself mirror Kirk's beaming smile. Shaking the man's hand, he knew a shitty mark when he saw one.

A Coke in his fist, cubes rattling, he went table to table in the Student Union Building cafeteria asking questions. The team name had just been changed from the "Red Devils" to the "Varsity Reds," this reportedly having something to do with Fredericton being a fundamental notch in the Bible Belt. The season started in two weeks, a road trip to Nova Scotia against Dalhousie, then Acadia. The coach was Michael Whetter, and he could probably be reached through the Athletics Department. He was believed to be quite young, maybe even late twenties. No one knew if he had played any pro.

Bonaduce had hoped to find at the helm an old crony, or at least someone who'd heard of Bobby Bonaduce. At worst, and this might be the case here, it was some youngster who'd kept all his teeth, played college and then gone to coaching school to learn the European stuff: the jogging with medicine balls, the five-man rotating unit, the playing flimsy and falling down howling if somebody nudged you.

It's not like you wanted to be handed a spot on the team. It's just that when you're not in the greatest shape it would be easier for all concerned if you were dealing with someone who knew what you could do. Because in training camp you don't go out and bash. These guys were going to be your buddies; you had their knees, shoulders to worry about; you saved the bashing for the enemy. This was a concern because, from the look of things, he might be forced to go out and impress someone, show what he could do. And what he could do was bash.

The meal had an edgy, formal quality to it, and Margaret seemed almost nervous. Nervousness didn't suit someone like her. Bonaduce suspected she'd gone backstage and campaigned to have everyone eat together tonight and welcome the new guy. Not present was the other woman, Joyce, who apparently almost never left her boyfriend's. So much for Bonaduce's mating-math.

It was him, Marg, Rod, and he was introduced to the two others. One was a poor guy named Toby who had a withered arm held like a fleshy hook against his chest. Toby was a smiler, but behind the smile was that brand of whatever hell it was to grow up with an arm like that. The other person, Beth, turned out to be Marg's sister, and Beth was even bigger, and six feet at least.

Margaret brought their plates out two at a time. Unlike the others, Bonaduce waited for her to sit before he began, though he didn't think she noticed.

Marg looked beautiful next to her sister, Beth. Beth wasn't

quite walleyed, wasn't exactly hulking, but those were words you'd use. She hunched over her plate, protective of her food. Her thin, tightly curled hair made Bonaduce imagine her bald when old. He looked at Marg and saw her being bald too.

"So where's 'Ralph'?" Toby asked Beth, taking some bored pleasure in overpronouncing this name. Bonaduce had heard Toby refer to the boyfriend as "Ralph the Forestry Ape." He'd surmised too that Beth doted on him, and that Marg was a bit worried that her sister's love seemed desperate.

"At a funeral," Beth answered, shovelling a forkload. "One of his profs." She spoke with her mouth full, and Bonaduce had to look away.

They were eating something Marg had cooked and called "student gourmet" — mac and cheese with extras thrown in. Bonaduce embarrassed himself commenting on what tough but tasty tomatoes they had here in New Brunswick, meaning this as a sort of compliment, and Marg having to explain about sun-dried.

"So. Robert." Marg cleared her throat for the rehearsed question. "So like, what brought you up here? To do English lit."

"Well, that's" — he chuckled for her, shaking his head — "that's a complicated one."

"Oh, the chain," Toby said slowly, mocking no one in particular, "of pain."

"Well, yeah, it's always complicated," Bonaduce offered. "But I guess here I could say it was either push rust in Utica, or English lit here."

"'Push rust' ...?"

"Sell cars."

"Sounds like a bad name for a band," said Toby, making a show of buttering with his good hand while holding the bread to the table with his bad elbow. "'Push Rust.'"

"No," continued Marg, "but like, why here? You've been all over. And apparently unencumbered. I mean, *New Brunswick*?"

"What you do is this." He smiled to tell them he was both joking and not. "You turn forty. You find an atlas, have a few beers, close your eyes and" — he closed his eyes, twirled his finger, then stabbed — "Hey, New Brunswick!"

He dipped his head and ate. Dinner would soon be over. Things would settle in a week and be just normally friendly. He had no doubt now that this was Marg's work. She had asked Rod, who'd been reading a book in his lap, to put on one of his classical discs. It played quietly now in the background, making you want to sit up straight. Toby, proud to know, announced Vivaldi. Bonaduce had heard it before, it was a common one, almost elevator. Toby announced further that they were listening to "Spring." When Rod told him it was "Winter," Toby said it should be "Spring," because those plipping sounds were so totally like icicles melting.

This guy Toby, amazing. Suggesting Vivaldi had gotten his seasons wrong.


It was Krieger who changed Bonaduce's outlook on hockey as a job.

Krieger was finishing his career in Kalamazoo just as Bonaduce got there. A basher and a crasher and the team captain, he was one of the characters you meet. He'd had his nose broken a bunch of times and was fond of saying that on windy days he didn't know what side of his face his nose would end up on. If asked about his scars, Krieger might say someone had put out his face fire with a shovel. If you sat next to him at the restaurant and displayed an appetite, you might hear your dining style likened to a starving man sucking a dog through a keyhole. Krieger's hyperbole.

Bonaduce's second year there, Krieger retired but stayed in town as a car salesman, which is what lots of guys did, cashing in on what local popularity might have accrued. Also they were essentially homeless otherwise. Certainly jobless. Bonaduce easily pictured Krieger selling cars, leading a customer around, nodding at the car's back seat and making some outlandish sex joke, and the customer feeling included in the panache of professional sports.

The team missed the bruising Krieger. Certain tough guys come to be mother hens more than anything else. When play stops they check for scuffles, concern on their faces, protective. They are respected and don't have to fight much any more. In any case, with Krieger freshly gone, Bonaduce said what the hell and stepped up his grit to fill the void. He had to try something. He hadn't climbed leagues and he was twenty-five.

Slash, spear, elbows always up. I'm meaner than you. Drop the gloves first, get in the first punch. In front of the net be a constant menace, a fucking monster. Your goalie's your helpless naked mother and nobody gets near. It wasn't so hard: you'd been living on the edge of malice to begin with.

Though the face got messier, the style paid dividends. That first year he came close to the IHL penalty record, he got the loudest cheers at home and the loudest boos away, the local paper said it was like he'd miraculously come out of nowhere, and once suggested that if Bobby Bonaduce ran for mayor, well, hey. Until he was traded again two years later, a few of the guys called him "Mayor," or even "Your Worship," which is what the mayor of Kalamazoo was referred to, politics being as full of hyperbole as Krieger. But even though violence didn't get Bonaduce the phone call from above, he was now a known commodity, a leader, a mature influence some team would need. He'd been made captain.

Though what had really fuelled his new violence, if the truth were told, was the sight of Krieger selling cars. Bonaduce drove past on his way to the rink and he'd see Krieger in the floor-to-ceiling window, sitting there at a communal desk, waiting for customers, Krieger's boredom clear even at this speed and from this distance. It was the "Used" lot — they generally stuck the ex-players there, the idea being that hockey fans were more the Used than the New market. Krieger would probably sell a few cars, but still.

What Bonaduce had seen through the window was that, when

you quit the minors, selling cars was about as good as it got. He'd seen a few retirees jump into assistant coaching, but they were the keeners, the hockey-Eddies. He'd seen others go into what turned out to be shady business deals. Some went into security, donning fake cop gear to walk empty malls at night. And he'd seen guys keep at the beer like they'd always done while playing, only now they ballooned, adding forty, fifty pounds in a few years. Some drank more than ever, more than beer, and some — you heard stories — got into dealing dope. Rumours of downtown violence, detox, bad guys from Colombia. Some of the names you heard had faces. You could remember crashing corners with some of them. You could remember the grace of so-and-so's stride, and you could understand the bitterness that maybe helped take him down, because he and everyone else knew he should have been in the NHL from the start but management was too stupid to see it.

You'd heard of other teams offering career counselling for older players. While it may have been coincidence, two weeks after an old 'Mazoo alumnus, a guy named Al White, was found dead in a Boston alley, such counselling was offered to a few of them, including Bob Bonaduce, who was now twenty-six, an *older player*. This was about as mood-enhancing as writing your law-school finals and on your way out being handed an application for employment at McDonald's. To attend a session was to finally admit you were not going to the bigs. No one signed up.

What Bonaduce did do by way of career enhancement was enrol in an English course.

His third prof he met the next morning in class. He stumbled in late and she rose from her chair in greeting.

"Jan Dionne" was all she said, giving him her hand in a clumsy, human way. Finally, a professor who didn't have to act like one.

"Jan? Bob Bonaduce."

This was "Creative Writing: Longer Narrative Forms." Bonaduce was registered in the creative-writing option, meaning this was his speciality, this was what he would do next year's thesis in. He had already decided to write a novel. According to her thumbnail bio, Jan Dionne was primarily a poet. This fact made Bonaduce sweat a bit, thinking of his application. But what were the chances?

He sat and took stock. A seminar, there were only three other students, and Jan Dionne, around a table. Hard to hide in this one.

The other male in the room looked maybe Jason's age, and he wore traditional artist's gear — tight black refuse and a glower. Name of Philip. Serious business, this guy. One young woman was uncomfortably pretty, blonde, with unforthcoming but potentially wild eyes, hard to read. Her name also happened to be Jan. (Bonaduce dubbed them "Big Jan" and "Little Jan," an age thing, because they were the same size.) And there was Kirsten. Glasses and, though she may yet turn out to be nice, she cast upon the room a constant lip-length sneer, one that wrinkled her nose and bared her upper teeth. They were never not bared. It was like she'd once been struck snarky by one of youth's big sticks and her face had set this way. Kirsten didn't look at him long enough for him to nod to.

"You look lost." Big Jan was smiling at him.

"Well, you know. I'll catch up."

"We can get a coffee after this and I'll fill you in?"

"Great."

Big Jan explained that they were doing "plot-building exercises" begun last week. She invited him to jump in if he cared to. She had given them a scenario whereby a person turns a corner and hears a scream. The idea was to come up with what happens next, the goal being something called "artful incongruity" — which Little Jan, perhaps seeing in Bonaduce's face something other than comprehension, explained was "some plot device that's unexpected but not so out there that it's just bizarre."

They went round the table with their incongruous plots and

Bonaduce heard nothing too good in any of it. Kirsten's was actually sort of stupid, in that a woman screamed because the guy was naked, which was fine, but then she had the guy wake up, it was all a dream. Big Jan pointed out that using a dream to end a plot was clichéd and a cop-out, to which Kirsten, lip lifting and nose wrinkling, asked whether fiction wasn't a cop-out by definition. To which Big Jan said, while that may be true, such discussion lay in literary theory, whereas this course was about craft, about what worked dramatically. When Kirsten fell into an unconvinced, talentless stare, Bonaduce found relief in the knowledge that her presence in the class would take some of the pressure off him.

This relaxed him enough to contribute when his turn came. They were about to move to the next exercise when he half-raised his hand.

"Bob?"

"This is off the cuff."

"That's fine. So: fellow comes around the corner, there's a scream and— First, your character's name? And occupation?"

"He's, you know, unemployed. Newly unemployed. Name of — Robert."

"What happens next?"

"Okay. First, it's his own scream. It's him screaming."

"Okay. Good. So what's he screaming at?"

"Well, everything. The details."

"What sort of details?"

"Well, it's sort of random. Just all the shitty stuff. All the details that sort of work at you—"

He put his hands up and worked his fingers like chaotic worms, half-noticing that those on the right hand weren't going as fast as those on the left ... *and depending on the pattern of plaque it'll be one hand or the other, one foot or the other, thankfully not both ...*

"—the details that suddenly get you. Make you scream."

"Okay, so what happens next?"

"He dies. Boom. Totally unexpected."

Jan's eagerness fell. "Well, cop-out. It's like Kirsten's dream, a convenient—"

"It's not the end. It's the beginning of a story about his afterlife."

Big Jan looked willing to be eager again.

"It's been done in movies and stuff, I know," Bonaduce continued modestly, "but if you write it really straight, the reader won't expect it, won't even know he's there, because there's no trumpets and stuff. That's your incongruity. That it's just ordinary."

"An afterlife ..." Jan Dionne shrugged at the size of this.

"Another incongruity is that the same shitty details are there, but now he knows what they mean. He feels foolish for blowing it all his life. His main feeling in the afterlife is embarrassment, and" — what was that word — "atonement."

Bonaduce took in the details of Philip shutting down, Little Jan's ass shifting, Kirsten's teeth watching him.

Jan laughed again. "You've done some thinking about this."

"Jan? You hit a certain age."

Jan Dionne would be workable. She was an eye-to-eye prof, one who began by respecting you and then you could blow it or not. Over a coffee in the English Department lounge, surrounded by some definitely non-human types, she filled him in. The course was a workshop. You brought in your stuff, everyone discussed it, you took it home and fixed it. At year's end she had to — Jan whispered this bit — assign your stuff a grade, but only because academe — she shot the others in the lounge a dismissive look — demanded it. It's a struggle for us here, she added, meeting his eye, the "us" including him, and meant "writers." Her gaze lingered into uncomfortable silence, and it was in this moment that Bonaduce became aware of her hairless chin, her facebones, her breasts, and the rest of her difference and unknowability — her as a woman. He felt this as both a bridge and a distance.

"I forgot to mention that I enjoyed your poetry," Jan said as they stood. So sincere she wasn't smiling. "Very much. I didn't read the whole portfolio, but enough to know it was extremely good. 'Eclectic' is right."

"Hey." A slight shrug. What were the chances. Don't meet her eye. Let her misread fear as humility.

"'Till Death Do Us.' The sex/cannibalism ironies were so layered. 'My flesh, the salt of your kiss, the teeth of time ...'"

"Hey." Jesus, quoting the stuff. He hardly remembered typing that one. "Do you remember one called 'Blades'?"

"No. Sorry." She paused apologetically. "But I remember lots. Have you thought about a collection? What I saw was certainly publishable. Here and there I was intimidated, to tell you the truth. That one, 'Aeolia,' my goodness, and so different from—"

"Stuff I worked at over the years. Long bus trips, not much else to—"

"That's right! I know! You're a hockey player! People are talking about that."

A shrug, a dull look away to deflect this direction. Afraid as he was, it was disappointing watching her turn into a hockey fan.

"Any newer work you'd like me to see? Poetry is my area."

"Actually I think I've packed it in. Fiction is all I do now. My new area. Writing a novel for my thesis."

"You've started it?"

"Thought I'd get the jump on it."

"You going to bring it to the workshop?"

"Why not."


To get into the creative-writing option, which let you do two fewer academic courses, he'd had to submit "a portfolio of recent creative work." He had no such work, recent or otherwise, save for two old poems, and no time to write more. He could write, he knew he could write. In the meantime, there in the college library in Utica were all these literary journals — *Mississippi Review*, *Ploughshares*, *Alchemy* — a slew of unread anthologies of unknown poets' unknown poems.

It took him an afternoon and evening to select and type twenty-eight pages of poetry. And his own two, "Blades" and "Black Hogs." Describing his work in the cover letter, he used the words "eclectic range," and "postmodern."

As arranged, he met Marg outside the library, where she'd been studying, and they walked out to the student parking lot together. An almost balmy night. He remembered that Maritime weather was nothing but change, consistent change. Also that the extremes could be entertaining but you got sick a lot.

He took off his sweater and carried it in his hand. His other hand squeezed two books. He had to get a briefcase. Time to hit the yard sales. Marg was bookless, her long arms dangling not quite in rhythm to her pace.

"Haven't quit school yet, eh?" he asked as she waited at the locked passenger door. He searched for the key.

"Not yet." She smiled as he opened her door for her. "You know, like, not a lot of people lock their cars here?"

"I've been in the States for twenty years."

"Especially, I mean," she continued, and he was already wincing with the punch line, "cars like this."

It was warm enough to ride with the windows down. Marg marvelled at the eight track, and played with the old air freshener. She brought her nose to it.

"I think this has lost its power."

"Well, it's acquired new ones."

"Oh — this is your rabbit's foot." She nodded and seemed happy, like this was her territory.

"That's it." He paused. "Keeps me a lucky mess."

She looked genuinely interested in the grey cut-out now, fingering it with respect.

Lucky mess. It was Fournier who had called him this. That accidental way non-native speakers make poetry. Fournier, his best friend ever? Who knows. And why decide such a thing. But Fournier, Fournier and his watch exactly three hours late. Ask the time and it took him that little calculation. It was one of those many-buttoned watches with beepers and such, and Fournier would go into pidgin English to explain how he didn't know how to set it. But it had been perfectly three hours late for years. Out of the blue, in a rare insecure moment, Fournier had confessed to him that he'd set it this way when he was still Vancouver property, playing for their farm club, Hamilton, three time zones away. He'd bought this watch and set it and kept it at Vancouver time. The silly hopeful bastard, it had probably cursed him.

It was eleven when they pulled off the highway into their gravel drive. A motion-sensing light over the kitchen door shone in their faces. Bonaduce envisioned a year of this: arriving home, this light, Marg beside him, the old-oil smell of the gravel. Arriving "home."

"You're limping."

"Stiff." He hadn't realized he'd been helping himself along, one hand on the car.

Inside she asked if he wanted tea and he said okay and took a seat on the couch. Rod nodded to him and went back to his reading. Rod was always reading. You could hear someone in the shower and, mixing with the musk of an old house, smell the distant steam and soapiness.

He may have nodded off. Marg delivered his tea. She put a disc on, some soft Celtic instrumental. He picked up the case, The Irish Descendants. Not your most imaginative name. What he felt like, he didn't know why, was some Shirelles. Even some Supremes.

"Do you play Yahtzee?" Marg asked.

"Well, I don't know."

"It's dice, but sort of like poker."

"I know poker."

Marg located score sheets and two pencils, and what looked like a handful of dice. This was okay, this student life. Late night, tea, music, good company, no real worries. Yahtzee. He'd missed all this.

Bonaduce asked Rod if he wanted to play Yahtzee. Rod declined, smiling. Rod said almost nothing but you could tell he was a good guy.

"Do we bet?" he asked Marg, who was rattling the bones, warming them up.

"We could bet."

The taskmaster morning sunlight of fall. It didn't sound like any of his housemates were up and there was no evidence of them yet in the kitchen. Moving quietly, still a stranger here, he plugged in the kettle. Or tried to, missing the socket, his eyes still fastened more to dream details than to those of the waking world.

It was the kind of dream that shapes your morning and fills it with feeling long after it's forgotten. Jason was a Jason the father hadn't known, a boy of a prime sixteen, and they were all in bed together: Bonaduce, Jason, Leah. Dad in the middle. He could feel their heat. They'd all been jogging, in bright white track suits, though his own was muddy-dirty. In bed they still had these track suits on, and they were covered with a heavy comforter. It was hot but Bonaduce kept the comforter gripped to his neck in case anyone wanted to throw it off. No one said anything. Jason seemed concerned with food, and Bonaduce and Leah shared a proud knowing look at their son's appetite.

Three adults lying in bed together. Bonaduce shook his head, smiling gently, blowing into his coffee cup. He took the coffee to his room and sat on the unmade bed. He put a hand down, the bed still warm from the heat of him sleeping, the heat of his dream. Out the window, the maples were hinting at red, the poplars at yellow. The start of their pretty death.

He had the name and number scrawled on a napkin scrap. This piece of paper felt so electric in his pocket after two days, he had to smile at himself, how nervous he felt, how like a teenager afraid to call the special someone.

He decided that when he did call he would leave a message, and not have to talk. Ashamed of this cowardice, he plotted nonetheless to call on a Saturday night, a time any healthy young guy would be out-and-about. Hey — the message would say, and its tone would be neither pathetic nor too clever — Hey, guess who? Well, you sitting down? I'm in town. And I think maybe here for a while. Anyway, got some weird and wacky news. Gimme a call. Let's have a coffee or whatever. Be great to see you! Hope things are good and all that. It's been a while, eh?

Something along those lines. There was no telling how he'd be, how they'd be, if the call happened live. Even worse, way worse, if it happened in the flesh, face-to-face. That could be a stammering, awkward disaster. Better get the boy on the phone, leave a message, let him prepare.

Noon public-skate. The Lady Beaverbrook Arena. He'd practised here with the Express a few times. Outside it reminded him of a swimming pool because of its low contours and walls of blue tile.

He hadn't public-skated since he was a child. Outdoors in Winnipeg, at night. Lights strung up, music piped through bad speakers — Juliette, Rosemary Clooney — and couples skating hand in hand. Once in a while the Beatles as a treat for the kids, and a sudden licence to go wild. The young Bonaduce flying around, near misses, showing off. He remembered being grabbed mid-wildness by the coat scruff, yelled at by some old hero whose wife had her hands hidden in a white fur muff, like in a Hollywood movie.

He laced his skates. The smells always got to him. The water-melt on wood or rubber, the Zamboni fumes, sometimes ammonia, the old socks or wet cigars, or just the after-stink of your buddies. You always knew you were in an arena. How long had it been, six months? This would hurt.

The wall sign said noon was an adult-skate, no kids. Through the glass doors he could hear piped music, "Maggie Mae." And it *was* late September and, hey, he was back in school. The nice coincidence, the teenage astrology, of music. A whiff of a song like that from the window of a passing car could make you feel her skin, smell her shampoo, see the bark of the tree she braced against.

You can smell ice. The broad white sheet in front of you. He stepped on, the tiny vertigo of first-time-in-a-while. Mostly middle-aged and old men, here for exercise, skating a slow circle. Two couples. No muffs, but both were doing the fancy hand-hold. Born of Holland. Maybe Hollywood.

It was cowardly coming here, public-skating before reporting to the Varsity Reds. But he had to get the worst kinks out. He'd never not been in shape but he had to admit he was forty. And doctors were sometimes right, whatever; something grim had indeed attacked him, who knows what. But the legs felt decent. Right calf wasn't all there but it seemed to be suffering no loss of thrust. Better slow it down in fact, some people were watching. Public-skate protocol. Awful that they might think he was showing off, like there was a need to. He pictured himself losing his mind, doing some bashing here at the geriatric noon skate, something out of Monty Python. "Berserk Skater Maims Twenty Before Turning Blades On Self." Did they still have the *Daily Gleaner* here?

Actually it was a challenge to skate this slow.

Nor was there any doubt now. She was fighting not to look at him. Marilyn Bauer. Had to be. The veiled way she was eyeing back. They'd partied together two decades ago. Leah's friend Marilyn Bauer. Husband Dale? Dave? Marilyn and Dave. Dave had been with Leah before Bonaduce arrived on the scene, then they'd continued as friends. This now-platonic connection had nonetheless given Marilyn coy reciprocal claims on Bonaduce and, that's right, they'd had that flirt once under the table with their feet.

Marilyn Bauer looked ready to break into a smile the next time he chugged near. Fredericton had suddenly shrunk. Bonaduce left the ice, an early exit he would not read about in the Sports pages.

Time to suck it up and make some phone calls. What could either of them say? He was respectable. He was a grad student. He was a published poet.

He'd actually often thought of writing. Writing something. And not just when bored — the road trips, the bus, Jesus, the endless bad TV in the what-town-we-in hotel. Sometimes he was simply inspired. He'd write a bus-poem, usually a funny rhymer, and maybe set it to guitar for later, or maybe he'd show it to the guy beside him, depending who the guy was. He wasn't hiding anything, it wasn't that, they already all saw him as a freak, it's just that only certain guys would appreciate the clever lines.

How many times had some guy, knowing he'd taken another English course over the summer, yelled at him across the dressing room: So when you gonna write a book about us? They'd laugh and mock him for the booky weirdo that he was, but in their eyes you saw that they did feel their lives were worth writing about, and that they hoped maybe he would.

Maybe he would.

Getting "home" that evening he saw tacked to his door frame, hanging from a leather thong, a many-coloured spiderweb thing in a metal hoop. A few feathers dangled from it. It looked Indian, and it was apparently a gift. A taped note said: For your window, Margaret.

He took it down and rehung it in his window. And in doing so realized that he'd be seeing sunsets from this room, here was an orange one now. It wasn't a bad view altogether, he hadn't noticed this. Early peerings out had depressed him a little because it had looked so barren — unkempt fields and stunted trees fronted by a neighbour's heavy-equipment trailer permanently parked there, the trailer barren too. Greys and browns and the dying greens of fall. The scene had made him think of Jan Dionne's term "emotional landscape," which was where the main character found himself, and into which the clever author would plant traps and rewards. Well, if this scene was his emotional landscape, there were no rewards in sight, and probably no traps either, and it looked like it'd been decades since any author had come scheming by.

He scraped a crusty smidgen off the glass with a fingernail. If you wanted to, you could see this lack of drama out there as simplicity. This lack of colour as subtlety. More fuzzy than stark, like a watercolour. You could see it as an empty stage waiting for something to happen. Birds. Deer. They had to come. In two months, snow. There were worse things to watch than an empty stage. For now, this decent orange sunset. This Indian thing from Marg.

In the SUB cafeteria he thumbed through the *Daily Gleaner*, Fredericton's rag, searching for Sports, wanting to check up on the stats and lives of a few buddies. He couldn't help but notice the spelling mistakes, and the wildly bad headlines — "Seniors Pursue Recreational Pursuits" — and letters to the editor, half of which quoted the Bible while railing against a gay group's attempt to hold a Pride parade. Where was he, Montana?

Today's paper had a Health section, which he scanned, trying not to read "Kidney Symptoms and—" "Bowel Disease the Scourge of—" You get into reading this stuff and you turn hypochondriac, fearful every time you pee and things feel a little off. "Pancreatic Cancer Rare But—"

That's what Coach Murphy had had. Pancreatic. A fast one. The Tulsa players had taken turns in groups, it was easier that way, Murphy being a coach no one liked. Half-dozen guys shuffling around, trying to hide behind each other, no clue what to say. How ya doin' Coach. Can we get you anything Coach? We lost to Phoenix again last night, blew it in the third. Lame jokes about who blew it, shoulders punched, Coach Murphy manages a smile. In it you can see his corny gratitude and terror both. He cries, or maybe it was just pain, his face squeezing up like a baby's. He looked so weak, completely used up, no say about whether he cried or not, a leaf in some fatal wind. It didn't exactly cancel out their former sense of him, all that macho dressing-room bluster — it just made it seem pointless. The last time Bonaduce saw Coach Murphy, his head was turned to the window and he was unresponsive to them. He'd fallen to an even more basic state. Though *fallen* wasn't the word. His intelligence as such appeared gone, but you could see that his feeling for what he looked at — the light in the window — was deep. A yearning, but not even that complicated. A plant's basic connection to the sun.

One *Gleaner* article that caught Bonaduce's eye had him actually laughing out loud as he chewed his last french fry, kept him smiling as he sucked his large Coke through a straw. Doctors, oh they'd be duking it out over this one. It was about red wine, how someone had found something in it that looked damn close to a cure for cancer. Bonaduce could see the hypochondriacs arriving even now, sick line-ups at the liquor store, fists squeezing necks of plonk. Responses by other doctors would be a week away, articles about the dangers of guzzling, about how red wine *caused* cancer.

Doctors — he glanced at the young types slouched over their fries and bookbags, as yet unstricken with any of this — doctors

were our gods. Doctors certain of themselves and lord how we're
glad they are. It's just these damned second and third opinions.

*... Unfortunately for you it was a pyramidal attack ...*

*... Good news: the attack was pyramidal ...*

*... Now on the other hand, if you'd had a pyramidal episode ...*

How, how could there be such basic contradictions?

*Mr. Bonaduce, multiple sclerosis is genetic, is hereditary. Bob, may
I call you Bob, MS is a matter of diet. Hello there, sir, pleased to meet
you, multiple sclerosis is viral, something you caught as a child, and it
flowers — I'm sorry, perhaps that's not a good word to use — twenty
years later.*

Well, doctors, I guess I don't really care how I got it as much
as I want to know, how do I fix it?

*Mr. Bonaduce, you don't. Your nerve roots are covered with a myelin
sheath, which has been damaged, and blocked with this white crud,
"plaque." It'll keep occurring, more and more. Bob? You fix it with
diet, visualization and prayer. Sir, you can do any of the diets if you
want, they probably won't hurt you, but mostly you rest, and take any
number of drugs indicated by any number of symptoms.*

Okay so I don't fix it. But if I have it — and I don't have it —
give me the scenario. Tell me what would happen.

*Bob, you will continue to experience deepening bouts of localized
paralysis. Double vision or spot blindness. Fatigue. Fatigue is persist-
ent. Pain. Later, aside from general immobility, of course incontinence
must be provided for.*

Incontinence? That's—

*Yes. But, strangely, there's another, final thing.*

What.

*At this point euphoria is a common complaint. Well, since it's eu-
phoria, "complaint" might not be the word to use in this—*

That's funny.

*But it suggests not only spinal and optic deterioration but also that
somehow the actual* brain *tissue is—*

He'd heard nothing more, frozen on the *incontinence being
provided for,* on the image of diapers, unable to consider them
and unable not to.

Sure, he probably shouldn't be drinking this Coke. Or having white bread, sugar, beer, Cheez Whiz, chips — right. Diet was one thing most of the gods agreed on, especially the alternative types. There was only one thing upon which all and everygod agreed: fatigue. *Don't, Mr. Bonaduce, Bob, sir, let yourself get overtired.*

Now how would a university student or hockey player ever get himself tired? Bonaduce rattled the cubes in his paper cup, sucking it dry, making the sound of a child finishing his milkshake. He savoured the dread possibility that Jason could come in here at any second. Bang, his son. His only blood family. Here's Dad hangin' in the SUB with a Coke, books scattered around. Hey Jace, how ya doin. Casual wave, like it hasn't been years, like Jason wasn't some unknown creature now, nothing remotely like the ten-year-old of their last handshake. Maybe nothing the same but the DNA.

Whoever Jason was now, he'd be thrown for the loop of his life. Off-balance and full of big questions. Frightened, in a word.

Well, better him than me.

Gail Smith's class was a secret hot room in hell Bonaduce hadn't known about. The intimate size of it, six, was extra-hell. Both black-mood Phil and glare-teeth Kirsten were in this one too.

Introductions were made for the latecomer. Bonaduce felt big and stupid already. In Winnipeg, because home room was French, if you were late you were *en retard*, and he hadn't dropped the association.

Gail Smith called everyone either Mister or Ms, and she herself was "Professor Smith." Bonaduce was about to witness her sitting up straight for three hours. He would not catch a smile, but to show she got a student's wry aside she did a thing where she turned down the corners of her mouth and jerked her head up and to the side, looking off into the sky with amusement and tolerance. It was like she saw herself as a seventy-year-old guy from Oxford. She could actually be kind of pretty except that she was so careful not to be.

Bonaduce would stay mum the whole time. The first hour was occupied by what looked like an argument, but probably wasn't, about what constituted "Britain." It seems that Professor Smith's inclusion of several South Asian writers on the list made Phil and Kirsten take offence on their behalf. Smith's point, that they were victims of British imperialism, and "forcibly adopted, as it were," seemed to rankle Kirsten in particular, in that she was certain the writers would be outraged at being thought victims. Smith countered that the only fact that mattered was that all these writers *had moved* — she almost shouted this. Which made Bonaduce wonder why she hadn't dropped the "British diaspora" thing and just called her course "Writers Who Have Moved." He also wondered if these writers — Vassanji, Ondaatje, Begamudré — would care what Smith or Kirsten thought. Luckily he didn't have to contribute this or any other musing, for these seminars were set up so that each week a different student did most of the talking, or "presented."

It wasn't as if Robert Bonaduce was afraid. Not overly. Humanly nervous in front of new humans. For all intents and purposes speaking a foreign language. People sat so alertly. Even Phil's dark slouch looked coiled and ready. Drawn blinds kept the sunlight outside where it belonged.

But all it was, really, was that these guys had worked up a decent act, all witty dash and brain-pizzazz. The ordinarys in the cheap seats could see this. But knowledge *was* power, and these types knew tons about which the poor Bonaduce had no clue whereof nor whatsofuckingever. Phucking Phil, today's presenter, began his Malcolm Lowry spiel with shrugs and hand flaps as if to suggest he'd thrown some thoughts together out in the hall. Then launched into a sentence beginning, "Now of course the temptation is to foreground a reading of *Volcano* with a reading of Lowry's *life*, but those narrative contrivances in the text — linearity, closure, what have you — subsume in their very *artifice*, artifice by which the text, as 'novel,' derives, shall we say ..." Phil was especially good at belittling certain notions by pronouncing quotation marks around certain words and getting people to smile, and Smith to jerk her head back.

The sentence continued for quite some time, and at first Bonaduce was spellbound. Then worried that this was the way you talked in this room. Was he supposed to "present" in this language? Then he smiled, enjoying the notion of *This is Phil presenting*. He remembered hearing the word used like this before, as a verb with no object, in TV nature shows. When a goat stuck its chest out, or a salmon turned itself bright red, or an antelope lifted its ass to another's face, they were *presenting*. Ten minutes in, Bonaduce was stifling his laughter — at Professor Smith's stupidity for allowing such a sentence to continue, at his own stupidity for not having a clue what was being said, and at Phil's stupidity for caring about any of this in the first place. He grinned picturing himself when his turn came three weeks from now, him with his upper dentures out, *presenting* with a sloppy lisp, dumb-on-purpose, saying "Well I theen the movie on thith inthteada the book but," and he was wearing his hockey gear, and three days' beard, his posture *presenting* so to threaten violence if anyone fell from wide-eyed attention at anything he said. He grinned harder and shook his head with an insight into the essential difference between his last career and this new one: if in the other game you disagreed with someone, you physically attacked him. What made him laugh aloud and got him reprimanded by Smith, who asked him, as if he were six years old, to "Please share it," was the image of him understanding something Phil said enough to disagree with it, then lunging across the table and grabbing Phil's little arm and snapping it. Bonaduce decided against sharing this and mumbled an apology. Thinking himself understood, disagreed with and laughed at, Phil glared at him, and Bonaduce felt instantly overtired.

The ordeal was finally over. They gathered books and notes. Bonaduce had drawn a few decent pictures of his station wagon. He decided he could maybe do this course if he got serious and learned the rules, and the meaning of "postmodern," and next time read the book. Leaving the room, Bonaduce tried to be friendly to the other guy who'd just suffered through with him, a teammate if you will, a bespectacled Mr. Webster. Filing out, it was like the siren had gone, and they had lost but hadn't deserved to; they were bruised and weary and going for a shower together. Pointing to the slouched, exhausted Phil, Bonaduce threw an arm over Webster's little shoulders and whispered, "Guess we're gonna wanna buy our essays from *that* guy." Mr. Webster didn't look Bonaduce in the eye and his smile was nervous, but he did seem to know it was a joke.

In the department lounge, as usual, the glances at the Bonaduce body as he scanned the bulletin board or stole coffee, dropping two loud nickels into the can instead of quarters. Young or old, prof or student, library nerd or nose-ring artist — up came whisperings of *professional hockey player*. Looking at him harder by not looking, Bonaduce the walking car accident. He'd expected this, body-people being exotic to head-people. Models, athletes, embodied some kind of ideal, so said the Greeks, though the notion had lately fallen from favour. And him doubly exotic — accepted into grad school, a jock who presumably wasn't stupid. These types were magnanimous enough to enjoy the little thrill of a preconception broken. But, hey, he'd show them: he could be stupid in ways they'd never dreamed of.

They wanted to know about the fights. Especially those who thought they didn't want to know. Those who so quickly shrugged off the ludicrous subject in fact looked a bit like deer alert to a trouble-noise. Or they were hungry for the information, if only to have theories refuelled. It had not been a surprise to Bonaduce that half the fans at a New York boxing match were intellectuals, many of whom were women.

Stupid rough hayseed hockey players. Bonaduce wanted to explain things. He pictured the guys in the dressing room, on the bus, in the bar. The levels of wit he'd heard. But mostly it wasn't words, it was the way a guy being interviewed taped a stick while spouting bad clichés on purpose, or waggled his ass below the gaze of the camera. It was shared looks at the swelling colour of a teammate's knee. It was hotel and nightclub and taxi savvy. It was sound public management of pride and envy, something academics were famously inept at.

Language, simply, was a route not many of them took. Should he tell these loungers that in 1968 Eric Nesterenko scored thirty-two goals for Chicago and published his first book of poems? But that would be falling into their trap, accepting their definition of intelligence.

On the ice is where it really happened. The brilliance of some. All senses sparking, working at the widest periphery, aflame with danger and hope both, seeing the whole picture, the lightning-fast flux of friends and enemies, the blending of opportunity and threat. Words didn't stand a chance here. Words were candy wrappers, dead leaves.

Bonaduce took his two-nickel coffee over to the main table, ringed on three sides by couches, seven or eight people on them. Might as well get to know some of these guys. Especially since half of them were young women.

"Can I wedge on in here?"

All the bodies on all three couches flinched to make room. He sat in the largest gap, smiling and nodding at the stiff young woman on his left and the nervous young man on his right. He grabbed up a *New Yorker*, chuckling at its cover, its tight little in-joke, an urbane mocking of the urbane, in this case a bunch of businessmen hustling to work in a demented way.

True, sure, dressing rooms had their share of morons. Guys who would say *libary* if they ever had cause to say it. The stuff he'd heard come out of guys' mouths. *Twats, queers, hosebuckets*, and half the room laughing. But a dressing room was your basic cross-section, this seemed only reasonable. The fact remained that half the guys in any dressing room he'd ever sat in could have ended up here in this lounge, thumbing *New Yorker* cartoons and being wry. They had for various reasons taken a different route, the body-route. The logic and joy of having it work like that.

Out of the blue and apropos of nothing except their being inches apart, he stuck his hand out at the guy beside him, whose head was down in a book which smelled freshly purchased. *Lady Windermere's Fan.*

"Hiya. Bob Bonaduce."

French fries in the SUB and then a long evening bent up in a library carrel, reading Brian Moore, in his head pronouncing it "*Bree*an," which coloured everything. Home by midnight, and on the kitchen table, weighted down with a buttery knife, a scrawled note from Marg: "Friend of yours called long-distance. Fornay? Fornier? French accent. All excited. Said you MUST begin something called a yeast diet. Said to tell you it's a cure? He's sending you a book on it. I assume you know what he's talking about."

You wake up with vision so fuzzy it's like sleep's dreamscape has continued, and then you find the legs don't work too well. Couldn't even bloody walk, he was a big nightmare puppet with packed rag legs. It wasn't some awful new injury, because he'd been feeling so weak and weird lately he hadn't even been playing. Rolling and flopping himself across the floor, it was almost funny. There wasn't a lot of pain aside from some deep nervy stuff he recognized as having been there for a while. The hands didn't work either. Despite dumb eyes and sleeping fingers, he eventually got Fournier on the phone. *Fournier, Jesus, you're not going believe this.* Damn if he wasn't slurring his words as well. He made a joke about the mother of all hangovers. Fournier promised he wouldn't, but an ambulance came and the boys in dull green, all intent on his survival, in no mood to crack a smile at the Bonaduce jokes, packed him up and away he went. Halfway to the hospital he was halfway better; a few hours later he could walk, he could see okay and he was feeling foolish.

But tests, tests, tests. Sitting in the blood-sample room full of sick people, holding a number, waiting for his name to be called, exhausting the *Sports Illustrated*s, endless baseball and basketball, in your stomach a drone of worry doing a dance with your trust in a body that had never let you down.

Passed from doctor to doctor. (After so many high-tech gizmos and scans, the test of choice turned out to be the cartoonish popping him on the knee with the rubber hammer.) Have you ever experienced double vision? Bonaduce pingponging his eyes from the doctor to the curtain and back, asking, Which one of you asked that? The doctor deciding to smile, but continuing, How about blurred vision? To which Bonaduce answered, actually serious, Do you mean concussion-blurred vision, or the kind that's just sort of usually there?

Waiting for tests, feeling better, he half-enjoyed the image of him in the corniest of scenarios. He was lying in a hospital bed, adult-diapered, limbs mobile as breakfast sausage, a professionally flirtatious nurse spooning vanilla dessert into his yop, and he asked the doctor (who'd be checking things off on his clipboard, brow furrowed, when everyone knows there's nothing *on* the clipboard): Well, Doc, does this mean that's it for the NHL?

The doctor is a wise-ass hockey fan. He says, Hell no, Bobby — there's always the Leafs.

Answering the questions, he was made to recall his body-history, which in his work was more or less typical. Finger, two noses, cracked footbone, a hairline in the right collarbone (the most painful), lots of sprains and cuts. About a hundred stitches in the face, all healing well and looking just fine except the rubbery scar-mess over the left eye, and those white lines crisscrossing his five o'clock shadow. Like Krieger, he'd had a job as a fencing mask in Heidelberg.

The only bad one had been the leg. In Rochester, which is a broken-bone kind of town, an innocent shove had conspired with a rut in the ice. Deep in the skull you hear and feel the snap. A beloved leg suddenly foreign, angling off into new territory. The senses falling in another direction, into a deep inner black, into fainting. Embarrassing, but no choice in the matter.

Then the strangest thing: coming to, what he felt was, what he even said to himself was, *I'm out of it.*

The war was over. Tonight's game, but also maybe the season, maybe hockey altogether, the career. Balled up there on the ice, Terry-the-Trainer's whisky breath asking if it was a knee, he felt the descent of a peace, he could even smile a bit in the wincing. He must have looked macho being helped off — smiling while the leg dangled so ugly. The tough Bonaduce. No one would see in the smile a little kid home from school sick, in pyjamas, TV all day, a warm bed, Mom's bustle in the next room.

The year-of-the-leg he was back for the playoffs and he played ten more seasons. All part of the job. Everyone played with pain. Injuries were unsurprising. In fact they felt nothing but appropriate. If you played the game right, you were in their arena, so to speak. You were sort of asking for them.

Waiting at home for test results, he began to see disease the same way. As life-injuries. We're alive, so we're in their arena, we're really just waiting. He thought about death and saw that being alive in the first place was sort of like asking for it. Waiting for test results you think all sorts of things.

But you can point your attitude one way or the other. He wrote everything off to a deep flu, to a stubborn virusy thing. The clumsiness was frightening, but viruses were getting weird, weren't they? He could still skate okay. Funny, he could skate better than he could walk.

It was like an injury that was taking time to happen. You could actually forget about it, forget it was still happening, until the dropped spoon, or the delay of the comb. Then you understood how big it was. You could feel how life itself had become a hovering that was nothing other than sick. The air around you an impending deadness. They said it was going to come back; relapse and remission were the poles of your new planet. The whole thing would, simply, get worse.

In hockey it was generally all nice and quick.

"Leah there by any chance?"

There. Done. Some things you have to just do.

"She is. I'll just go and locate her."

That would be Oscar. He sounded okay, kind of funny, mocking his use of "locate" as he said it. Oscar Devries. She was still Leah Miller, like she'd always been, eschewing the tuneful Bonaduce moniker on their wedding day, contemporary gal that she was. Phone to his ear, he could hear Oscar walk away, wooden floors it sounded like. Oscar was a lawyer with NB Hydro or something. Probably an elegant old house, reno'd from the rats to the rafters.

"Hello?"

"It's your best nightmare."

"Bobby?"

"So that was Oscar, eh? You still with Oscar?"

"That *was* you! You're in town!"

In her voice excitement and fear.

"I am."

"Marilyn called, said she saw someone she thought was you. Remember Marilyn Bauer? 'It *had* to be him, and he was *skating*, it *had* to be him.' So I guess it was! Is!"

"Here I am."

"You here playing?"

"No, hell no. Packed it in. Old age, eh? But don't tell Jason. That I'm here. Surprise."

"Sure. So — you here for a while?"

A definite note of concern behind the cheer.

"Could be. It's kind of a long story—"

"We really have to get together, but, look, I'm out the door.

I'm really late. We're having a party Friday night. Oscar will tell you about it. 'Bye."

And Leah was gone. Leah who would never for as long as she lived ever have to apologize to him, because he was the one who'd left. Leah who felt that the distance between them was now great enough for her to be excited over the phone in front of Oscar, with no fear of anyone misinterpreting. For her to invite him to her party, easy as could be.

But he'd heard what he knew he'd hear. Not in her voice, but in her silences, and the way she breathed. He knew she'd been holding the phone with both hands.

"Hello?" Oscar again. "Now you'll be wanting directions, is that it?"

You could hear him smiling, an ironic, friendly guy.


It was a decent little bed, and something conspired to keep him in it. His first single bed since he was a boy.

Maybe if you just stayed put, lying down, and eased your mind in the right direction, this pure and gentle going-in that almost erased you, a tender secret muscle the size of your body that turned you to air if you flexed it right — if you stayed here like this, you could be one of those people, and he knew they existed, one of those people who know only what matters, who can play life like the game it is, who know its movements — its tides and wind and forest smells — and understand all the efforts of the heart. You would know to keep in mind that everyone's lost and no one's to blame. You would be able to lie here in bed like this but be content with it, content to look out this window to see those birds leaving that branch, moving off one by one in a sprung rhythm that suggests music.


This morning he found his roomies at the kitchen table, puzzling over heating and phone bills and such. Rod was wondering what had maybe been paid and what could be "left again till next time."

It was raining outside, cars were *whooshing* loudly by, a tableful of roommates were talking house matters. Things had a homey, practical feel. Toby already had a beer going. Bonaduce rummaged through his assigned half-cupboard, looking for the can of smoked oysters he was sure he'd bought. He was politely invited to take part, so he shuffled over, and he listened to Toby's suggestion that he take his turn and pay the phone bill. He decided to hold off airing the logic that this particular bill, some of which was long distance, covered a time previous to him setting foot in this country, let alone this house. He wasn't sure how things here ran yet, so he wrote out a cheque. Doing so, he briefly eyed Toby, who openly eyed him back.

Then went to his "room" and searched his "closet" (six hangers hanging on a string strung between two nails) to "get ready" for tonight's party at "his wife's house." What did you wear to such a thing? Were they rich, casual, stiff-necked, hip, what? And did he want to fit in, or did he want to shine?

He went to the bathroom. Sitting, he looked toiletside and noticed dark, flame-shaped stains of wet rising from the floor up the wall. The drywall was permanently damp and thickened with it, whatever it was, a rank ecosystem of climbing swamp. Instead of paying a phone bill, he'd love to come in here with a sheet of drywall and can of paint. Point this house in a new direction. He would discuss it with them. In the meantime he had Leah to get ready for. He picked up a paperback *Hamlet* someone, probably Rod, had left lying upside down on the floor, beside the swamp.

He lay naked on his bed, looking out the window at the stars. The party wasn't until nine and he didn't want to be early. He was already tired. Hard to kill time this time of night.

Red, white and blue rubber balls in both hands, you squeeze

until it hurts, get the ligaments popping out in the wrists, and on the forearms blue veins almost the width of a cigarette. You do lose a step or two, but keep the wrist strength up and you always had your shot. He'd seen oldtimer games, and some of the old boys could still rip it pretty good. Forty feet out, a flick of the wrists and, bingo, the biscuit's in the basket.

These stars in this clean New Brunswick sky were a treat. The whole eastern seaboard of America had basically erased its stars. City lights and a bit of carbon burning was all it took. Fournier, who'd gone up hunting in Labrador, had a story of a Japanese girl visiting Goose Bay and pointing in amazement at the night sky and asking her host, What are those? The smiling host, about to explain the wonder of the aurora borealis, looked up and saw none. And then realized she was pointing at stars — she lived in Tokyo and had never seen stars.

Squeeze the balls. Look at the stars. Tyger Tyger. Looking at stars is a feeling that's probably identical to what a dog gets looking at the controls of a stereo. Twinkling stars. Feel them pull at your little mind in that gently eager way they have, let them remind you for the first time in years that what you are looking at you are incapable of truly seeing and that the only honest response to this is to drop to your dull and sorry knees.

Loud stars. Hungry stars. *Synaesthesia*, grad-student word for the day. This jazzy darkness. Your citrus heart. Sweet and sour Leah.

Montreal traded him to Toronto in the middle of the season, just after Christmas, so he'd had no time to get his affairs — such as moving, such as abandoning his wife and son — in order before reporting to the Rochester Americans.

His plan was agreed to by Leah. At least, that was his memory. He'd go check out the town of Rochester and ascertain his status there. Because everyone involved was fully confident he'd be getting called up to Toronto sooner rather than later. One little injury to one Leaf defenceman was all it would take. Why move Leah and Jason to Rochester when they'd only have to move again? Leah was still in school, third year, so she should stay put, stay in Fredericton.

There were lots of reasons why this plan was agreed to. No one dared raise the main question.

Sex was great, it was always great. But between sex and the next sex was that edgy lack of purpose, a waiting which seemed most of all to be a kind of vacancy. They did share some vital loves: the same food, the same luscious colours in a picture or a sunset, a French horn for the way it came lording in. Smells. And of course sex, its textures and pace. They shared the senses, the runes of body. He'd even understood her eating the dog food, understood her after she'd been caught so embarrassed with the can of it and she told him it was like eating meat from the centre of the earth. They were joined perfectly in bodies' routes of need and terminals of pleasure. But with most else — friends, politics, questions of whether happiness came more from a Cadillac or a hike — on little could they easily agree, and it was so loud a problem it never had to be discussed.

Jokes though, they could share jokes. They could always make each other laugh. At a party, eye contact to confirm something scandalous they'd laugh at later. Sometimes they even joked about real things, about which they had no business laughing. What's your name again? Smiling sadly at the truth after they asked, Do we even know each other? Have we been properly introduced? No, though I believe I've just been Bonaduced.

Their joking was probably something close to love. As she tucked into a steak he could gently bark and whine, even in company, though she'd quit the dog food by now, and she'd laugh. She understood; they both felt the loving comment on her carnality, and her deeper needs, which seemed funny in the midst of a boring chatty party and their bed waiting upstairs.

He made attempts. He did. He tried and tried to expand his love, and to harden it against the hard times to come. Now and then even falling to the corny — flowers, a necklace for no reason, once a poem set and sung to moody music. But finding himself stooped and corny, he could never follow through. Couldn't stay pure, had to screw it up — he'd mock his flowers while handing them over, and the poem he wrecked by tacking on a spontaneous raunchy verse. Or when he fertilized her lawn for her. He'd seen on a lawn across town how green a chemical fertilizer could make grass — careless spreading had left a dark green spaghetti-drawing on a field of yellow. He got a spreader and commenced to write a message in fertilizer on her rented lawn. But the bag was empty after the second word, and the *I LOVE* that appeared several days later was messy and lopsided, and read more like a saint's axiom than a corny guy's love note, and Leah laughed but wasn't roused in the larger way he'd intended.

Ten o'clock, Grey Street full of parked cars, a party. The cars mostly newer though nothing too luxurious. Their house was a pleasing old place not in overly tip-top shape. Something about it shaggy at the edges, though it was brick. Oscar, smiling and ironic at the door, said, "Big Bob Bonaduce!" Leah must have described him. What words would she have used, she who hadn't seen you in ten years, or loved you in twenty.

"You must be Oscar."

He seemed okay. He wore the constant smile-of-a-host, but his was gently wry, and he had a shagginess to him as well, a slight sloppiness that Bonaduce liked in friends, though he was never that way himself. Both of them were wearing jeans and a sweater, but Oscar's jeans were faded to weakness. He wore wire glasses, was getting bald, with the round face baldness gives. A deep, croaking voice for that small body.

And not an ounce of nerves. Apparently no fear of losing her back to the hockey guy.

"Your old wife's somewhere in that." Oscar hooked a thumb back toward the main crush of people. "Beer's in the fridge, everything else's on the counter. I fetch you your first one." He raised his eyebrows in question.

"I guess a beer. Thanks." Bonaduce was already looking in over Oscar's turning shoulder, and there she was.

Leah. Even the name. There she was. Even the word *she*, the way it divided the world in two. And then ripened and rose in the blood.

She was lifting a dipped mushroom to her mouth, tense in the shoulders, pretending not to have seen him yet. Her body as aware of his. Frightening how clearly his body remembered. Seeing her confirmed how exactly remembered. Her skin, its planes and hollows, both hidden and seen. The feathery hair on her neck. The way she held herself, even when relaxed every motion verging on the next, more than ready.

Panic in her shoulders told him she remembered as well. The only question was, would she hate him all over again for this?

Maybe this wasn't the only question.

She was wearing jeans too, and a fuzzy black sweater, mohair, the kind you'd get at a Used store, mildly campy and showy. A thin, almost invisible gold necklace draped her collarbone and then fell on into the sweater. A bit of makeup it looked like. Funny how they'd spent years and miles apart, but something of them had stayed front to front, talking loud and clear. The mushroom was in her mouth and she made as if to consider something as she began to chew. The choice of a mushroom wouldn't have been deliberate. She was staring off, composing herself, or revving up, one of those, because he could see that once she stopped chewing she was going to swing his way, lift her face and see him.

A teammate in Tulsa had a weird wife, weird in that she had written a book. Bonaduce learned it was self-published, but that didn't matter to anyone: Buddy Simon's wife had up and wrote a book. As Buddy described it, looking vaguely afraid, as if listening for something behind him, the book was about "ideas and philosophy and that." All the guys' wives or girlfriends received one at the Christmas skating party.

Maybe the weirdest thing about the book was that it was actually pretty good, pretty entertaining. Bonaduce relieved his jealousy scoffing Julie of her copy and thumbed through it, a collection of homespun theories about this and that, most attributed to local farmers and off-kilter thinkers and old almanacs. Why cows lie down before a storm, a talking albino crow, Native prophecies about drought and pollution, home remedies — one of which, the inside of a banana peel rubbed vigorously on a bee sting, the author herself had seen save an allergic teenage boy's life.

One idea, a few pages long, its source "a naturopathic healer in our general vicinity," made Bonaduce see himself, the distant Leah and twelve-year-old Jason in a new light.

The idea was that ideal mates were brought together by a combination of looks and gestures, and to a large degree smell. The result was that, when two compatible people got together, it felt like good sex. (Bonaduce provided some adjectives of his own: *dirty* sex, *breakfast-lunch-and-dinner* sex.) What the two bodies communicated via their smells and such was genetic compatibility, which would lead to superior offspring, kids strong of limb and agile of brain. (Buddy Simon's weird wife noted that "one might see a mix of both Darwin and Hitler in this view.") But the gist was that if Nature's purpose was the best baby, its slick lure was the best sex. Two naïvely compatible parents led blindly grunting along the path to procreation.

Lying on his latest couch in his latest apartment, reading this sex theory in Buddy's wife's book, two hours before a game, Bonaduce thought of Leah. It was no effort to remember her. Her body, with its imperfections that were perfect to him. The little gut, showing that her body knew how to enjoy itself. The fingers on the stubby side, but strong and curious. Thick ankles and calves, to better hold that body up for more curiosity, more pleasure. And her soft skin — her skin was the best, it was the place where giving pleasure and taking pleasure were one and the same thing.

Her eyes, her bright eyes. You looked in and saw she was smarter than you but also that this wasn't a bad thing. You could also see how she felt her body to be not quite hers, or not quite her. She could hold her body at arm's length. You could see she respected her body, but also that she saw it to be a kind of playground.

Smell — said Buddy's weird wife's book — was the key. Here he was in Tulsa and he could still smell Leah. Her body's *root*. Even now it made him ache. I would climb the highest mountain, swim the widest sea. The smell was urgency itself. Mixed with heartblood, and with grace. They'd been helpless with each other. The very first night they did it three times and, not that kind of girl, she hated him for it, as early as that. He knew even while inside her that in his life he'd feel nothing else like this. It took them a year to catch their breath and begin to suspect that their bodies had duped them.

Lying on the couch, considering this woman he hadn't seen in years, Bonaduce might have masturbated had Julie not been there in the kitchen, plus he had a game. He closed his eyes and pictured Jason. Perfect Jason. Healthy, tall Jason, possessed of that symmetry Nature indeed seemed to favour. With the hard Bonaduce jaw, and noble nose; with Leah's light hairlessness, slightly feline eyes, wide smooth face.

The times he did come through Fredericton and saw Jason, one problem was what the mother and the father did for a living. How it defined them. Nothing was ever said but there it was: Leah the social worker, helping refugees settle in the Maritimes. Aiding victims of war and torture, far from family and home, their lives ripped from them like skin. Leah's days were filled with their stories and, in retelling them, her heart was so overfull she would sometimes have to cry. On a few occasions she told them to Bonaduce, a man who had dedicated his life to working violently hard at preventing people with different-coloured uniforms from putting a puck in his net.

He'd be in town a single night, now playing for the visiting team, and before or after the game he'd drop by. Jason would be off having a snack or something while Leah cried about someone she'd met that day through her work, and Bonaduce would see as if in a mirror the trivial ugliness he represented. Hockey. It wasn't as if Leah was asking him to consider who was the right or wrong role model (there being no question), but rather which one of them Jason might want to follow in the way he lived his life.

When he visited it wasn't always clear what she was crying about.

He visited when Jason turned six. He'd been looking forward to talking with his son, reasoning with his growing boy, his kid, and he came away surprised at how naïve he'd been. The whole bus trip up he'd dreamed of what they'd do together, visions of skating on the river, himself showing off a little. Maybe a movie, he'd ask the mother. But they would definitely talk and talk, two guys wild about seeing each other. *Jason, I love you. Jason, what's it like being alive and six? What does life look like stretched way out like that in front of you? Hey, what's it like being my son? I'm sorry that I cannot live with you. You see, life is a tragedy for some. But we are connected by our blood and so it doesn't matter where or when we ...*

Jason looked at ease in the shades of olive and mauve Leah had dressed him in. Bonaduce smiled, no yellow and purple for this kid. Jason was also at ease seeing him, more excited in the gift of the toy ambulance than in his dad, then quickly pouty because the toy didn't take batteries or "do anything." Clearly, Leah, who had after an assessing pause in the doorway left them alone, hadn't done enough to prepare the lad as to the significance of this visit.

Bonaduce couldn't help staring at his boy's body, couldn't help the out-and-out butterflies at seeing how the little arms turned in their shoulder sockets, how the lungs puffed in and out, and how fast the kid scrambled under the bed and back, how he *knew* the tarantula gun was under there in that mess. And how quickly Jason's moods went screwy and sought only the silliest things. How what at first seemed a respect for adult stuff — yes, for *fatherly wisdom* — was nothing of the kind.

"Is lightning the biggest thing?"

They were in Jason's little sky-blue bedroom, Bonaduce sitting thrilled on the boy-sized bed.

"Nope. It's not."

"Gareth says it is."

"Well it's not."

"What's bigger?"

"Well ... air."

"No way."

"Well, it is. Air is way bigger. It—"

"Lightning could *kill* air."

There was nothing to say to this, and Jason waved the eight-barrel gun in the father's helpless face.

"If this had real bullets it still couldn't kill you."

"Really?"

"No way way way."

"What's your favourite season? Do you like winter?"

"No ... But bullets fit. Do you think if the bullets will fit it could kill you?"

"You don't like winter? No way! Don't you like Christmas? Playing hockey?"

"Know what I'm getting for my birthday? *Laser bullets*."

"Hey, good stuff. You know lasers, they're a kind of 'ray,' like a space— But your birthday's not for eight or nine mon—"

"Or night-vision goggles. Get me night-vision goggles for my birthday."

A mischievous laugh, looking the dad-man in the eye, aware of his own greed, doing exactly something Mom told him not to do.

"I'll send you a surprise, but it won't be night-vision goggles, so don't be dis—"

"I'm way stronger than you."

"You're probably right, big buddy. You — well — wait now — you probably shouldn't hit. You really — I mean it now—"

No doubt real fathers learned the key. But when did a kid start making sense? Bonaduce had no memories of being stupid himself.

But there were also times to cherish. It was never hard to find the good.

Jason was eight during the next visit, and it must have at some point occurred to him that his father was a pro athlete, because he dearly wanted to impress Bonaduce with what his body could do. His friend Luke had a tramp and Jason could do a flip, *C'mon and see me do it.*

It was late fall and it had snowed and Bonaduce couldn't imagine who would have left a trampoline out, but he borrowed Leah's car and turned corners where Jason pointed. Jason described his flip and variations of it, and then it became a double flip, and he was the fastest skater on his hockey team, and he could do lifters that sent the puck right over the net, almost taking the goalie's head off.

"But if you shoot it over the net, you can't score a goal," wise father explained, then instantly regretted it, seeing he'd tossed some damp into Jason's fire. It wasn't about scoring goals.

Nor was it about trampoline flips. After too many wrong turns, always followed by what Bonaduce came to see was a too-theatrical puzzlement on Jason's face — "Gee, I thought it was over *there*" — he realized they wouldn't be finding Luke's trampoline. And though he remained curious about whether Jason could in fact do a flip, he saw it wasn't the point and never had been. He was only mildly saddened that he had been following a route of Jason's untruths, that the boy had thought it necessary to go this direction to impress the father when it hadn't been necessary to go anywhere at all.

But it would be great, Bonaduce decided, it would be fucking great to have the time and place to get out and play hockey with his boy. Skate fast, take a goalie's head off, whatever. Everything, even standing up all wobbly, would be great. Holding hands through mitts, Jason glancing up at him, them gliding fast enough to scare him a bit, Jason's bright-eyed look full of body's pride and thrill. And it would be the one time they'd ever truly *share*, because what did kids really know — in fact what did people really know — other than the feelings in their bodies?

How many times, on a bus, with a guy, had the subject come up? How many countless quiet talks about getting married and having kids, wondering together about that kind of future? Most guys saw it as a given, and it turned out they were right. But how many times had Bonaduce sighed deeply and announced, "Well I've actually *got* a kid, up in Canada. He's seven now." Or eight now, or eleven now. The sigh before the announcement was a complex sigh, not just a sad one. There was even a bit of pride in it. Under its tone of melancholy at having fucked things up, there was also a hint of satisfaction that, because of this son's existence, life would never be empty. His son was no longer a little kid, he no longer had a kid's blind respect for feats of body so he no longer blindly respected Dad. He was being pummelled by adolescence, sussing out life's many green routes, alive to and aware of Bonaduce only in some unknown measure.

But how often had the *fact* of his son saved him from the depths. Thanks, Jason.

He understood it was the cheapest immortality any man had ever clung to. But there it was, a comfort.

• • •

He'd survived Leah's party. It was time to see Jason.

He'd been antsy all day with the good butterflies, those of spirit rather than fear, those that helped a sharp performance. Only amateurs aren't nervous.

This morning, feeling the phone in his hand, the black plastic against his head, he'd called. Timing it right, nobody home. He left a simple message: "Hey, I'm in town. See you later today at the rink."

But funny how his nerves were as much about hitting the ice this afternoon and playing some hockey as they were about seeing Jason. It was just that these young guys were going to be in top shape and Bonaduce wasn't. He'd gone for ten runs now, and public-skated three times at the Lady Beaverbrook. One leg laboured a bit, but you wouldn't call it a limp. He was almost over whatever it was. Doctors were the first to admit theirs was an inexact science. Hey, he was going to play with his boy, he was going to play for the Varsity Reds, he'd be charging out from behind the net, he'd spot Jace circling to split the defence, he'd send him in alone with a perfect bullet on the tape and Jace would score a fucking beauty and then with the rest of the guys gather smiling in a huddle on the bright white ice and Jason would whack Bonaduce on the ass like a buddy.

All these years he'd made little of the fact that there'd never been a divorce. That on paper he was still married to her and her to him. He'd mentioned it once in an early letter, offering her any route she wanted to go. But she never mentioned it back, and in the meantime you couldn't help but wonder why not. Women were generally so keen on clarifying anything to do with relationship status. Perhaps not Leah.

But why were they still married? She was Catholic but, except for the wedding, she'd not gone to church in the time he was with her and he couldn't fathom her being bound by those laws. Was it instead that she cared so little for the piece of paper that she couldn't be bothered? Had she married him in the first place to satisfy her parents, and him? A shrugging traipse through a dead institution? Leah was contemporary and left-leaning and this might indeed be the case. Did she care, had she cared, so little for the marriage in the first place that divorce didn't even occur to her?

Strange to think that the marriage meant either too much or too little for her to end it, and that he didn't know which.

Skates in hand, he stood twenty-five rows up in the stands and watched. He told himself this wasn't hiding. There was Jason down there flying around. Good strides, low centre of gravity, fast. Professional speed. Not great with the puck. Shitty shot, actually. But good sense of position, a decent head for the game.

All this took Bonaduce about a minute to see in his son. What was sad, this was his son's chosen career he was seeing and any scout would see just as quickly that this youngster didn't have the goods for the big league, or even the next-to-big league, the one the father had made. Father watched son swoop past a check but then lose the puck for no reason other than wooden-handedness.

He continued watching, mesmerized. The way Jason leaned on the boards, catching his breath. The way he turned to hear a buddy say something, nodded curtly, said nothing back. Bonaduce found himself thinking the words "Scorpio. Bedroom eyes. Soar like an eagle or crawl like a lizard." Then saw himself and Leah standing over their magic little son, Leah reading aloud about Scorpios from a book some friend had given her. Neither of them believed, though Leah seemed for the moment open to it, her new-mother's hunger for information of any kind. Still it was fun thinking of a one-month-old having bedroom eyes, or that he would grow up either noble or flirting with the ditch.

Hard to read someone from the way he played hockey, but the young man out there on the ice seemed maybe kind of bland.

He and Fournier used to mock this goalie, René Leblanc. Over two seasons they'd noticed Leblanc going over the other teams' programmes before games. Tightening his skates, he'd shout to his defencemen — "Hey, watch Peca, eh? Watch Peca, Peca an' Smythe, they gonna have good game. Stay on 'em." And after the game, if Peca or Smythe had scored, he'd give the guys shit. It turned out he had the whole astrology thing memorized, and by looking at players' birthdays he knew how they were supposed to do that night. After being found out, Leblanc eased off because Bonaduce and Fournier had taken to warning everyone that Number 6 had Pluto in Aquarium and he'd be throwing elbows tonight. Leblanc, a believer, did not crack a smile.

Bonaduce pivoted away from the pillar. Time to strap on the blades. Say hi to his young eagle down there. Time to do his Gordie Howe thing. He found the stairwell. It wasn't exactly a limp he was suddenly into, but he had to use the handrail and he had to laugh at the timing of how our bodies hate us. Pimples the night of the date.

In the lower corridor he searched for the Reds' dressing room. He had a notion. If the planets and whatnots actually did stamp a code on us, it wouldn't be at birth but at conception. The baby that came out pissed off and howling had obviously been long stamped, it'd been in there hiccuping and with its own style of punching Mom in the gut from behind. If you got stamped at all it was when you were a quivering single cell, a tender jelly wild with newness. Leah's parents used to embarrass her with their story of a train berth somewhere between Ottawa and Montreal, this her start. Two cells meeting in the middle of a rocky night. Nature's biggest deal, the merger of chromosomes, the trading fire for fire. Bonaduce couldn't remember the precise time of Jason's coming, but it would've been in Leah's old room there on Charlotte Street. He could picture the sky-blue room, the morning light through its small window. It could have been any night of many when something stamped the ooze that came to be Jason.

He rapped once and pushed in the dressing-room door. Liniment and sweat, it smelled like most. A young guy packing rolls of medical tape into a metal cabinet stopped to look at him.

"I'm Bob Bonaduce. I talked to Coach ah ... I guess the assistant coach. Said he had some gear for me?"

"You talked to me. And I forgot."

The trainer went to a locker and started pulling gear out. He tossed it on the floor in front of an empty stall and pointed to it. Then he startled with a thought.

"You cleared all this with the coach, right?"

Looking down, Bonaduce gave him the thumbs up.

Just like at every training camp, the nameplates above the stalls had been removed. Make the team, your name went up. They'd need initials this time. J. Bonaduce. B. Bonaduce. Where in this room would they seat themselves? Bonaduce would enjoy it side by side, but it might be too embarrassing for the boy. J. Bonaduce.

Hey, obviously Leah stayed married so Jace could keep the good name. "Jason Bonaduce" was a good hockey name. Though it wasn't a great hockey name. "Bobby Bonaduce" was a great hockey name.

Was it an accident so many great players had the great names? Short muscly ones, gold on the tongue: Bobby Orr. Bobby Hull. Syl Apps. Others, despite their names, hadn't made it to greatness: Bronco Horvath. Morris Titanic. Merlin Malinowski. Others, like himself, who despite the great name hadn't made it out of the minors: Hal Cabana. Vic Pitt.

In this working-man's poetics there was the perception that a "Jason" was either spoiled or rich. A kid named "Jason" had grown up with brand-new hockey gear, had gone to summer hockey schools. "Jason" was almost grounds for other teams to run at you, or for your own coach to bench you at any hint of you being lazy, or selfish with the puck.

The gear was stiff with someone's old sweat. Blood swelled in his face when he bent to his skates. He couldn't quite work his right ankle, nor did the toes on that side have their power. Hey Jace, how ya doin there, thought I'd come out for a dangle.

He himself was a Leo. Leos can purr or they can roar, but they're best at shining quietly, knowing they are admired.

Leah, delicious Leah, there at the food table, nibbling. He joined her and it was the two of them chewing away, food to nourish their bodies, they'd always loved eating together. Damned if this wasn't also like seeing your best old friend. You hit a certain age and you find certain judgements have worn away or gone underground. Nibbling, happily pressed close together by the crowd, they talked about nothing serious. You're looking well. Nice house you have here, is that oak? Beside him her body. The small paunch. Her skin. He pictured her twenty years ago wearing his leather Express jacket, way overlarge, like wearing her big fella's own tough protective skin, in the manner of Fifties sports guys and their gals. Much more aware than him that it was the Seventies, she'd humoured him. He did like her in it. Maybe she'd liked it a little too, though he remembered her erect posture in it, her look of patience and independence.

For Oscar's sake he tried not to stare at her. Good pâté, he said, nodding as he chewed, though he'd never been wild about organ meat. She laughed and told him, Guess what? She was vegetarian now. And they both laughed perfectly, knowing without saying that it had gone from dog food to this. He'd never forget it, he'd known her all of two weeks, catching her spooning it right out of the can into that cute little face. Leah horrified at being caught, but Bonaduce had felt strangely touched, not because he'd found a weakness but because something in this ultra carnality was akin to her hunger in bed, a horniness which felt so good to be a party to. Plus, Leah being refined, and petite — well, dog food was a contradiction that deepened her immensely. During that evening twenty years ago she came to know him enough that she could laugh about it. A few months later she said that telling him — he was the only one she'd ever told — had helped her drop it, her weird craving. After a year she reported in all seriousness that she was down to the occasional Gainsburger, which she ate more or less out of nostalgia.

Vegetarian now. He shrugged and she shrugged back, as if saying to each other, *Of course* apples become oranges.

"A minor shift from the Alpo diet." He pointed at the carrot she turned in the dip.

"My history is *not* for public consumption." The hissed mock-panic, a nudge of the shoulder into his chest.

But it thrilled him that maybe Oscar didn't know.

"You know Jason is too?"

"What, vegetarian?"

"It was actually him who got me into it." She went ironic, sounding just like Oscar. "I mean, the kids these days."

"Jesus, why?" He wanted to say "how." How do you play vegetarian hockey? His body felt sure that no meat meant a lack of something powerful.

"I think there's something moral going on. But I don't know what came first. He just stopped eating it, around fifteen, said he couldn't stand the taste. Except for chicken in Chinese food, then that went too. So how long are you in town for?"

"You still drink? Can I get you a beer or something?"

Leah stayed put while he sidestepped and squeezed his way to the kitchen. Oscar was there, laughing and chatting, and it was weird drawing a beer out of his fridge for his girlfriend.

A woman friend was talking to Leah in low tones when Bonaduce arrived back. Eyes down, half-smile, she zipped away pretty quickly. He wondered what, exactly, the talking was about. Ex-hubby hockey guy. Leah's Jason's daddy back in town. There was a rich and tangy high-school taste to all of this.

"I've moved here."

"You—" Her face quickly shut off, became unreadable. "Did you get traded again? Traded here?"

"No, hell. I've retired. Actually ..." He'd decided beforehand to be perfectly straight with her because she would find out in any case. And there was the chance she'd be an ally. "I'm going back to school, a master's degree. You know, English."

No response. Beautiful Leah, paused with celery stick. Unable to decide what dip, or wishing her celery was metal, sharpened.

He'd said "English" with a respectful weight he wanted her to hear. Sure, he wanted her to think of him in other than hockey terms, why not. But also he had changed his mind about English. Something good had happened in his bathroom that evening, him sitting there with *Hamlet*, the wet flames of swampwater crawling the wall beside his leg.

Arriving in Fredericton he'd been prepared to defend preconceptions of his violence and stupidity by mocking English literature itself. Hey, it's nothing special you're doing. In fact it's perverse. Your face in the blinders of a book, indulgently gorging on words despite this dying world, the starving masses. Someone you know is gasping in the terminal wing and you sit reading *Lady Windermere's* fucking *Fan*.

In the bathroom he'd thumbed the paperback *Hamlet*, remembering maybe liking it back in high school. Sitting on the toilet, free of any pressure, free of having to do something *with* the stuff — maybe that was why it clicked. How could you not be cowed? Here you were perfectly described, here you were crawling between heaven and earth, a dirt-bound angel. Caught helpless by the demands of heaven, yet helplessly mired in earth's crude gravities. Animal stink wafting up between your legs. Noble yet snuffling along for the next sandwich. Dull angel or special dog, take your pick.

This deepened the way he said "English." He wanted to free Leah of her celery and meet her eye and explain to her his new feelings about it. How our struggle can feel only tedious until someone like Shakespeare renders it worthwhile, and for their good words we must thank writers everywhere. English. You read *because* people are in the terminal wing and your turn is coming. Maybe you even read *Lady Windermere's Fan*.

"Why here, Bobby?"

"Well, the whole thing's wacky, but I'm going to play hockey here too, with UNB. With Jason."

This got her. Tucking back, giving herself a double chin, she began shaking her head. "Well that's ... that's ... I don't know ..."

"What don't you know?"

"What to think. For one." She managed a little smile.

"Jason doesn't know what to think yet either — I haven't told him." Tiniest of jokes. "So, could you maybe not, you know, if you see him ..."

"Hey."

Leah put both hands up as if warding off the food table. She wouldn't look at him. In the side of her eye he saw a flash hinting at what might be her reservoir of anger.

"He's an adult. You can both do whatever you want."

Funny, the last bit. Father and son as co-conspirators. Her uncontrollable boys. Bonaduce wasn't at all unhappy that she summed up the situation in this way.


Standing at centre ice with the coach, Bonaduce registered the instant Jason spotted him. It now became intensely difficult trying to talk some sense into this young fellow Whetter when you knew that, over your shoulder, catching his breath after a drill, the long-lost son was staring at you in bewilderment and who knows what else. He tried to listen to Whetter while sneaking sidelooks at Jason, whose plumes now gradually quieted. The lad was a plugger even in practice. Bonaduce shot him a wink he maybe didn't see.

"Thing is, our first game's in a week and a half." Whetter had his elbow cocked, whistle ready in his hand. He kept shaking his head, kept toeing a pylon with the point of his skate. He had on four-, five-hundred-dollar skates. Why did coaches need the best skates? Up top he wore glasses, and looked like a broad-shouldered accountant.

"You're not in shape and—"

"*Game* shape, no."

"—and the guys have been at it since August, dedicated from the start, and cuts were made a month ago ..."

Whetter let the last bit rest, content with bureaucratic cowardice.

"You gonna make the playoffs?"

You hated saying such an arrogant thing, but time was awasting. Almost smiling, Whetter gave him a *touché* look, point taken. Bonaduce shrugged. The shoulder pads were too small and the helmet rode up too high. He whapped at it with his glove, then threw his head to his left shoulder, popping the vertebra that had been getting stuck since he couldn't remember.

Jason wouldn't come over as long as he stood talking to the coach.

"Bob, the other thing, maybe the only thing, is the pro rule."

"The pro rule."

"The sitting out a year."

"The what?"

"A pro comes back to school — it does happen — they have to sit a year out, don't ask me why."

Bonaduce felt the cold sweat of foolishness break out. He didn't respond because he couldn't.

"So first we have to find out if Utica — East Coast League, right? — if Utica constitutes pro."

"Of course it fucking constitutes pro." Now feeling himself turn red.

"Well okay, and if that's the case, you sit. A year before eligibility."

Say something. Focus. Ineligible? It was a creeping, bureaucratic word, nothing to do with this game. The hockey he knew, the best guys played, the others sat.

"Actually I wasn't playing, I haven't played since last

December. I was injured. So — hey — maybe I'll be eligible in December."

"If you were still under contract I doubt it but—"

"Well actually the contract got all screwed up too. So maybe I'm free to play. The owner, this unbelievable sleaze, he just—"

"But anyway, hey, we'll get everything checked."

Whetter turned, bringing the whistle to his lips and saying, without looking at Bonaduce, "If you're ineligible you can't practise with us either, we'd get dinged. Get the gear off."

Whetter blew the whistle hard three times, skating away from him.

Hard not to move his body, dance around, as he waited in the concrete tunnel outside the dressing room. Hard not to plot hellos, hugs. It was all so—

Jason. Here he was, coming out through the door with a smile already set, breathless, flushed in the face. He stopped five feet away. Steam rising off his soggy longjohns in the slight cold.

"So what the hell," he said, almost yelling, much of Leah in his smile, "what the hell was *that*? A cameo? What you doing in town?"

It sounded rehearsed, but now they shook hands easily. Jason had become more slick in performing the rite than however many years ago it was Bonaduce had last had this pleasure, this hand in his.

The father smiled back. He should speak, but found himself taking in the son's lanky body, the shoulders not so wide, Leah's shoulders, they could take some added muscle and he'd still be mobile — he hadn't peaked, he could do more. Weight training, he'd make a decent power forward, bash the corners, crash the net, you don't need the good hands.

"Well, actually I thought I'd stay the year."

"Wow, no kidding!"

Bonaduce — as casually as he could, shrugging and smiling

with self-deprecation, leaving out all medical news — explained his plans.

At first Jason said, "Really?" Then in the clutch of nervous laughing his eyes pulled away and something bubbled up in his tight gut — you could see it — and buckled his spine. Jason's stuttering inbreath filled the hall with his confusion. The boy just standing there, yet moving so fast. Looking at his father he brought a clawed hand up as if cradling and juggling a ball, a very Italianate gesture. Bonaduce could see Jason's grandmother in this.

Trying to laugh the same laugh again, Jason couldn't look at him now. Nor could he speak. His face went a new red.

Speechless and in trouble himself, Bonaduce watched his son spin away for the dressing room, double-palming the door with more violence than he'd shown on the ice.


That night, for the first time in his new home, he broke out the guitar. Slow picking, with interludes of languid strumming, at his feet a case of beer. At some point into the room came Margaret, Rod, Toby, and some other guy whose name he did not catch. They heard some Bonaduce versions of blues standards, some Howlin' Wolf stuff. They were patient with and then mocking of his dip into country, which was fine with him because humour went well with the genre, and Toby knew a few and warbled mockingly along. They were briefly intrigued when, beer done and time to think about bed, he dug deeper into his time-bag for Muddy Waters, then way back to Woody Guthrie, the room falling quiet for the simple good politics. Or maybe everyone had left. When he looked up and saw that all but him and the roaring Maui surf trucks had found their way to bed, he started his secret string of tunes from that alltime hardcore ragtop heartbreaker, Roy Orbison. And damned if Bonaduce didn't lose a tear or two, there at the end, head down, the candle casting a light less sad than perfect in the way it put a glow on the front of the guitar.

II

Societies differ mostly in how each culls its herd.
—F.A. d'Amboise

*Why* kill yourself to win? Sure as fuck not for me.
And not for the fuckin' money in *this* league. *It's the guys*. Look
at each other. Look around. *That's* why we put the fuckin'
biscuit in the basket. *Now get out there*.
—Coach Murray Murphy, Tulsa Oilers

MARGARET.

At the sink she repotted plants. Like so many other jobs in this house, this was hers by default. (She wondered, trying not to be too judgemental about her roommates, whether it was more a case of "not noticing" than "letting things die.") One plant (mother-in-law's tongue?) was all roots, pale clean roots woven tight, shaped exactly like a pot. Amazing how it survived, just on water, with maybe the decay of its own skin as nourishment. She should stick it, potless, back on the windowsill, see if anyone noticed.

Her back was to him and, because of last night, as he brushed past she half-expected a pat on the rear or some sexual tease. He looked the sort but apparently wasn't. He was a kind she really hadn't known before, a boomer who hadn't done the hippy thing or the business thing but instead had played sports. He seemed the least Sixties of anyone in this house, which was ironic, him being the only one alive at that time. All the same there was a sort of restless *On the Road* feel to him — she'd read Kerouac in Hawaii — but you weren't talking Sixties now, you were talking Fifties. Beats, the boys' club of the day, bunch of dads gone wild. There was also something about Robert more basically Fifties: you could see him with slicked hair behind the wheel of a smooth rod with stuffed dice dangling from the mirror and deep purple hoor-lures framing the back window. It was effortless to see him so. His smile, a smoke or toothpick in the James Dean mouth.

The dreamcatcher, he'd thanked her but joked about it, how this fancy new air freshener didn't smell hardly at all. When he saw she took it a bit seriously, and after she explained the psychology of it — how knowing it's in the room can trigger lucid dreaming — he seemed to reconsider. He wanted to know if it could affect luck. In fact now he seemed a bit in awe of it. The man's been out of the picture for a while.

It wasn't like someone's father living here, but it was close. The creased pants and polite manners and constant corny announcement of his limit of two-drinks-a-night, though after dusk he sometimes slurred. His lame "Time to hit the books, eh?" and then you could hear him snoring through his closed door. The others were still a little mad at her for renting the room to him, unable to kick all the way back with a guy like that around. Until his helpful ways and that goofy guitar night showed his harmlessness. That and the fact that he spent so much time in his room. He seemed generally tired.

But he didn't belong. Where did a Robert Bonaduce belong? In this he was a mirror for her because she was hanging on in this house by a thread herself. This house out on the highway, the traffic roaring east or west without doubt, and her life lacking any direction. The bare halls and rooms felt like a stage upon which she was acting out her limbo-life: between men, between jobs, between journeys. It was unhealthy to be banking on memories of Hawaii, to be nostalgic at twenty-four. She was at the wrong university to service her fading passion for archaeology. Which was probably good because she'd been understanding that bones and such were maybe best left buried, and that to search backwards in time was exactly what she should not be doing. In that school of thought, the whole world was a crypt.

When he'd driven up looking to rent, Rod had huddled with her and laughed, No way, looks like some sort of mafia guy. She'd shrugged and said, So what? Her whim was to give the house some range. Bonaduce might be a spark, a bit of colour. And a practical joke, why not. Rod's I-can't-believe-you're-going-to-jump-his-bones look put exactly that idea in her head and made Robert doubly interesting. Maybe a bizarre romance, Christ, who knows. He was old but in a dented way cute, and a grad student in literature, so smarter than he looked. He would have stories to tell.

As it turned out he would keep his stories to himself. Behind the corny cheer he carried a weight. He'd sit staring in the living room, then grin hiyas and howdys when he saw you. He worked his face a lot when people were near. Good in public, bad alone. Her opposite.

Toby didn't like him, but at least there was some strange respect. *Grudging* would be the word. In a way they were similar, stuff going on underneath they tried to hide. Indirect. Toby was funny with his new description for Robert every morning. "He's Moose, Reggie, Archie and Jughead all in one." Or, "He's what I would have been were it not for drugs." Hilarious him straight-faced saying that, his tiny body a hundred pounds less, his withered arm. Robert could tuck him behind an ear like a pencil.

Robert must have had some fine injuries — he'd grab his feet or legs as if to check that they were there. She caught him punching himself in the foot and he made a madman joke of it, punching calf, knee, thigh, tongue hanging out. He could be funny. Some days he limped and bumped hallway walls. He didn't like to talk about hockey unless to run an anecdote by you for the novel he's planning.

Then last night he came to her. It was way after midnight. He asked softly at the door if she was awake. He sat on the end of the bed. It felt fine that he'd come. He was shy. They both dropped their joking and she welcomed this. She tucked up her legs to make room, but then slid a foot back to tickle his thigh through the covers, she didn't know why, didn't know if she wanted this from him yet, or ever. The physical part alone might be okay, because he didn't seem selfish, and he had a worldliness and humour. But it seemed very likely that he'd go gushy on her. Thinking she needed that. And thinking he meant it.

He seemed not to feel her toe's welcome. Then, destroying

all romance within a million miles, he asked, How close do you feel to your parents? At first she tried it out as a joke, a Groucho Marx sexual thing and a way to acknowledge their ages, but he didn't smile or waggle his eyebrows. Jughead Archie Reggie and Moose had asked her a serious question.

She thought a moment, then told him she couldn't put it into words. She apologized for being so lousy with words, thinking how he must always get that apology, being in English. He said she was great with words, and asked other questions: Did she think it was automatic for a child to love a parent even if the child didn't see the parent much. Did she love one parent more than the other. Animals were connected by smell and such — did she think humans had anything like that as well.

She spoke her thoughts to him for what they were worth. She didn't ask why he was asking. It was pretty obvious he had a kid somewhere. One thing she said made him stiffen and fall silent. What she said was, "There're plenty of assholes out there, and lots of them are parents," but she'd only been talking about her own situation. She worked her toe harder to get him out of his worry.

"You have a kid?"

"I do. Yes."

"You're not an asshole, Robert."

"Not to you."

"I doubt it's even possible."

"Oh it is," he said, and in the dark she could hear him shift his shoulders, could hear his tired smile. "I contain multitudes."

An old hockey guy, quoting what was probably literature.

§

In the department lounge someone whose name he didn't know had invited him to Rye's Pub, see you there. So now Bonaduce —

get out of that sleepy little room for a change — found himself downtown in a bar, celebrating some guy named Murray's oral defence of his PhD being over and done with. Kirsten and Phil and others whose names he didn't know had claimed tables. Some surprise at seeing him. Sure, he didn't know Murray, or his "thesis area," or exactly what an "oral defence" was — if the subject came up he would resist his joke about spitting. Something in the air had told him that grad-student socializing was encouraged, which was not a bad thing at all, hang together. Maybe as the bar was closing they'd get in a brawl with those History bastards over there.

His mood was definitely better. He'd decided Jason didn't hate him, nor was it a snub. Jason was shocked. What else could you expect? He'd basically abandoned the boy. A beaming, *Hey! Great, Dad!* from a dumb-knob son would've been unnatural and disappointing. This setback showed Jason's dark depths. What parent wanted a child who was uncomplicated?

He was good at patience. Maybe there was nothing he was better at. Though let's not bring up the pathetic side of this, his twenty years in the minors waiting patiently by the phone.

Eventually Murray arrived, accompanied by Professor Daniel Kirk, who was Murray's thesis supervisor and who Bonaduce hoped wouldn't remember him, for he hadn't yet made it to class. People shouted and raised glasses to Murray. Murray was a homely tall-and-lanky, like a weed that towered over the garden. He looked myopic behind his glasses, perhaps partially blind, lenses thick as porcelain. He smirked cynically by way of general greeting. Bonaduce had the sense of Kirk trying not to look his way, which was good, let's both do that. And they both did, though when Kirk sat they had only Murray between them.

It proved a strange little time. A poor team party. Half of them left after a single beer. After the one bland toast there was a jerkiness to any conversation, a lack of tone or build. The table-talk broke into shadowy murmuring pockets, Murray not even in one. Bonaduce felt bad for him, though as the minutes crawled by and from Murray's few blurts he came to suspect that Murray was an unliked loner and the cause of this rhythmlessness to begin with.

It took Murray ages to get his first beer halfway down, at which point Bonaduce ordered him a second. When it came, instead of a thank you, Murray glanced at it with what looked like annoyance. He dutifully poured some into his glass, glugging the beer from straight over-top so the foam rose fast and some spilled.

"In Germany the mugs are tapered at the top. Which" — Murray demonstrated with his hands as God might squeeze a volcano top to contain the eruption — "quells the climbing head."

"Ah." Bonaduce smiled. "So you did the beerfest?"

His damaged recall of his own Munich visit didn't include tapered mugs. Maybe he hadn't made it to the classier tents. Murray turned his head to him but didn't look up from the table.

"I haven't been to Germany, but I collect."

"Ah."

"My father travels. He gifts me with steins."

This was pretty good, *gift* as a verb, one of the better ones in the new language he'd been learning here. Other verbs he didn't like so much. *Dialogue*. Let's dialogue. Hell, why not get Sally and trialogue. Eight of us at Murray's lousy party, octaloguing away.

He went to the bathroom, to urine. Coming out, wondering if he shouldn't just go home, a waitress gave him a stern look and asked if he'd washed his hands. She was good, her coy smile delayed just right. She was attractive enough to make the joke racy and it all a bit exciting. Late-twenties, countryish, maybe a little wild. "Coral," said her name tag. How to answer. Coral, no, I didn't, I thought you liked them dirty. Coral, could you come and show me how.

He looked witlessly down at his hands for her. "You mean these?"

She made to snap him on his ass with her tea towel. She'd made it all a little dance, already moving off and smiling at the next guy.

Another one or two had left. Murray was talking loudly, to Kirk.

"—no. It's not racial, it's cultural. The reason there are no philosophers from the equator is because they allow *desire*."

"Nonsense."

"They have sex at puberty! What more could you want? What's left! What's left to puzzle at after that! You net fish for the kids to eat! Think about it for God's sake."

Murray was actually fairly funny. Ballsy too. Here he was lecturing Kirk, professor. Now he turned to Bonaduce to lecture him as well, though Bonaduce could see from the eyes swimming in their lenses and staring past his ears that he could have been anybody.

"*We* sit up in the northern climes, *squeezed* with unfulfilled craving. Of all kinds. So what we do is sit and *think*."

"But education has its—" Kirk began.

"No. As long as we continue to privilege restraint, restraint over pleasure, we will remain, as it were, 'philosophical.' And they will remain childlike and happy, happily non-abstract. They do what they *want*, for God's sake."

What are you thinking, trying to fit in with these types. *Privilege* as a verb now.

Coral came by to empty ashtrays and wipe their table with her snapping-towel. Her manner was a bit theatrical, knowing she was being watched by the likes of Bonaduce and whoever else. Wiping in his direction, she leaned over so far that — hey, she was probably only doing her job but it was the kind of thing you can construe as an invitation.

Nothing was clear tonight. The heav'ns felt rotten, or something. When Murray left — big stein-expert man making it through almost two beers in one sitting — those who remained started jabbering about him like he was some sort of genius. Murray was squeezed all right, just like Kirsten and Phil and all these guys, thinking so hard and long they'd thought themselves into some fancy corners. From the sounds of it they were in awe of Murray (well then why weren't they nice to him?) because he'd "tossed off" his thesis while working harder on his real interest, which was a journal.

"I heard him refer to it as his" — Kirsten dropped her voice to a whisper — "his 'commentaries.'"

"He's been prolific as hell," said Phil, with the most respect Bonaduce had seen from him. "Three volumes." He shook his head in amazement. "Three volumes."

"How long has he been journaling?" Kirsten asked, her airy teeth for once looking more beaverish than judgemental.

"Since coming to Fredericton. Five years."

*Journaling.* This was getting good. *To journal. To beer.* Let's really beer tonight. Hey: *to verb.* Let's verb another noun.

The only question here was why did these supposedly smart folks admire a guy who wasn't thirty who'd never been to Germany or anywhere else, yet who was insane enough to have written three volumes of what was for all intents a fucking autobiography? "Prolific" just means you don't get out enough. Three books about himself. Sitting in a fevery hunch in the library, in love with his own brain and chewing at it like a worm. Egoing like crazy.

Coral swept by again, giving Bonaduce a look, knowing that at this dead table she had a good audience in one at least. She made as if to dab at her forehead with her little towel — Whoo ain't I hot an' workin' hard? — and giving it some sexiness to boot. Then gone, smiling at the next table, good at it and knowing how to have an okay time at a shitty job. Coral was a trueheart and a relief. He could handle a Coral.

He could Coral all night long.

· · ·

## Post Game
### by R. Bonaduce

After violently winning that night, they went to the strip club. Canary Singh, a wiry little centerman not born in this country, but part of the Asian hockey diaspora, sat a row back of the action, while the other guys had their usual handhold on the beaver rail. Their hoots and hollers occasionally brought Singh's head up out of his newspaper and cup of tea.

"Hey buddy! Hey Canary!" a few guys eventually called out to him. "What ya think of *those*?" They hooted and pointed in glee at the bounteousness of Darling Doctor Gail, two parts of whom were looming over them.

"Well, I think that those would feed a great many people in my country," said Canary Singh, gently rolling his head like they do.

Those of the guys that heard this stopped smiling and instead looked slightly sickened.

"'Tis not a mysterious thing, these entertainments of yours," Canary continued, sitting up now and pointing at Gail. "The bull is but of course made stiff at the sight of the sacred, what, the sacred *oo*ders? ooders of the cow. And just as it is with the cobra, in its rising to—"

A fist knocks Canary Singh's face out of the picture, and another fist flashes through but you can only hear the smack. The guys turn back to Doctor Gail.

Rolling his head more slowly, fingering the stitches under his eye, which had been sewn in just that night but now were popped, Singh picks himself off the floor, spits some gore and a coupla teeth onto the butt-burned carpet, flips open his paper again, hoping his buddies haven't gotten any of his blood on the sports pages. His name is in the summaries tonight. Two assists. He always sends the summaries home to a cousin in Calcutta.

. . .

Marg had offered him the loan of her laptop, leaving it here in the living room. With a hundred books to read and family relations to repair, he'd opened the thing, shaking his head at the foolhardiness of deciding to begin his novel, a project he wasn't supposed to even think about for a year. And as if he'd still be here.

The beers from the PhD party had him a bit goofy, and any serious intention was gone by the time he got the machine figured out and the title tapped down. Years ago he'd played a few months with a guy named Singh, an arrogant bastard. Singh had been both a fighter and a lech, a cruel loudmouth in strip bars. It was fun to turn him into Canary. The rest of what he wrote made him smile, dumb as it was, the fault of another beer and the echoes of Gail Smith's class that morning.

The second class hadn't gone any better than the first and he verged on dropping the course. Or having it dropped for him, the more likely scenario. He had to find out if taking only two courses kept his student status full enough to let him play for the Reds. He also had to maintain a certain grade. He should find out what that grade might be.

His little quip this morning hadn't helped. They were hashing out the "diaspora" definition again, arguing whether certain names on the reading list deserved to be there. While it was gratifying that no one else appeared to like Gail Smith either (in the lounge he had heard Phil whisper acidly that "Smith's reading list is nothing but whimsical"), the day's discussion was another round of grand language and hooded spite.

Bonaduce made two contributions. Neither his first, "Well, a good book's a good book," nor his second, "Hey: we're all just mutts from away," seemed to secure his position as worthy participant.

It was really too bad about Smith's class because he did like Canadian lit. During the long and scattered path to his BA he'd managed to find CanLit courses in, of all places, Kalamazoo, from the sound of which you'd expect courses in Popeye, or Aztec Cooking, not books by Canadians. During the classes he'd decided not to pull rank by revealing his nationality. But he felt he had insights into the material that the others lacked. Reading her novel, he'd felt a shovel-the-snow kinship to Atwood, though her tough-shit sharpness made him nervous; and to Davies, though he was a stuffed shirt. But you could just tell they'd both shovelled driveways.

And Leonard Cohen, his CanLit favourite. You couldn't quite picture Lenny shovelling out a driveway, or even having a driveway, but here was someone who knew the body and its deepblood longing, and he wasn't afraid to sing it into sweet words, hard for a guy. He could have been Irish-Italian. He even looked Irish-Italian.

The first time he came "home" and walked in on their game he thought he'd lost it, thought he'd left his brain in class. Going about their domestic business — which for Toby meant lounging, for Rod reading, and for Marg and her sister cooking while washing enough dishes to eat off of — his housemates conducting a conversation that went like this:

"Lobster trap," Toby said, for some reason.

After a moment's hesitation, Marg said, "Handicapped parking."

"The concept," said Rod, focused on his book, "I'm struggling with."

"Hell," offered Marg's sister.

To which Toby shouted, "Nope!"

Marg's sister, slouching in thought, stirred spaghetti sauce, looking a bit nervous. "Heaven!" she said next.

"Better," said Toby, "but, nope. Heaven's still a concept. C'mon."

Marg's sister looked angry now. "Fuck!" she tossed at him. "Cunt!" she added in defiance, while Toby, supercilious, nodded at her.

Toby settled grandly back. "Some of the Flemish painters," he announced.

"Let's stop growling," said Marg.

Toby and Rod looked at Marg, then at each other, in some sort of agreement.

"His future varicose vein operation," said Rod, nodding toward Bonaduce.

"Hiya," said Bonaduce.

"Howdy," said Marg's sister.

"Nope, nope, nope," said Toby.

Not looking up, Rod asked Toby, "Nope, what? Nope 'Hiya'?"

"'Hiya' was fine. Nope 'Howdy'."

"I was saying hello," Marg's sister explained. "Don't insult me."

"*That's* better," deemed Toby.

"Brad Pitt's bum," said Marg's sister, to which Toby closed his eyes and subtly shook his head, for some reason not pleased but deciding to let it go. Toby had lately begun to make Bonaduce think of a hamster cage. The seedy hair and the way it fell, and the frayed collar, and the colour of his skin, gave you the combined feel of dank and dusty shavings.

Understanding now that this was a game which, at a minimum, involved coming up with something weird, Bonaduce decided he was up for some fun. He was decent at weird. He jumped in.

"Trained hamster you keep tied by a string around your neck that's trained to, whenever you start choking on a chunk of food, it goes down your throat and eats whatever's stuck."

The housemates looked at one another for a moment, then explained to Bonaduce the notion of "non sequitur," how you had to say something that absolutely didn't fit. There could be no connection at all. Even opposites didn't work, because they had the connection of being opposite.

"And make it short," added Toby.

"Toby? Was that your turn?" asked Marg's sister.

"Was that yours?" Toby answered back.

Bonaduce had another go, answering a pretty good "Kangaroo high-jump record" to Marg's "Is the Lord's Prayer punctuated?"

But then he sidled off to his room, to read. No wonder these guys were good at irony — they came home at night and *practised*. They worked out like pros. They had non sequitur relationships, lived non sequitur lives. They even had a non sequitur diet: doughnuts, tofu, fresh basil, moonshine. Bonaduce recognized now why he'd found them in some way smarter even than the grad-school types: not giving a shit about normal stuff, like conversation, gave you a sort of intimidating power.

In the days to come the game continued on and off, in spurts, and Bonaduce understood that he'd been witness to earlier versions of it but hadn't cottoned on. You never quite knew when it might start. The next morning, in fact, he was in the kitchen putting on his shoes to this scene:

"Any of that left?" Rod asked, gesturing to the frypan Toby held with his good hand while scooping out bacon with his bad. The room reeked of old oil and scrambled egg.

"Tuesday," Toby answered.

"Melanoma," said Rod.

"I wasn't doing it," said Toby.

"Clinton didn't resign eventually," offered Rod.

"*I wasn't doing it. Tuesday. We have nothing. We shop tomorrow. Tomorrow is Tuesday. Today we eat shit. He*" — Toby pointed at Bonaduce — "*ate the last egg.*"


Quit your fooling around. Quit your moaning. Get off your ass.

One shoe on, pause, breathe, take a gander out the window

— Mr. Neighbour should really paint that old trailer of his — pull on the other shoe, work at getting that frayed lace licked and in and through that damned eyelet. Time's a'wastin'.

It all comes down to, what do you accomplish within the clumsy grab of the day. What do you do between the calloused hands of dawn and dusk. What do you need, and find, and use. The squeeze is on.

You could say it's a duty, either to others or to yourself. But a duty all the same.

Oscar Devries answered the door, waved him in, and as he ran upstairs shouted something about Leah being called out on an emergency, just make yourself at home.

Bonaduce removed his shoes and wandered into the living room. A Beatles song was on, but he noted an odd roughness to John's voice, then a harmony that shouldn't be there, then laughter — it was an outtake, this must be one of those anthologies. Great, let's hear it. The party here a few weeks back, he recalled the wafts of music, old British-invasion stuff: Animals, Who, some Kinks you didn't normally hear. Now some connoisseur Beatles. He liked Oscar even more. This was a friendly house, a sweater dropped in the very middle of the living-room floor, and three dirty cups and orange peels on the coffee table.

He sat deeply into the couch and took note of his old man's sigh. Man he was tired ... *Of course you will find that fatigue is the biggest day-to-day impediment* ... and this fight was not the good fight, because the enemies were big and shadowy and there were too many to see. He put his feet up on the coffee table, nudged a cup with a toe and wondered if he would fall asleep here in his wife's house.

He might have. Last he remembered he was really liking an *a capella* version of "Because," and now here was Oscar coming in with coffees, and the cups at his feet were gone.

Leah had been called away to a church in Sussex, where a

Guatemalan family, facing deportation, had last week taken illegal refuge. The little daughter had developed a fever and earache, and they'd wanted Leah's help, only Leah's, in getting a prescription filled.

"It's after hours, it's Sussex." Oscar shook his head, blowing into his coffee. "We can assume our Leah's having a red-tape kind of day."

Our Leah.

"So I'll call her tonight, set up another time?"

"No, she called and said she'd be back soon. She wants you to wait. She apologized profusely." Oscar smiled. "Actually, she didn't apologize. Nothing comes between her and their suffering. Her priorities are clear."

"Guess you can't blame her."

"Oh, I manage to." Oscar keeping up the smile.

The coffee was the strongest Bonaduce had ever tasted. Why did it feel odd to find out that Leah had ended up with a nice guy? Kind, with pleasant wise-ass tendencies. Balding and shortish like an Oscar should be, but also not caring about this, an Oscar worth his salt. Bonaduce felt revved up in his presence, could easily fall into friendship with this guy. Jesus, what would Leah make of that?

"Actually, she was on the news last night. Did you see it?"

Bonaduce shook his head.

"They mostly interviewed the father, who was typically tearful and amazed at our Canadian hospitality, and then there was Leah, large as life. They let her have a few sentences. She came off quite well."

"Hey, did you tape it?"

"I should have."

Proud Oscar. Leah the celeb. Bonaduce recalled the times in Fredericton they'd watched him on local sports highlights and a couple of times interviewed after games, major five-o'clock shadow, sweaty hair plastered to his forehead. Him wincing to see and hear himself, Leah joking not to worry, last week Tony the goalie had sounded even stupider. And there was the time he'd propped up a football-sized baby to see the screen. *Look, Jace! Look, Jace! See Daddy's pass?*

The Beatles finished and Oscar went to the CD rack. Bonaduce had come to talk to Leah about Jason, to see if the boy had said anything. To solicit Leah's help. At least advice.

"Any preferences?" Oscar asked, flicking plastic against plastic.

"Well, I'm definitely into the old stuff too. I liked what I heard at your party. Hey — so anything." He paused. "So how well you know Jason there, Oscar?"

Oscar was into a drawer of cassettes and he held up a hand for Bonaduce to wait. He popped one in, made some equalizer adjustments, and on came "Here Comes the Night."

"Hey. Early Van."

"You know it?"

"Sure, it's great. 'Them.'"

They sat and listened for a moment, attuned as much to the other man's listening as to Van Morrison's young throat hitting its raspy limits on the chorus.

"The Brit guys were pretty innocent, eh?" Bonaduce offered. "They all did the big attitude." Acknowledging Van's Irishness would only complicate things here.

"Sorry, I'm not following."

"It was all an act. Like the Stones. Everybody was five foot two and in art school."

Oscar smiled, his shoulders leaping in a silent laugh. He looked happy for this guy talk. Should have him out for a beer.

"Oh, now, well, I think the British have their fair share of tough guys, and psychotics."

"They love a stage is all I'm saying."

"You think" — Oscar pointed at the stereo, pausing then shaking a finger just as Van Morrison went into one of his wails — "you think that's an act?"

"I know it is." You could picture the wee guy in a booth, headphones on, holding the mike the exact proper distance for an undistorted howl, this his third take, he's warmed up now.

"You don't scream like that for real unless, I don't know, you're watching your own blood pour out of you."

"Okay, I suppose." Oscar, enjoying this, searched for something to counter with. "But on TV, videos, you see these bands that look evil and I tend to believe it."

"They've had to think more, you know, visually. Can't just stand there and sing any more."

"Well, I guess, sure. Learned to act." He paused. "Okay. Have you seen Iggy Pop?"

"Hang on, I mean Brits. The *Brits* are the actors. All they did was put American R & B on stage. Iggy Pop's real."

"Oh, I see."

"No, it's true. Go ask any Brit superstar, go ask the Beatles who turned them on and it's always Chuck Berry, Elvis, Jerry Lee Lewis. Even Carl Perkins, for Christ sake."

"I suppose."

"Oscar? Americans couldn't fool anybody. They don't even try."

He was up with Oscar now, hunched shoulder to shoulder and peering into the music titles. Oscar was indeed an Anglophile. Stones, every Beatles you could think of, even Petula Clark, housewife with a ditty. Elton John, well of course, and Supertramp, the whiners. Lots of Moody Blues, who were The Lettermen on drugs.

"So you have it down to a kind of British-versus-American thing."

"Oscar? How many American bands can you recall who wore the matching, you know, 'outfits'?"

You had to admire the Brits for their imagination, but, well. If Jerry Lee Lewis was mad at you he'd shoot you in a second. If David Bowie was mad at you he'd put on a costume and stare.

Oscar had been thinking. "You got me."

"The Byrds did, for a while."

Bonaduce tried picturing Oscar and Leah together. They weren't a likely mix. He didn't feel jealous, in the way he sometimes did over sexy women he didn't even know, couples he passed in the street. He saw Leah being cheerful with Oscar, efficiently going about her day, threatened by nothing in the man at all.

"So the Brits only *look* like they suck blood from animals," Oscar mused, mildly imitating Bonaduce. "But they're in actual fact just — clarinet wusses." He grinned, pleased with himself.

"There you go."

"In all probability Ozzy Osbourne doesn't bite chickens' heads off at home, true."

"That was great coffee."

Bonaduce slumped back on the couch. Two regular guys sitting here talking music. Oscar was getting more comfortable. Good thing he hadn't thought of Paul Revere and the Raiders. Or Kiss, Alice Cooper. It would've been all over.

"This body piercing's pretty spectacular though." Oscar shook his head in a kind of admiration. "How far is *that* going to go?"

"It's a contest, isn't it."

"I saw a nose ring the other day, not the usual tiny little thing in the side, but a big, thick hoop" — he pinched thumb and forefinger into both nostrils — "like a bull. She couldn't have been fourteen. And man? I saw a bone once, in Toronto."

"Hey — guy in Wheeling has one. Or had one. I mean a hockey player. He—"

"Nose ring?"

"Nose ring. He attracted some attention. Guys trying to get at it with their sticks. Guy had balls, I guess. Hockey player with a nose ring ..."

Oscar smiled appreciatively.

"Earrings have been around," Bonaduce offered. "Guy can have an earring and still be a stud."

"The code." Oscar nodded to himself.

"That's right." Bonaduce lifted his cup, forgetting it was empty. "So. So how well do you know Jason?"

"Not well." He shook his head with self-judgement.

"Ah."

"Considering we lived together for three years. I mean, I can tell you what he doesn't like for breakfast."

"Right."

"I came in at a touchy age I think. Fifteen. I just made myself available if he needed me for something, but he never did. Well, the car, a summer job, that." Oscar pulled a bullied face and made as if to go for his wallet. "But emotionally, no. He's such a private kid. But you know that."

"Right."

No, you don't know that. You don't know that at all.


Hard sitting still at the highway house between classes, between *jogs*. Between the last thing and the next thing. Breaths.

The Maui trucks made it harder. Something adhesive in them, you could get dragged out of your thoughts by a big truck, get towed on down the road. Maybe it was just that he envied the driver his destination. Here he was, stopped, while so much of the last twenty years had been a road trip. Buses from Rochester to Muskegon, to Springfield, to Portland. Portland Oregon *and* Maine. On those endless purgatorial all-nighters he'd often be sitting up awake, eyes on the black window, generally unaware of but held anyway by the bus's constant muffled roar. No one else on the road except the big trucks, working the interstate. Catching up to one, buddy-buddy alongside for a while, the truck's whining, roaring insistence would blend in with and double that of the bus. You can see the driver lit up ghost-green behind his wheel, staring straight ahead, both of you rushing in the same direction. What's the guy nodding to, what beat? You try to guess the tape he's listening to, you almost hear it through the noise, hey it's Beefheart, no it's Johnny Cash, no the decades have flown by, it's Vince Gill now. You know in all likelihood it's Abba, or funk. Though a guy likes funk you don't automatically hate him, despite his obvious deficiency. At least it's not disco, or *Belafonte's Best*. It's probably Anthony Robbins, or Sri-somebody, the driver's probably nodding yes, inspired to be all the trucker he can be. Actually you can tell from his intent face that, like you, he's alone with nothing but his own rambling thoughts. Beside you on the road, in a sixty-mile-an-hour chair. The guy like a teammate you'd never meet.

Reaching across the table with his good arm, Toby poured the wine. He usually poured because the wine was usually his, homemade red bought from a friend for two bucks a bottle. The friend made a fifty-cent profit per bottle, so Toby didn't feel guilty.

Bonaduce lifted his jamjar for Toby to stop pouring.

"Studying tonight." He smiled but didn't know if he was joking or not. At night he'd been accepting the glass of wine Toby always offered. He always stopped at two.

It was a decent domestic scene. Rod, never much of a talker, sat in a corner sipping and reading. Despite the slightly froggish set of his lips and eyes when he read, Bonaduce liked the look of Rod, the relaxed alertness as he sat, the graceful way his spine arced out of his collar. Tonight Rod was reading something by the Dalai Lama, and occasionally he would mutter a quote, some kind of gently wise truth you'd expect. Bonaduce and Marg had taken to keeping the Yahtzee game at permanent readiness on the coffee table and played it nightly, as they did now, a dime a game. Toby talked.

"It's not the best," Toby said, as usual, after topping up everyone's jar, "but it works. And it's cheap. Bloody booze tax. It's all taxes. Fucking, government, monopoly."

Bonaduce had lived with Fournier for much of the last decade — five, six years? — but otherwise alone. He'd forgotten that roommates weren't always a bowl of cherries. These young types were okay in general and Marg here was a jewel, but Toby — Toby was getting on his nerves. From the first he'd noticed that Toby had a certain nasty air about him. Then it dawned one night, listening to Toby speak, that every single thing Toby said was negative. Life was taxes, government monopolies, sleet. Even when he smiled it was hooked by a sneer. His chicken arm hard against his chest, blocking open laughter.

"Well, taxes, yeah." Bonaduce gave a little shrug. "But then we don't pay medical here."

"Yeah, right." Toby rolled his eyes and looked away, possessing information Bonaduce did not.

"Well you ol' *luck* bucket," Bonaduce exclaimed to Marg and her large straight. Marg liked his cowboy talk. He scooped the dice and rattled them loudly up at his ear. "Baby needs a new pair a feet."

You don't want to avoid the people you live with, skulking off to your room in the evenings like some kind of loner. You want to participate. But evenings, while drinking Toby's wine, you couldn't help but get his constant dark slant on things, his voice being the dominant one in the room. Some complainers you understand and forgive, others you don't. If Toby were to lean in and look you in the eye and say how God had given him a shitty arm and a shitty life, you could sympathize. But when a guy complains constantly, constantly, about the bad things we all shared — weather, politics, good food too expensive or cheap food tasting bad — it got a little tiring. Thank you, Toby, for always reminding us, for always making clear the lowest shitty denominator.

"Free medical? The drug companies charging sixty bucks for a bottle of pills it costs two bucks to make?"

"Yeah" — Bonaduce made himself nod — "I guess it is pretty bad that way."

"AIDS medicine costing thousands a month?"

"Right. That's wrong."

"Wrong, man, it's criminal. We're afraid to die and people cash in on that. No one should make more money than anyone else. It's immoral. With health it's criminal."

Bonaduce nodded absently, thinking about the drugstore today, where he'd gone for vitamin C, devil of a cold or something coming. He'd found himself in the geriatric row — walkers, trusses, canes, all beige and ugly-practical, easy to hose off.

He'd had to force himself to walk the aisle, pretending he wasn't noticing the twenty feet of adult diapers, a whole fucking section for them.

"And everyone *knows* it's criminal," Toby said.

They'd had an argument once, almost a fight (Bonaduce had actually been able to picture them fighting, Toby attacking him with both arms, an ugly image). Toby, who was on unemployment insurance, had been ranting that the government changing just the name, from "unemployment" to "employment" insurance, was typical in that their solution to any problem they couldn't fix was to euphemize it. Toby was right, but Bonaduce made the mistake of joking that the government would soon be calling death "Afterlife Canada," and to this Toby said, "It isn't funny, man," and glared at him until he was forced to get up and go to his room.

Toby was uncorking another bottle of wine, as usual making a display of it. Bonaduce didn't like thinking it, but he suspected these one-handed shows of non-disability were why Toby had gotten into his wine habit to begin with. Toby was opening wine and staring accusingly, and it felt like gritty déja vu. Bonaduce sighed and looked away.

"That's how it is, I guess."

He hardly heard himself. He'd been halfway into a sip of wine when his own ditty, "We don't pay for medical here," came back to him, echoing. He stopped his sip at the possibility that on some deeper level he hadn't chosen Canada so much as he'd fled the medical bills of the United States.

"Your roll, there, Robert," Marg drawled. "Howse about a quarter a game? My ol' *luck bucket*'s gettin' full of your dimes."

OSCAR DEVRIES.

When, out of the blue, Bob Bonaduce called on a Friday night near the end of November and said in his way, Hey Buddy, let's do a pub crawl, Oscar was surprised and impressed with himself, first that he agreed and second that he felt glad for it. And when Bonaduce pulled up in his wreck and honked, he was actually doing it, he was pulling on his coat, smiling and shrugging to Leah, waving, going, incredible. Doing the male thing. Poor Leah, she no doubt had some complicated feelings about all of this. His "Honey, I have a date with your ex" seemed to get to her somehow and hardly let her smile. This outing apparently wasn't quite what she had in mind on those occasions when she suggested he go out and find himself some friends.

The idea was to hear some music. Over the phone they'd agreed on a bar called Chevys, which Bob had heard played nothing but oldies.

Considering they were middle-aged men who didn't know each other, in the car it was surprisingly smooth. Just two fellows venturing forth with what looked to be adolescent drinking intentions. He'd been made aware, during sessions with the counsellor he and Leah had seen, that with men his own age he was at ease only when the roles were clear, when the sign "Client" or "Employer" or "Sales," or what have you, was shined up and pinned to a chest. Oscar had nodded politely at the woman's exaggeration, but he did take her essential point home with him.

Declaring just how fine a beer sounded, Bob Bonaduce grinned, nodding at the windshield, and Oscar understood that he was going to a dance club with someone who was "ruggedly handsome."

So, this was the man Leah had married. And this was the father of Leah's son. Most of all, though, in the air was the fact of Bonaduce having slept with her. Twenty years ago or not. Leah had described it as "adolescent passion," as if these words dismissed it. On the contrary it made him consider this thing called animal magnetism, it made him remember how at the party Bonaduce had looked at Leah, the simple but profound gravity in his eyes, and it made him consider his own lovemaking, which was infrequent these days and which — under the glare of true animal magnetism — might amount to little more than feeble.

He glanced down at their two pairs of blue-jeaned knees. To his knowledge he had never been alone with someone who had slept with the same woman. It was a vague and queasy thrill, the proximity and palpable sense of their two laps side by side here in the car.

"Decent night," said Bonaduce, head tilting back in meditative satisfaction. "Decent fall."

Oscar agreed.

He had feared a heart-to-heart, some confession or plea from this man who couldn't help but have unrealistically romantic notions about Jason. The cheap pathos of absence. According to Leah, Bonaduce was orphaned at some young age, the father leaving, the mother dying. In any case Leah said she feared unresolved father stuff surfacing here in Fredericton in some kind of overblown way. What words had she used? "Walt Disney way." Play catch with me Dad, golly jeepers, atta boy Son.

But once in the car Oscar saw that Bonaduce would neither blurt nor plead. No, the man had slicked-back hair and he opened his window in preparation for lighting a small, thin cigar with a comic flourish. Bonaduce kept smiling. He exhaled luxuriously and announced with corny pleasure, "Only on special occasions." Which made Oscar feel good, to be called a special occasion. The fellow had some social grace. No doubt in his career he met people all the time. The smile appeared genuine. He could have been a successful minor politician, that small-town charisma. The clothes, the relaxed athlete at the wheel, the casual vanity of the man. Looking over at you for no reason, smiling and meeting your eye as if something were transpiring.

Other than ask directions to Chevys, Bob Bonaduce was happy to go on about nothing remotely serious. As with his blather about British musicians and nose rings. Tonight it was questions about Fredericton, about nightspots, about when Oscar thought the first snow would hit. He asked about "your lawyer job," nodding politely to the litiginous intrigues while not listening. He really did need to talk but the need had nothing to do with content.

Chevys revealed a side of Fredericton Oscar hadn't seen up close. Everyone was between forty and sixty, which was a nice surprise, and which made sense given the music. In the first ten minutes they played Young Rascals, Elvis and Dusty Springfield. But he'd be damned if this wasn't a singles bar. Tables of ladies sitting wide-eyed and available. Men standing posed in shadow with arm crooked, their beer bottles held pointed in comically suggestive angles. Quick, serious swigs as if suddenly considering something. Swallow, as an afterthought. Ripple your jaw muscles.

He couldn't help but smile — he had never felt so stared at. Women in their forties, even fifties, made up to the hilt but in tight jeans like it was 1975, giving him a hungry unblinking come-on. Oscar Devries, piece of meat. Great stuff. Bonaduce didn't seem to be noticing, though he was getting double the eyes. Well, the man must be used to it, scenes like this. What else does a man do? In Kalamazoo.

The volume went up for an old Doobie Brothers, and if it was hard to talk before, now it was impossible. He and Bob had more or less guzzled their first beer (it seemed to Oscar that they'd each been trying to keep pace with the other) and now Bonaduce appeared with four bottles, two for each of them. Oh-oh and oh well. The DJ behind smoked glass spun a slow platter next, "Ruby," that Kenny Rogers cowpat about a good old boy home from 'Nam sexually disabled, him watchin' his Ruby goin' out to git herself laid, poor him waitin' up, drinkin' the wine. With this song the mood changed as if the DJ had pulled a switch, some kind of perverse romance suddenly in the air, everybody's face taking on the cartoon loneliness and tragedy. The guys swigged with inner torture now, and the gals were stricken in their chairs, eyes wider than ever. And Bob Bonaduce — oh goodness, look at this — there was Bob Bonaduce, eyes downcast, disabled, suffering the same.

Oscar tilted a beer and decided to climb off his arrogant perch. This blue-collar watering hole had lain hidden somewhere in his oddly polar world of executive suits, on the one hand, and

Leah's impoverished refugees, on the other. Despite the manipulative music it was elitist and hypocritical to stand here in disdain of the tabloid loneliness of Middle America. For apparently Middle America crossed the border. And you couldn't help but visualize the wanton middle-age sex. By the looks of things this bar would lead to a lot of it, all these divorced old—

"*This is great, eh?*" Bonaduce shouting in his ear.

"*Yeah.*"

"*Good music.*"

"*Yeah.*"

Except for the ubiquitous "Satisfaction" and the Hollies' "He Ain't Heavy," there'd been precious few good tunes. All Top Forty, the expected Motown, Creedence, nothing remotely obscure. Bob seemed bored too, eventually. He didn't seem interested in the women, of which, from the looks of them looking at him, he could've plucked his choice and taken home with the effort of one waggled finger. He'd already refused two women asking him to dance, but now accepted a third, she a rotund sixty-year-old who made her request a self-deprecating joke.

Weird being here. Leah's early husband. Weird watching him down there dancing. The grace of an athlete, the stiffness of having muscles like that. Somewhat flinging his arms around in humour and confidence, and also implied threat, though that would not be deliberate. How much of any dancer's dance was deliberate, exactly? There were questions he wanted to ask Bob now, because Bob was quite possibly not as uncomplicated as he seemed. Living across the river in a house of twenty-five-year-olds. Middle-aged grad student in English but who spoke and looked like a fellow who — what, owned a gun shop? ran a gas station? Apparently he was serious about the hockey with Jason. Jason had reacted negatively to the idea. How was that developing? Leah had not returned from Sussex the day Bob had come over to discuss it. Maybe they'd spoken since on the phone. Who knows? He was staying out of it. He thought the father/son hockey a sweet idea, but so completely innocent. Let's play catch, son. A given that Jason would find it awkward. "Lame" is the word he'd use.

"*Wanna head out?*" Bonaduce, puffing, limped up. Lame.

"*Sure.*"

Bonaduce led him out of Chevys. In the car he said he knew another good bar, Rockin Rodeo, which he then disparaged as "kind of hick." Oscar, who had just experienced the hickest scene of his life, wondered what was in store.

"I've had four beers, probably have the same there, we cab it after that," Bob announced, clicking on his seat belt.

"Taxi's on me." Oscar smiled because both of them were still almost shouting.

"Sounds good." He flashed the Bonaduce smile. "I'm on a student's salary these days. This is my big night out."

What salary would this man attract when school ended? An English MA, in his forties, God help him. Oscar had done an English BA, but only as a route to Law, and perhaps one shouldn't mention this. Bob Bonaduce had basic problems he wasn't dealing with. This constant good mood of his clearly strode on rickety stilts. And if any serious conversation was going to ensue tonight, now was the time, and maybe it was his job to start it.

"I've wanted your side of this and now I can ask you: how come you and Leah never did get divorced?" It wasn't that he didn't believe Leah's version. And he hoped this didn't sound in any way jealous, because it wasn't. Leah wasn't speaking fondly of the man.

Another Bonaduce smile. "I guess we weren't on good enough speaking terms to get one."

Oscar chuckled appreciatively.

"Yes, well. It goes with the territory. We've had some problems ourselves. An early affair ..." He shrugged, content to leave ambiguous an affair that had only been Leah's.

"Ooo, hey, it happens."

"But — I love her, Bob."

Now, hell, what was this about? He'd shrugged as if casual

but hadn't it come out like a plea? Four bottles of beer and he'd turned to pathetic mush, telling about affairs — he'd never told *anyone* else — and now confessing his love.

"That's good to hear, Oscar."

He and Leah did have a good one, a good relationship. They'd healed and worked through. They had an unspoken understanding of where they were headed, of what was *utmost* in a relationship.

"That's really good to hear."

Oscar looked over to him and smiled, though Bonaduce was staring straight ahead, driving carefully. His poise at the wheel. Big carnivore in graceful repose. He could picture Bob Bonaduce with Leah. To picture this was also to understand that, when sex was mindless, when sex was inevitable as gravity, *utmost* had no chance.

He waited a half-mile before asking the next one.

"So is this hockey thing with Jason important to you?"

Bob either shrugged quickly or suffered a neck spasm of some sort, it was hard to tell in the dark of the car. The man who had been an orphaned adolescent didn't otherwise answer the question, though the car was going faster.

Oscar regretted his question for what he now saw might be its latent cruelty. But Bob's silence was so turned in on himself that Oscar wasn't made to feel awkward. In fact he felt freed of any involvement. Outside, it had begun to sleet. Mixed with road grease and bugs already there, the windshield turned the colour of mud. Bonaduce didn't appear to notice.

"Can you — can you see? Do you have any wiper fluid?"

§

Bonaduce remembered the washer fluid running dry about an hour out of Fredericton on the long haul up, seemed like ages ago now. You always try the wipers anyway, make that same greasy mistake. He found a wad of paper on the floor, pulled over, got out, spit, wiped a face-size hole in the mess. Old Oscar could ride blind. I love her, Bob.

Too bad they didn't have a couple of road beers.

"Bob, can you see?"

"No. Why?"

"Good. Excellent."

Windshields were one of those things you don't think about until they make themselves known like this. He'd completely forgotten, but recalled now when this windshield had last entertained him, the reason he'd run out of fluid: the firefly. An hour out of Fredericton, middle of the night, he'd seen off the highway what looked to be a cloud, a swarm, of fireflies. He'd never seen a cloud of them before. Hundreds at least. Marvelling at the auspicious luck of seeing a cloud of fireflies just as he was embarking on a new life, a sudden *splot* woke him up, a double-take wake-up because the fresh-dead bug was a firefly, its guts phosphorescent green on the windshield, eye level, right there.

The bug was dead but its guts were alive. Bright, bright as a tiny flashlight. Green fire undiminished. Again, and though not a nice event for the bug, he saw it as his luck. A neat little story to tell, and some science to boot, a firefly's light outlived its life. The fire came first, and it was bigger. So what was the human equivalent?

All kinds of thoughts swirled as he drove at speed. He'd quit the bungee music for now and had rolled up the window. You could stare at the little green sun and at the same time see beyond it to the road. He was awfully tired, road-delirious, and his thoughts about luck took a turn. Because when the bug's light finally did start to fade, he saw this as the true image of his luck. So swirly and dream-caught was he, that it being a green light cemented the bad-omen deal, green being not only Irish but also part of the Italian flag. He watched it fade, he watched it fade, using the wipers to get it away, his luck draining, running out, bad choice coming here, bad sign this setting-sun fly, just go away. And there was no human equivalent.

Oscar silent beside him, he drove peering through his faced-sized hole. He knew he was superstitious. Firefly, dead air freshener, dreamcatcher. The luck of the Irish. Italian. In voodoo, scientists say, it's your own superstition that kills you. If that was true, what a truth it was. Because, if you could kill yourself with belief, it meant you could also fix things — anything. Well. Of course it was foolish to ponder these big questions, even when what might be an evil disease was shouldering you in that direction. Life throwing its gloves off, staring you down. It was even more foolish not to ponder them, even if you know there are no answers. You let twenty years slide by without considering the big questions, you obviously haven't been doing enough wrong, or right.

He drove, enjoying Oscar's nervousness. He'd thought he might get into this stuff with Oscar tonight, but wouldn't. A good guy, but Oscar was simply too cynical about too much. Marg had the better ear for it and, incredibly, the better words. Lapsed Christians had a good take on things. In fact, watching her, it had dawned on him that, since there are no big answers available to the big questions, maybe the key was to go smaller. Ask questions less huge, questions not aimed *directly* at the big stuff. Not what is *the* meaning of life, but where is *meaning* found. Not *what* is the answer, but *how* should I ask it. Where to locate yourself.

Love, of course, was a place to start. Which was sort of why he was here.

At the instant Bonaduce thought this, Oscar asked a question about Jason, which startled him. Coincidence packs a jolt. Coincidence felt like religion's messenger-boy. Startling as well was the next insight supplied by his beer-fuelled reverie: Superstition was the only religion he'd ever had.

Another beer would be nice. Expose Oscar to a bit of country twang. He seemed to have a decent sense of humour.

Oscar.

When they pulled up in front of Rockin Rodeo and studied its neon sign replete with lassos and boots, Bob broke into the most superb westernisms. "Thar she be, Randy-buck. Settin' thar all purty as a rivershell." It seemed that in his years south his ear had absorbed some of the essential American tongue.

Bob found a parking spot a block distant. It was a beautiful night now. Decent indeed. A hard white moon had come out. Overnight would be cold enough to start ice on the puddles. He had not in a million years thought he'd end up in this country-and-western joint he passed with no curiosity each day on his way to work. What was disturbing was that after only four beers Bob — big beer-drinking Bobby Bonaduce — staggered walking the block to the bar. He actually didn't seem drunk; but Oscar felt offput, and then a little custodial. As they neared the bar, once again his friend launched the lunatic drawl, a cowboy rant that mixed cheek and nonsense.

"Why, this'n here hombre's dirt-mad enough" — Bob was pointing into the face of a scowling woman leaving the bar — "to take and kick the ass-tanks off'n a bull in a toad storm. An she'all knows it, too."

The blonde hombre decided to smile as she climbed into her taxi. Bob kept up the showoff as he pushed in the double glass doors, then the fake saloon doors, talking louder and louder over the music. He stood surveying the place. He pointed at various women.

"*She* was so purty that, wellsir, ever' bigbone weevil from all hunnert counties took and went on a stomp for her benefit, and her benefit too, and hers'n — spree the likes a which six yaller dang bitch coyotes couldn't howl 'nuff to keep *tam*."

Everyone was in jeans, half wore cowboy boots. Even a scatter of cowboy hats. One fellow in a shiny aquamarine cowboy shirt, thumbs hooked in his belt loops, stomped the floor with his big heels, quite serious. Oscar told himself that this was not unlike walking into a meeting place of the Klan, then he understood he only wanted to see it this way for the thrill of it, because he was already bored. This was loyalist New Brunswick and it was dress-up. Though there might likely be fights.

Bob Bonaduce was loud enough that a few heads were turning, and while Oscar smiled broadly to show everyone it was all a joke, he really wanted Bob to stop.

"Well thar, mister, watcha thank of this'n har line-dancin' dude-pit?"

"If you shut up I'll buy you-all a beer, Big Bob."

Rockin Rodeo was fine from the point of view of studying exotic culture and its music, but two beers later it was very much time to go. Then it was later still and he'd had too much to drink, having stupidly agreed to the cowboy-macho thing of two tequila shooters back to back. Coupla manly men. It was fun drinking in this bar with this man but not worth sitting hung over in tomorrow morning's light. If anything it made him realize his love of Saturday mornings. Him alone with his coffee and paper in the sunroom, Leah sleeping in. The click of his cup, the smell of the coffee, and newsprint.

Outside, impatient with the task of getting a cab for each of them, what with these womenfolk flirtin' their way in front, he was foolishly manly again and drove Bob's wreck to Bob's house way out on the northside highway. He was afraid Bob would've driven himself if he hadn't. Bob's legs weren't working right, and his tongue was thick and slow. *Helll. Owwe. Ahhh-fisss-errr.*

Stupid. Cops did love to catch a lawyer. Why was he doing this?

Bob snapped on the radio and sought music, music being the string through this night's beads.

At Bob's house a clutch of kids dressed in black stood in the gravel parking area, staring into the sky. They yelled at Oscar to turn the car lights off, they were looking for the Hale-Bopp. Bob launched into a string of puns about Halley's comet and bebop music and Bill Haley and the Comets, none of which the kids seemed to understand or want to.

Oscar somewhat self-consciously stepped through their midst and into the house to phone a cab. But Bob Bonaduce took the phone from him and mannishly replaced it with a beer, screw Saturday. Some of Bob's tapes were truly classic, the fellow did know music. He had a big cardboard box packed with tapes. In his funny little room. Bob was enacting some sort of student-hell parody, living with these vampire kids, but he seemed to be enjoying himself. The box had Musswell Hillbillies, early Who, Fairport Convention, these the only good Brit stuff, for Bonaduce was indeed married to the early American white boys. Jerry Lee, some uncommon Elvis, Gene Pitney, Del Shannon, and anything pre-Dylan. Pre-complexity? The Brits had always been into complexity perhaps because, well, to give Bob his due, they were already at a remove, copying the Americans.

The gang of glowering youth came in from their comet and sat in the living room drinking tea and talking softly, more than likely stoned, definitely not wanting two drunken old men in their face. There was a small laughing argument about what went on the stereo, Bob laughing that he'd sue, and then goddamn renovate this place and everyone in it, he had his own lawyer along too. Oscar for one would have been more than happy just to stay in Bob's room and flick through the tape indexes, sit on the bed and talk about whatever, but Bob had a guitar by the neck and insisted Oscar stay in the living room and sing. Bob bragged that he knew how to play every song off the first album of some band called Los Lobos. It was unclear whether or not they were about to hear every one of these songs.

This wasn't to be the case, but it was still largely awful because Oscar was forced to sing. This only after the young people had drifted off, and only after much ridicule and another beer, and another beer. Some of it wasn't bad funny-singing, Bob "doing Oscar Devries doing Mick Jagger," and then a spontaneous ode to the Hale-Bopp comet, except that some housemate asleep above started pounding on his floor, and Bonaduce, hissing how he didn't fucking like that one-armed gimp, pounded the ceiling with the head of his guitar. Oscar was drunk enough that it was more amusing than scary to see Bonaduce's anger fire his muscles like that, the speed of it and the teeth-clenched smile, a rage that may have served his profession but rage nonetheless. Bonaduce left dents in the ceiling, and the guitar was sprung out of tune.

§

His eyes blinked, stayed open. Sure, this morning had to come. He realized he'd been expecting it. A morning when the truth dawned clear and hard and woke him before the sun did: There was nothing to do with his life than the thing he was doing now, and no one wanted him here doing it.

All he could manage under the weight of this truth was to go up on an elbow and look out his window. Scan the stage. It was grey, windy, shitty out. Nothing else. The comet had left for now. Right, he'd seen it last night, his first comet, and it had surprised him. Paler than starlight. It was fuzzy and playful, like a child's crayoned happy-thing. He'd read in the paper the previous day how comets were regarded as harbingers of doom, and standing with Oscar beside the car he'd had doom in mind as he searched the sky for the comet. Toby had impatiently grunted, There, and Bonaduce got behind him to sight along his good arm. His eyes found this softly glowing fuzzy-bunny thing. Now instantly doubly sinister. You are shown the face of death and it is Shirley Temple's.

Up on his elbow, Bonaduce could feel the entirety of himself gaining, by the moment, a dark and precarious weight. He knew he was one step away from going down and staying down. He willed the eyes to stay open. He looked through the rainbow threads of the dreamcatcher. Marg had called it this, explained its reason for being.

He looked through, seeing what he could, eyes zooming through blurring threads to focus on the distant treeline, the empty stage. Dreamcatcher in reverse. Hey, out there. Catch this one.

Well, with any luck you can find something specific to blame a lousy mood on. And he was a bit hung over. Quite a bit hung over ... *and of course fatigue* ... Lucky him, he could blame a variety.

Last night had been all right though, his date with Oscar, ending up back here for some tunes and a nightcap. The guitar, right. Toby's stereo had been eating and ruining his tapes for a month and Toby refused to demagnetize. His young roomies had nothing but CDs themselves and unfortunately it wasn't the right kind of music. In this he and Oscar had been in agreement.

But now how in anyone's hell could a successful lawyer in his forties be shy about singing the good oldies in front of a bunch of kids? They wear black and nod their snarky little heads to Nine Inch Nails but so what? Even Marg he didn't like last night. Young types who give no credit to anyone but themselves for anything. You laugh at the purity of Del Shannon, it's your loss. Live your lives in a snarkier-than-thou postmodern house of mirrors, go ahead.

Despite what it was speeding toward, there was something okay about age, there really was. Last night, him and Oscar like buds here in this romper-room house. At the writing workshop he and Big Jan sometimes caught each other's eye and almost smiled after a blurted youngism. In the halls at school, nineteen-year-olds ambling smug with all the latest trendy torn cool junk on their bodies and on their minds — it was stuff you knew nothing about, but you couldn't help feel sorry for them, looking down from your perch of age. Because you knew, and they didn't, that what they so absolutely believed in right now, what stiffened their spine and curled their smirk, would in twenty years be gone. You knew, and they didn't, that in twenty years they wouldn't know anything at all, and feel just like you.

Imagine telling this to Jason. Imagine the look.

He opened the fridge. Toast, toast would be good. With jam. Or maybe meat, this looked like meat, liverwurst. It didn't smell off, too much.

"There's a giant hole in the bathroom wall."

Here was Marg, standing in her big white terrycloth robe. The whole idea of her was hard to look at.

"Was that all that noise last night?"

Shit. That's right, the bathroom wall.

"Well, Marg, it was all rotten there. I decided to fix it."

"Looks like you kicked the wall in."

It came back now. He'd fallen hard against it for no reason and dented it with an elbow. Then he'd lost it a bit and started kicking, starting with the swamp-wall beside the toilet.

"It was all rotten." It was. Some of it the fist had gone through easy.

"But I mean we're renting. That's like, the landlord's job."

"So where is he? It was all piss-soaked."

"Well, now we have this totally screwed-up wall."

Marg's face was slack, her voice was monotone. She wasn't into reasoning.

"I'll fix it. I just couldn't stand it. I hated it. Can't see how anyone could sit down beside that and take a—"

"*He* might hate it, you kicked in his wall. It wasn't rotten all the way to the bathtub like that." Marg turned her back on him and started doing something fast at the counter with her hands, grabbing up papers or something. "I just cleaned it all up, so I know."

"Marg? I'll fix it."

.   .   .

# THE HOCKEY NOVEL
## by
## R. BONADUCE

It is not only species of animals that die
out, but whole species of feeling. And if
you are wise you will never pity the past
for what it did not know, but pity yourself
for what it did.
—John Fowles, probably talking about
old-time hockey

Oscar Devries, immigrant baby, was given his first pair
of skates at age four weeks. Outside their sod hovel the
prairie winter wind howled like a she-devil as Father
laced Baby Oscar's skates up tight. So tight that blood
began beading up at the lace-holes. But little Oscar didn't
cry. He cried only when they removed the skates and he
kept crying until they laced them back on, tighter. They
taped popsicle sticks on for shin pads and stuffed his
little rig into a thimble. Helmet? No helmet, Oscar
thrashed his head until they gave up trying to put one
on him, he wouldn't be a fancylad. And fuck the
mouthguard too: he already had no teeth. They noticed
he had come into the world with several facial scars.

Oscar's first game he played naked, save for his bleeding skates. His foul temper kept him warm and red and
his skin unfrozen. He went goalless but, using his adult-
size stick, he sent six players to the Winnipeg Regional
Hospital.

. . .

Bonaduce poured himself his second glass. Red wine, hey, I feel a tumour coming on, pass the red. He wondered if Toby would miss this bottle, if he kept count. Downstairs, Toby kept his bottles stacked dusty on their sides as if it was a fucking wine cellar, not a rat cellar.

He was having nothing but trouble coming up with anything for Big Jan's workshop. He'd whined to her and she'd simply said, Write what you know. So he'd joked, Hard to write about nothing for very long. And she'd said, Nonsense. And he'd said, Nonsense it will be!

So, sure, he could write about hockey. But what? A pack of anecdotes? The exotic stuff? He'd seen a goalie's artery slashed. He'd seen teammates shit their pants during a game, one guy — who was that, O'Dowd? — forcibly trading the dirtied pants with a frightened Russian rookie, O'Dowd the satanic joker. (Here ya go, Jan and Phil and Kirsten, good stuff, eh?) Or Donny Carter, his nervous breakdown between periods. That nervous little look, the glancing around like a timid baby, not talking, took a few days for anyone to catch on, then a year on the sixth floor for Carter. Or should he just write a stupid Rocky story about a guy who overcomes the odds? Everyone liked that crap, maybe even Jan. Bill Spunska, clumsy immigrant, barely makes the team but scores the winning *yadda* with *yadda* left on the clock in the *yadda yadda* finals. Do you do the social-comment, team-as-microcosm thing? Modern gladiators, boxed vicarious bloodwar, testosteronic bugs in a bell jar. Do you write for an audience at all? Or do you just scribble for yourself and hope someone else gloms onto your heartbeat? But how to convey the subtleties of a thing, how do you hold the good mirror up to the rink's old wet-cigar smell, or the sound of tape tearing off the roll as distinct from ripping off an ankle, or the kaleidoscopic personality of a dressing room? Or the game itself, the fresh ballsy chugging, the deepgut serenity of a solid hit and the guy going down. Or the danger of it all — you have the puck and you're lugging a bag of gold to market surrounded by fast bandits.

How do you know if anyone will care?

Tonight at the laptop, once again he'd begun with a legitimate beginning, the Fowles quote, then fouled it up going right into the Oscar joke. Well, Jan's other advice had been, just start writing, no goal, freeform. Maybe he'd try again tomorrow. Maybe he'd shove this in Oscar's mailbox in the meantime, why not. Too bad it wasn't this fun writing essays. Humour — humour was the antidote for all that wasn't humorous.

His first piece of mail. In the student general mailbox a message from Professor Daniel Kirk regarding the "New Traditions in the Carnivalesque" seminar he'd registered in but so far had not attended. Hard to say how old the note was because he hadn't been checking the box. Come to think of it, he'd passed Kirk in the hall a few times and the guy's stick-up-the-ass response to a friendly hello Bonaduce had written off to personality rather than circumstance. Sorry, professor, my mistake.

A word in the last sentence was underlined:

<u>What</u> are your intentions?

Nice, a catchphrase for him to go to sleep to and wake up with, a jingle for life. Come on, *what* are they?

His second piece of mail was old news. His grant had been turned down. He was to subsist on the assistantship alone. Once a week he met thirty students, Engineering types mostly, to work on writing skills. It was strange. The course was called "Aspects of the Novel." A Professor MacAphee, whom he hadn't met, gave twice-weekly lectures on novels the class was supposed to have read, then on Fridays the lectured-to students broke into groups for a session with a grad student, to work on essays about these novels. Bonaduce had questions about this. If they wanted these guys to learn how to write essays, give them subjects that mattered to them: movies, computers, sex, whatever. They lacked the tools to say the right things about the novels even had they read them. They wrote MacAphee's lecture insights down as best they could, and it was Bonaduce's job to help them hammer these notes into essays. He encountered poor slobs trying to work in "Apocalypse now was of course but the bastard celluloid son of heart of darkness the masterpiece," not knowing if this meant it was good or bad.

Bonaduce figured he was a decent teacher, because in their tongue-chewing labours he saw himself mirrored in Gail Smith's. He got on their good side, even the back-row sneer-doctors in the ball caps, by clapping his hands and saying, "Gotta do it so let's do it, let's fuckin' go get 'er, ya wanna be as dumb as ya look?" It at least got their attention. The only reason they bothered to stoop to try to put fancy sentences together was to pass the course, get the degree, the job, make as much money as possible. Bonaduce had chased rubber for twenty years, but compared with these guys he was a philosopher and bohemian. If teaching this course was depressing, its social forecast was scary. What had happened to the liberal fucking education?

Regarding his first piece of mail, Bonaduce decided his intentions hadn't changed — that is, he had no clue *what* they were — and he left Kirk no note.

That night, there it was, in the centre of his window, the comet. The Hale-Bopp happy face, all plague-spewing innocence. It had an intensity you could almost hear. Having it in your window was funny and not-so-funny. It was hard not to feel singled out. Apparently for the next month this comet would be exactly right there.

What can you make of a ball of nasty dirty ice millions of

miles away framed perfectly in your very own bedroom window? Monster pulling a gaudy dirt-tail longer than lifetimes. Hanging there in your window utterly still — yet moving at a speed your mind can't take.

Absolutely no sound out there, ever.

*What* were its intentions?

## THE (HO)KKY NOVEL
### by R. L. Bonaduce

The history of hockey is actually herstory. Not many persons know this.

In 1846, on the outskirts of Halifax, little Gail Smith picked her nose out of her book and cast her steady regard through the window at the mess of boys playing out on the pond. Slipping and sliding in their boots, they chased a frozen turd around, batting at it with their bent sticks in hope that it might careen betwixt two wooden pails. "Score!" they would shout with glee, as if it mattered, whenever this occurred.

They had rebuffed her again. Not that she wanted to play. But they'd made a point, when going their smelly way out-of-doors, to make sure she knew she wasn't allowed. Their taunts, directed at her size, her gender, her appreciation of books, only privileged her steely resolve. To the sounds of their faint, wolfish shouts of "Score!" she went to the cellar for the knives.

It had taken her a week of evenings, working away with file, with hacksaw, with Whitmans auger. Her one pair of boots were ruined — but sacrifices were necessary.

When she appeared on the pond, bent stick in hand, there were the expected hoots of derision, but these were now laced with anger at her daring to challenge. Those that weren't engaged in red-faced yelling might have noticed that she was newly taller; those with the keenest eyes may have had to squint at the glint of sun off something excellent and unimagined beneath her feet. But all noticed, and were struck dumb, when little Gail Smith swooped in amongst them, confiscated and held onto their turd, performing defensive twirls and offensive thrusts, dancing the turd back into their mass and out again, just to taunt them. And in the end, all the boys and girls — many of them were girls after all — all lying in pain on the ice, dismembered, impotent, deconstructed, she casually nudged the turd 'tween the buckets with her shiny toe, and shouted not the crude word the others had used, but stated her own, fairly and without closure:  Hello

MARGARET.

It was morning when Robert's French friend from the States called again, waking her up. Referring to himself only as Fournier, asking for "Bobby," then all sorts of guy jokes. How's the big Bonaduce doin'?

She went downstairs to get Robert. The call had become mixed with the dream she'd been having, just as the phone rang. She re-pictured it, a dream so obvious it was silly. She had seen a shirtless Robert coming toward her, crawling toward her. He was emerging from some sort of hay loft, he was above her and grinning as he crawled out of the hay, his muscles glistening and defined by shadow, bits of straw clinging to them like beauty marks. He needed a shave, which was fine, which was even better, and as he grinned at her, crawling closer, his black hairiness turned blond and then longer, now great curling locks cascaded in rivulets in the valleys of his wet muscles, which got even bigger, and his smile grew even more perfect, and suddenly it was one of those strange ones where the dream is obviously goofing around on you, almost mocking, and the dream knows this before the dreamer does.

Robert wasn't in his room, and his coat was gone. Fournier, when told this, kept joking around. "Hey, so where is the guy, you hidin' 'im? You his wife? How many wives he have now?" All with a flirting edge, just in case. The kind of guy who knows no other way with a woman.

Fournier calmed down when she had no answers to any of this. His questions turned general and sober. So how was he really? His health. Was he walking okay?

"Well, he'll like, bump into the fridge if he doesn't see it coming."

"Jesus H."

She'd meant it as a joke, exaggerating Robert's clumsiness, his occasional shoulder hitting a door, which might send him into a little stagger. His friend's concern surprised her.

"I just want to know, did he get the book I sent up. The yeast book."

"I don't know."

"Maybe it got stopped at the border. The herbs and pills and stuff, eh? Jesus H, I told this to Kim. He didn't get it then?"

"I don't know. I mean, I didn't see it."

"He didn't get it then."

"He keeps to himself. He might have gotten it."

"You gotta tell him to do it when he gets it."

"Sorry? Do what."

"What the book says. When he gets it, you make him to follow it to a tee. He's a proud sucker but it's important, eh? For sure he can get better. Kim's instructions for the herbs and pills are in there too, eh?"

"I'll tell him." And make him do the herbs and yeast and pills. Okee-dokee.

"Bobby'll laugh — my girlfriend Kim, she's into the alternative stuff, right? — Bobby'll laugh, but she says you can snip it in the bud if you get on it early."

"Robert has like a disease or something?"

Silence on the other end, Fournier finally sussing.

"He has, he has MS, eh?"

"MS. That's …"

"Jesus H. Didn't tell you, eh? He's got multiple sclerosis. Can kill the stupid bugger."

"He didn't say a word to me. Wow, that's awful."

"Hey, it's the shits. He's pretty depressed about it."

"Well, yeah," Marg agreed. Picturing Robert in his room, aware of his presence in this house as if for the first time, she added, softly, "He is."

"He didn't tell anyone?"

"I don't know."

"Didn't he tell his wife?"

This was getting good. Marg couldn't help smiling.

"Which one?"

Fournier laughed.

§

## HOCKEY NIGHT IN THE KREMLIN

What has the game become? Money. In a brief time we have seen the game change to its corporate, crumbling state. The way owners buy winning teams, the way the players change teams …

It will get as bad as baseball, the money hunt. What are young kids making of this, seeing their heroes' sights are set on anything but loyalty?

To win, a team has to work as one body. Gone are the days you would kill and die for a teammate. Guys hardly know each other now. All the Europeans, even in the minors. Foreign guys sitting lost in the dressing room, no much eenglish, touching fingertips to their freshly stitched wound, wondering what they've gotten into.

Nor can we understand them. Look at the those Detroit Russians, who our game privileged with the Stanley Cup this past year. Them taking the cup to Russia and right into Lenin's Tomb. How can you understand people like that? If it's humor, it's different from ours. What it looks suspiciously like is loyalty and tradition, and of a sort we no longer have, if we ever had it at all. Father, Comrade Father, we have successfully deluded them, they think we are like them, we now have their money and their cars. Father, look at this trophy, we will touch it to your face. Wake up, Father, we've won.

He didn't try to conceal the Salvation Army store bag. He laid it on the kitchen counter, took out the can opener and put it in the utensil drawer, which was otherwise filled with broken spatulas, crumpled bills, gummy screws, widgets. A month had gone by and these guys were still opening cans with a hammer and rusty hunting knife, no doubt another ploy of Toby's to force everyone to watch how dextrous he was.

In his room, it was time to lie down. But first he took out and once more tried on the leather coat. A classic: wool-lined, ass-length, a little beaten up. Buffed at the elbows and lapel, where you could see past the dye into the old cow herself. Forty bucks, but winter was coming, and it was a coat that would last many more years. He hung it on the biggest nail.

His favourite book growing up had been *Robinson Crusoe*, and his hands-down favourite movie had been *Swiss Family Robinson*. As an adult, the main positive in getting traded (aside from sometimes getting a raise, or escaping a brainless coach) was the fresh start, with nothing. Survival of the freshly marooned. Later trades especially, he'd taken this idea completely to heart and jettisoned everything — furniture, car, dishes, even the bulk of his clothes.

More often than not, a trade involved a player coming your way from the other direction; a pissed-off or elated phone call from the guy often came the same day you got your news. But Bonaduce would politely decline the offer of the ready-made, furnished, dish-stocked apartment. Instead he hoteled it for a while, then on a free day found himself something small, clean. The first week he might buy a couple of pots, maybe a solid chair. Goodwill and Used stores were fine if the stuff was well built. Adding to your nest bit by bit, this was the Crusoe feeling. Locating the best little grocery was Crusoe finding the bread-fruit tree beyond the hill. The dented pewter mug was the half coconut shell, the yardsale carving knife was the fish hook fashioned out of a bent ship's nail. Comforts growing. Bonaduce would sometimes even think *coconut*, and *survival*, as he drank his milk out of the mug in the morning.

He would picture women in his new place. And eventually one would come, to help him with curtains, with dishes for four, with a rack of spices Bonaduce would have no clue when to use. Women seemed to like shopping for him in this way, maybe it was his dumb-dog trust. More than once he had a woman help him with his Crusoe-shopping before they'd even slept together and, generally speaking, this little burst of shared domesticity would lead her into the sack. Not that that had been his plan from the start, not exactly.

The Crusoe routine shifted when he was bought by Tulsa, and he met and roomed with the goalie Fournier. The arrangement was expedient and stop-gap. Here he was in Okie, the middle of nowhere, truly. Road trips were so long you were never home. In Tulsa it was common for four or five guys to room together, foamies and cots in the living room, save some bucks waiting for the next road trip or trade or call-up. Bonaduce saw how the guys here banded together more than usual. Oklahoma was a deeply strange place for a Canadian to be. Dust, heat, Okie-talk, pickup trucks downtown. Strange to be the home team here, trying to beat the shit out of a busload of fellow Canadians while all the cowboys in the audience hollered. They didn't shout here, they hollered, and sometimes they yipped. On the scoreboard the word *HOME* could tear your heart out. Within days of arriving in Tulsa, Bonaduce had all the lore about guns pulled out in bars, about places not to go. Safe in the dressing room, they enjoyed constant mock cowboy talk. *Well-sir, I reckon it's 'bout tam we should take and work up a lather out thar on the frozen ceement pond ...*

It was common knowledge that all goalies were weird, no matter where they may be trying to fit in. But with his accent and Montreal suave, Fournier fit this place not one bit. His English wasn't great, but the glint in his eye leapt easily over language. He had a way of smiling at your subtle question, looking at you with understanding but saying nothing. If you persisted, he might wave it away and say happily, "No matter!" But he was the kind of guy you gave the benefit of the doubt to, both because you wanted to and because he may have in fact understood. He read so much. He and Bonaduce had more books scattered about their place than the rest of the team put together. Maybe, they joked, the league put together. Fournier was a little hippyish, and had "two professional-hippy brothers" in Vancouver who sent him flattened hashish in letters, which he used in moderation. Fournier frowned on cocaine or drunkenness.

A three-year veteran of Tulsa when Bonaduce met him, Fournier was desperate to get out, had been from day one. Immediately he'd bought furniture, car, and all the rest of it, riding the common superstition that as soon as you plant roots you get traded. When this didn't work he went the other extreme, making almost a religion out of his bare fridge, cupboards, apartment. Once he'd gotten to know Bonaduce enough, he stated shyly that his lifestyle was in keeping with the tradition of Zen. He shopped "only for the food of one meal." He had two sets of clothes, one clean, the other on. If he needed a car or a tennis racket, he borrowed. No TV. He was usually the best-looking guy on the team, and French to boot, but he avoided the bars and tended to meet his women in the grocery or library. These women tended to be Zen or health-food types themselves. They talked that talk in any case, though in those unlikely cowgirl accents.

But Fournier was a good guy and Bonaduce went along. It felt okay to go out in the morning to buy that day's food. (Not unlike a hunting-and-gathering Crusoe.) Made you feel focused, life so simplified. He kept his closet lean. (The ship would be coming soon, take him home.) No stereo, so he bought an old guitar, learned the basic chords, started making up his own ditties. Where the rest of the guys went into debt for a muscle car, he walked or took taxis. For all this he felt lighter, more ready for the game, party, movie, or call-up to the bigs. He felt this leanness gave him speed. It was Tulsa where he began playing naked under his gear — longjohns in the heat made no sense, they soaked up your sweat and you carried these extra sopping pounds by game's end. Naked, skating blew you dry.

Here in his highwayside house in freshstart Fredericton — which in the minors was called Freddie Beach! — he had two shirts, two T-shirts, jeans, cords, sneakers, dress shoes. Underwear, socks. Guitar, box of tapes. Skates. He'd bought a towel, now a leather coat and can opener. He'd been given a dreamcatcher.


## A Mirror

We're a rack with meat hanging off it. Sometimes you get banged up or sick and the meat separates from the rack a bit. Things puff up or flap or dangle. Sharp hurt or bruise hurt or weird hanging-nerve hurt. Sometimes in the crammed dressing room after a road game you look at the other guys over thirty, those few that are left, and they look like you feel. You sit there actually laughing at what you have become, at how you feel, how at this very moment a shoulder and a lip, and a few ribs, and a foot, and maybe a deep organ somewhere to the left, are smashed numb or throbbing. Shaking your head in amazement, you sit there dripping sweat. You can smell yourself, the naked body there below your nose. You have a herpes flare-up and a cold. You are being yelled at to hurry to climb onto a bus, which you will ride all night sitting up.

Beside you a younger guy stands whistling, still eyeing the NHL, and one foot from your face he's flicking talcum powder onto his balls.

It's all more funny than not.


He woke in an instant. Brain abuzz. It was definitely the middle of the night. The room was dark but somehow vibrant. Effervescent, but beneath sight. He could hear that the highway was still. He wondered if it was this pregnant silence that had woken him. No, he sensed something alive outside. He went up on an elbow to see it.

There. Fierce, bigger than the sun, the full moon rising over the treeline. Huge, loud as kettledrums you couldn't hear. Its light stolen, and more powerful for it. You could feel all this, important, in the blood.


When he arrived, Leah and Oscar were in the living room together. The curtains were closed. She was on the couch drinking coffee, feet tucked up under, the Saturday *Globe and Mail* spread around her. Hard to say, because he'd never seen them together before, but the room felt stern, jagged, as if they'd been fighting. Though maybe this sternness was their comfort zone, the kind of air they breathed. He had no inkling of how they got on. Or who Leah had become.

He'd called a few times, and Leah could never manage a

time to do it, to get together to talk about Jason. Today, crossing the bridge into town, he'd decided to just drop by. The friendly Maritime way. It was Saturday and sunny so he stopped en route at the farmers market and spent the last of the month's money on a block of Emmenthal cheese.

Along with his leather coat, he handed the cheese gift to Oscar, whose thanks was a surprised raising of eyebrows. It actually even looked like a gift — a square wrapped in butcher's paper, tied neatly with string.

"Thanks," Oscar said. He hesitated, then smiled cautiously, not looking up. "And thanks for that little — I don't know what exactly you'd call it — that 'hockey story' about me. It was ... strange."

"Fiddling around, thought you'd get a kick out of it. Hope it was okay I sent it to where you—"

"My secretary found it *extremely* strange. She opens my mail. She might want danger pay from here on in."

"Hey. Wait'll she reads about Oscar-the-Teenager."

"I had no idea I had such, ah, *robust* beginnings."

"You smaller guys are the meanest. There was this little guy, Amis? You wouldn't—"

But, laughing, Oscar had already turned and walked.

With Oscar fetching a coffee in the kitchen, Bonaduce turned to Leah and got to it. She'd been pretending to read the paper, but looked up as soon as his question was ready.

"I was wondering about Jason, if he's talked to you."

Leah actually seemed serious when she said, "Bobby, if you want to play hockey with him, why don't you just play outside? One of the rinks, they flood the tennis courts, always by Christmas. Take your sticks, you see lots of fathers and—"

"No. Jesus. That's not—"

"You'd really have as much fun just—"

"No, it has to be—" She really had no idea at all. "That's kids. That's just fun. It has to be way more, you know, I don't know, 'serious.'"

He shook his head, surprised at her. It had to matter. Danger.

A team. Together, rushing the prize pig to market, bashing through deadly bandits, loving these guys who ran the gauntlet with you. Glory, laughter, sloshing tankards of ale at the inn.

Leah was quiet for too long. With no further word she un-curled off the couch and left the room. Oscar, who had returned, who had been wearing his ironic smile all along, shrugged and said, "It's a tricky one!" Then he fell to silence as well, staring at the floor, looking glad to be free of having to have an opinion.

The hall toilet flushed and, while Oscar didn't appear to hear, Bonaduce felt a little shy of it, of what it meant. He pictured Leah pulling up and zipping her jeans.

She returned and sat. In her stern silence the mother's love clearly reflected the son's troubles. Well, Bonaduce was here today to try to fix those. First he had to find out what they were.

"I came on too strong with him I guess. It was a little much."

"A little."

"Old Gordie," he said, smiling, "probably had a family pow-wow first, see how they all felt about the old guy coming to play." He looked up. Not even an indulgent smile from her. "Gordie Howe?"

"I know."

"I guess me coming here to live would have been heavy enough."

"Coming here to *visit* would have been heavy enough."

"Sure. I guess."

"And Gordie Howe was totally different."

"Well, yeah." Though what did she mean? "The principals raking in big money, the sentimental thing for the fans, sure, that really adds—"

"*No. Shit.*" Leah clapped her hands, once. He remembered seeing her do this to get Jason to listen. "He had the *right*. He was a goddamn *father*."

Oscar, rising and trying to flee gracefully, dropped the CD case he'd been handling and it clacked on the coffee table, an-other rude clap.

*A goddamn father.* What could you say to such a thing?

Nothing that wasn't feeble. I want to try to be. I have to start somewhere. Maybe we could all just.

"Well, Leah, I'll think about that." Think about what, exactly. Maybe she wasn't wrong, but she certainly wasn't right.

"I mean, Bob, do you have any clue at all?"

About fatherhood? In Tulsa there was Cynthia, with Lisa, her seven-year-old, and the three of them did almost a year together. He knew Lisa's homework, what she ate for lunch. Lisa had let him hold her after she'd fought with her mother. He had never exactly lived with the two of them but—

"Do you have any clue what Jason wants, or what I want?"

Ah, that's what you meant. No, I guess I don't.

"No, Leah, I guess I don't." Do you have any clue what I want from Jason, or from you? Yes, you probably do. "I guess you got me there."

He shrugged softly from his chair. He waited, then aimed a little smile at her, like a wedge into her hardness, an invitation to the intimacy she was working like hell to avoid. But she wasn't looking his way.

He got up to go. Leah did nothing to stop him. In fact she pinched up a section of newspaper to get on with her morning. She was that mad. Jason was that mad.

The sun came out from behind a cloud and flooded the window behind her, backing her in bright light, turning her black. He could no longer see her clearly without squinting.

He left then in thudding awkwardness, not letting her see his eyes. He was aware of his legs in their long walk to the door, and then the sound of its opening and clicking closed.

He stepped out into the sun and the draining knowledge that, of the two people he had journeyed back so far to see, he was now on speaking terms with neither.


MARGARET.
It was a week after talking at length to Robert's French friend.

She still hadn't mentioned anything about it to Robert, finding neither the opportunity nor the nerve. Nor the feeling, not really, that it was hers to do.

Though maybe tonight. They were alone in the house together. In the spirit of devil-may-care they had declared all the food in the house fair game and were preparing something good. There was her own angel-hair pasta, plus some nice hot Italian sausage from what looked like Rod's spot in the freezer, and the rest of her over-dry sundried tomatoes. Robert found some half-good garlic at the bottom of the vegetable tray along with a romaine with enough crispy leaves in the middle.

Standing with him at the sink, washing and ripping, almost touching shoulders. Here she was, making dinner with a man who was deeply sad but who did a pretty smooth job covering it up with cheerfulness, a man Fournier had called *one of the world's greatest guys*.

It was ridiculous that Robert made her think of her father, they were so unalike. Maybe that was why! Her father had never stood at the sink with her like this, she couldn't remember once. Or if he had, he would have made a big deal out of it: Let's everybody smile, here I am at the sink with my daughter, what do you all think of that? His spotlight for a moment including her. Her father had taught her in the end that there were many styles of insanity, many of them acceptable. One style let you have a business, a family, respect, and then let you disappear — well, San Diego — with a cliché secretary. He had no conscience, none. She was unclear in herself if she ever wanted him to call, say, at Christmas.

And here was Robert, appearing, from the States. Let's not take the equation any further please.

Fournier had been amazed at a few of the things she'd been able to tell him about his friend — He goin' back to *school? No!* — which told her how private Robert had been with Fournier too.

He'd found a jar of beets, which he held out to her in question, and which she suggested might not be appropriate for the meal. Her adding that they were Toby's mother's seemed to decide it for him. He winced and bent his knees opening it.

"Can't beat Harvard beets," he said. She couldn't tell if the stupid pun was intentional. "We can crank the stereo, play some Yahtzee later," he said, hands in the sink, jerking his head in the direction of the living room.

*But he's a bit of a loner, eh?*

Yes and no. Last night, again just the two of them, he'd brought out his guitar. She was ready to be embarrassed for both of them, but he wasn't a bit shy as he sang. Occasionally he'd look up and smile at her. One song he said was from Lovin' Spoonful, "You Didn't Have to Be So Nice." This one he sang right to her, smiling coyly, holding her eye, meaning the words. It was all so ordinary and simple she thought her heart would break. She realized then that he was the best she'd ever seen at looking at you, and almost meaning it. He finished, saying how that song had made him buy an autoharp, which sounded like "an angel's guitar," and that it was too bad John Sebastian had turned out to be "creepy and a sheep."

She tested the sundried tomatoes and they still wouldn't bend. The water they soaked in had turned to thin brown blood. Robert hummed as he melted butter and found the sugar and scooped in a "guesstimate" — she was starting to like his corny words — with his cupped hand. She tried not to be obvious as she watched him move. He looked practised in the kitchen, no stumbling, almost graceful. Mincing the garlic, the way he set down a plate. She didn't add to her beet-criticism when he brought out the Louisiana hot sauce, which was all vinegar too and wouldn't fit Italian either.

*He really should not eat certain things, eh? And the main thing — don't let him get stressed, or tired.*

Okay, Fournier, I won't let him.

Marg had been staring straight into but now noticed the frost pattern on the window in front of her. It was truly spectacular, backlit as it was by the kitchen porch light. A thousand prisms, shifting if you did. Framed in the window, it was a display, a happenstance gallery. If you had the time, you could watch it grow. Intricate patterns, hundreds of geometric storylines. No artist could do that, Marg didn't think. An artist would miss the precision or else go overboard into foliage and elves, something human. But how could beauty be so obvious and so painfully subtle, both at the same time? Some saw beauty like this as proof of God. That was too simple, though calling it an accident was too simple too. Not that that window display was proof of an intelligence, but more that it was what created expectations. And what made us try. That window display was what made us think there was something better. In store.

"Robert. Look at the window." She pointed, shaking her head, the prisms shifting colours as she did so. "I mean, *look* at that."

"That's pretty cool."

"Remember when you had the time to like, look at stuff like this? Magic Jack Frost?"

He nodded but didn't look convinced. She could see him take her comment and go within. Memories, worries, what. He smiled and looked at her. He had his hands up in front of him, dripping and limp at the wrist, fingers turned toward his face.

"I do have the time. I call it 'time to kill.'"

No dishcloth in sight, he wiped his hands on his pants. Then went to the fridge and, drawing out two bottles of Heineken beer, fell into his cowboy talk.

"Some especial-occasion-type beer, little lady?"

"Great."

"Crack the heads off'n a couple foreign weasels?" He waggled the Heinekens at her.

"Go to it."

He looked suddenly speedy and impatient. *And, hey, you really don' wanna make him mad.*

She hadn't liked hearing that one. The build of the man. His blocky hands ripping salad like it was air. Though Fournier had said it in an admiring way, and added, *Oooweee.* When she asked what he meant exactly, he said, "Ask the people of Kalamazoo, they tell you, eh?" and laughed. To her silence he'd actually laughed and added, "Don't worry, you're safe."

The bathroom hadn't been safe.

How mad would he be getting? The day after Fournier's call — and it wasn't like she'd hurried to find out, she was in the library already — she looked up the disease. And read about it, horrible. What must be going through Robert's mind? The thing was, anything could happen to the man now. Including nothing.

As she began to serve up, Robert told her to wait, mumbling "Hang on, hang on." First he fussed two tea towels into napkins. Then he cleaned off the table with his hands, one hand brushing crumbs carefully over the edge into the other. Disappearing to the living room, he returned with a Christmas candle, a foot-high Santa with only a half-inch of his red toque melted down. She decided against telling him this was Toby's special candle. She watched him light it.

"*Mah* Oklahoma," said Robert, sitting down finally and jigging hot sauce on everything, including the salad, "includes fancy eatin'."

The accent was totally believable, and went with the way he tucked in.

§

## WHAT IT TAKES
### —By BoBo Bonaduce

There are three kinds of toughness.

The second kind is the famous kind American fans like, the toughness of the big guy who can fight. Each team has at least one guy like this. If he's won enough fights early on, he can skate through the rest of his career

with his head high, face calm, sometimes even that cul-
tivated look of boredom. Cocksure as a dog who gets
paid to piss. Even the guys on his team fear him, sometimes hate him a little, because his job is to punch a guy's
lights out with no provocation and if you get traded he'd
do the same to you. Still, it is sad watching these tough
guys topple, when the younger tough guys start beating
them up on a consistent basis. The father bested by the
child. It means the end of a career, at thirty, and these
guys aren't going to any Hall of Fame.

The third kind of toughness depends on everyone's
fear of the unknown. The game of hockey is license for
some truly crazy men to inflict pain. These men can't
be summed up or described. They're all different, because one aspect of crazy-toughness is that it's a kind of
genius and it doesn't repeat itself.

He stopped typing. Picturing the guy's face, what it felt like to
go into a game against him. Even thinking about him, the feather
of fear tickled the gut. Shorty Amis. Bonaduce had seen no better practitioner of this toughness than Shorty Amis. He'd been
on the receiving end of the rodent's abuse more than a few times
himself.

The thing was, Amis and his kind were beyond tough. As in
Amis's case, it often had to do with the shoulder-chip venom of
being a little guy, but it was more a general condition of having
an eagerly sick spirit. Amis had no teeth, and his assaults were
two-voiced — a piercing shriek overtop a deeper, honking, ragged attempt at words. Guys fifty pounds heavier were unnerved
by his voice. Before, during and after a tussle, Amis yelled at you
and continued from the penalty box, shrieking until he lost his
voice. Bonaduce had seen him shriek till he retched.

Amis had once been called up by Philly to play the Bruins in
tough old Boston Garden, a kind of experiment probably, a let's-

unleash-it-and-see-what-it-does. Amis knew why he was there, and his NHL career lasted less than a minute, during which time he speared one guy (sending him to the hospital for a spleen), started a fight with the guy who avenged the spear (Amis getting beaten up), finished two more fights (getting beaten up twice more), shoved the linesman (getting tossed for this), spit at a fan on his way off the ice, and spanked the hat off the head of a cop for gawking in disbelief.

Amis would cut your face for no reason other than the colour of your jersey. He'd cut Bonaduce twice. The first time, Bonaduce fought him and, literally adding insult to injury, lost to the wiry prick. The second time, Amis's stick missed his eye by a hair, and Bonaduce was bleeding badly and too protective of his eye to fight. Other times they'd gone into corners together and ended up gloving each other's face and whatnot, and in the box the weasel-faced shit wouldn't stop shrieking. "Fuckin' stick your fuckin' eyes out, fuckin' chop your head off, fuckin' *shit* down your fuckin' *neck*, fuckin' *kill ya, I'll fuckin' kill ya, I'll fuckin' FUCK ya.*" Retch.

Once, Bonaduce realized the shrieking had stopped. Feeling like an air-raid siren had ceased, he chanced a look over. And he caught in Amis's glaring back something like humour. Bonaduce met his eye. When he saw Amis's quick wink, the hair actually rose tingling on his neck. He sat back and caught his breath, and later looked over at Amis and studied his calm profile. He looked quite bright. If Amis hadn't been born in Timmins but, say, in New York City, he might've been a poet.


He cradled the green plastic pot in the drive-way wind, the spindly plant brushing his chest and tickling him under the chin. He hustled it to his room. There are plenty of substitutes for blood kin. Anyone who forms bonds with pets, plants or inanimate objects knows this. The crone and her cat, the boy and his dog. The guy and his car. Even the *engine* of his car. Even a new engine *part* can be your special buddy.

Sure, it was a pathetic gesture to try to add anything to this little room, to try to make it more like a home. And a weakling plant like this one — a drooping pine-thing that lay somewhere between a bonsai and Charlie Brown's Christmas tree — a weak-sister plant like this could go the dangerous other direction and confirm a tawdry, lonely life, and cause fits of uncontrollable weeping, tears coursing the beard.

There was nowhere to place it but on the floor. He put it in the far corner, though nothing here was far, wedged it in tighter with his foot, and wished it well. It had been inevitable; at some point he always bought his house a plant.

His favourite, in Tulsa, he'd brought in under Fournier's wary gaze the day after teammate Lonny Miles went up on the rape charge. The rape charge had upset him, he wasn't sure why. The girl — Jennifer — was in fact a girl, or looked it and acted it at least, being only seventeen. He'd met her at a party the night before the alleged crime and liked her, perhaps because in certain ways she reminded him of Leah. It wasn't the clear skin and large-eyed cuteness they shared, it was more the brain-package, the depth and brightness and humour in the eyes, the basic read on the situation that made you wonder what she was doing with a bunch of hockey players, himself included, and Lonny Miles in particular. A crunchy little detail, one Bonaduce would be willing to offer up if he was called as a witness at the trial, was that, from the look of them sitting there on the couch, Jennifer didn't seem to like Lonny much. It looked like she wanted to be at the party but not stuck with Lonny, thin-lipped, brash, loud laugher Lonny.

Bonaduce sensed some connection between yesterday's rape news and today's walking down the sidewalk with a new plant. He'd liked Jennifer, however briefly, and he'd never liked Lonny Miles. What made him like Lonny Miles even less was the way he'd smiled when he'd said this morning at practice, "She got into it." He'd spent the night in jail, been bailed by the owners, came to practice almost gloatingly. When asked by the guys what the hell happened, he picked up his head and superciliously scanned the room, which fell quiet, uncharismatic Lonny Miles from Sydney Mines getting maybe his first spotlight ever. The little smile was an arrogant smile and, when mixed with the Clint Eastwood–like "She got into it," worked to suggest a whole slime-bucket full of things: he was irresistible, she couldn't help liking it, the bitch was deranged and the rape charge was absurd and wouldn't stick, he was so hot-damn he didn't care anyway because all that mattered was that she "got into it."

The piece of slime that stuck to Bonaduce was the literal meaning of those words. For the words did admit to rape, or something close. Because they said this: at the beginning, she wasn't into it. How not-into-it she was was anyone's guess — and Bonaduce couldn't help remembering her looking at Miles with something between tolerance and disgust — as was the degree and kind of seduction, more like coercion, probably physical force, used by Lonny Miles.

Bonaduce realized that this — even *wanting* sex with a woman who wasn't into it with you, who was very not into it and didn't fucking even *like* you — was foreign territory to him. Jesus, who'd enjoy that sex? Why not go stick your dick into some gravel?

Thoughts such as these walked with him down the sidewalk with his new plant. It was almost three feet tall and rustled beside his ear. Her age wasn't an issue apparently, perhaps this being the South. But in the newspaper were blatantly disparaging remarks about hockey players and Canadians, and the fact that hardly anyone went to see these games anyway, as if the converse would somehow have excused the rape, as if the star quarterback from Oklahoma State would be above such charges.

He brought in the plant, and Fournier, man of material simplicity, looked up like a lean wolf, instantly alert to excess. Bonaduce had recently joined his religion and yet here he was carting in this extraordinary bauble. It may as well have been a neon sculpture or ornamental barber's chair. Fournier watched him place it on the floor under the living-room window.

"Who will water this when we're gone?"

"I'll get someone."

This is all they ever said about it, Fournier being as sensitive as Bonaduce had always suspected.

It was called an umbrella plant. It was bushy and looked nothing like an umbrella, and he had no idea where it got that name. He looked down on it, fiddling a leaf between thumb and forefinger and on the verge of meditation, Fournier holding his tongue.

Here, this little Charlie Brown fern — Bonaduce had decided it was a fern — would not likely grant him the depth of friendly relationship the umbrella plant had. He'd kept it alive over the remaining Tulsa years, and bundled it off to his next stop back east, violating his own rule about starting fresh. It had uneven patches and rust spots now, but it stayed his buddy until, in his new place, a girlfriend poisoned it with tequila. He knew it was her and he knew it was deliberate. She secretly wanted control of his decor and didn't like that plant, or maybe it was his pure and simple affection for it.

## WHAT YOU NEED, CONTINUED

The first kind of toughness — it's what you need just to play the game. More a state of mind than body, you learn it as a kid or not at all — though you can see its birth in some Europeans over the course of a few seasons. It lets you play with a broken foot bone and not complain; it gives you dignity as you walk your chin to the dressing room to get it stitched, no freezing, so you miss no more than one shift. It lets you see pain as just another pebble in your shoe.

That's the key: it lets you see pain rather than feel it.

It's not as macho as it seems. In fact it's a trick. In the clash and speed of a game, things hardly hurt anyway. (I once took a skate on the forearm and didn't even know it until a guy smiling on the bench pointed at my blood-soaked sleeve.) But it's more than that. Like in war, where it's said a soldier's biggest fear is fear of cowardice, so it is on the bench surrounded by the guys: it's harder to show pain than it is to just sit on it.

In this way your pain is absorbed by the team. It's not a bad little trick.

And this first kind of toughness: when you walk into a bar, say, even if you aren't particularly witty, or sexy, or tough even, it lets you believe you're all of those. This belief shows in your face and in the way you speak, and makes people think you are those things too. Not all people, but enough so you get the rewards. You see this in guys again and again. You see complete schmoes almost become what they believe they are. It's not a bad trick, actually. It's one more thing you can do.

A hard and hurtful sun cut through the narrow ice-house windows, its rays deflecting off the saliva of Kirsten's bucking teeth into Big Jan's poetic goddamn hair, which baffled and trapped it.

God he was angry. He couldn't blame his mood on his little two-wine hangover. Nor could he blame it on this writing class. At least he wasn't afraid in it. People spoke English, he could hold his own. Though the day was coming when he would have to bring in a smash of work for them to tear apart. So far all he had were snippets, nonsense attempts at a novel that wasn't looking like a novel at all.

He even liked where the class was held, this old renovated ice house. It had thick stone walls you could lean your chair back against. It had *rafters* — how often could you use that word any more? The best part was this ancient oak table, must be fifteen feet long, for all to gather around, the kind of table you could imagine royalty supping at and tossing bones to dogs from.

He'd even almost enjoyed what they'd done this morning,

spontaneous drills to sharpen their "artful incongruity." The more twisty and stupid-on-purpose he got with his stuff, the more Jan seemed to approve of it. This morning he'd come up with lines that went nowhere and fit into nothing:

My nose points to what isn't me

It was a shit-climb to the mountaintop, upon which sat a shit-shaped rock, which could well have been shit's temple

Life is a Cyst in Death's Immortal Flesh

Who put the Hale in the Bopp-shoo-Bopp-shoo-Bopp?

But this morning, because he suddenly liked Jan less, he liked his lines less, and the class less too. He'd thought her an ally, all her talk in class about getting at real stuff, the heart, and fuck everything else. Quote unquote. You trusted her saying this. She would've made a decent coach.

Before class they'd congregated in the lounge for coffee. Despite the hostile potential of Phil and Kirsten, something like camaraderie had been tempting the spirit of this group lately, maybe due to their "creative" as opposed to "academic" status. They'd begun referring to their academic counterparts as "inmates," this evolving from Bonaduce's joke that you didn't see those types much because they'd had themselves committed to the library. He'd said "libary," and they seemed to get it, appreciating self-deprecation though never going near it themselves.

The little creative team had huddled at the lounge bulletin board, sipping, reading a fresh notice of a PhD thesis having its oral defence. Bonaduce crowded in — some of these things were amazing, the language in them. This one you could understand. It was on Shakespeare. But it wasn't about themes, or poetic language, or characters. It was *speculation* about *possible* uses of the *trapdoor* in *early versions* of *some* plays Shakespeare *might* have written. The thesis was more than three hundred pages long, and Bonaduce suggested while hunched there that they should find this inmate and rescue him before he wasted the rest of his life. Phil supported Bonaduce with a snort, but otherwise no one said a thing.

Sure, maybe he'd been arrogant in saying it, and maybe you shouldn't make jokes in a public place about wasted lives, since the inmate in question turned out to be Kirsten's boyfriend. He couldn't blame her; in fact he admired her balls when she turned to him, the scabbard of her lip lifting to reveal her sword of teeth. She said simply, "Shakespeare's a waste of time. Hockey isn't. Oh." Her eyes were already dull, having dismissed him in advance.

He was ready to do sheepish and admit he was a pot caught calling her kettle-boy black, but before he could, Jan jumped in to lead Kirsten away by the shoulder, leaning into her like a friend, with a stage whisper for everyone's benefit that "our Robert has given up chasing his silly pucks, though perhaps a little late."

Well, now stop. *He* could belittle his life and his game, and it was only fair that Kirsten had her little whack at him, but Jan was not allowed. So, in class, still pissed off, ignoring most of the creativity drills, he wrote and reworked this:

Not that they ever will, but if anyone ever asked me which was more important, playing hockey or reading Shakespeare, I will declare free from doubt:

When you read a book you are nothing but a fan. And fans of books have nothing — nothing — over fans of hockey. That a puck is an utterly meaningless thing to chase is exactly the point. They might never think of it this way, but hockey fans are drawn to the spectacle of men who are the best in the land at using their bodies to fulfil *pure desire*. Pure, because these are guys who will basically kill to get at a puck, this chunk of dumb rubber

the perfect symbol of worthlessness. It is so abstract, so
pure in its meaninglessness, it is almost Japanese.

It got him thinking about them — fans. Generally, players
didn't like them and didn't think about them much. But they
didn't like to think about that either, about not liking the people
who paid your salary, admired you, in some cases adored you. It
was pretty simple, really. How can you respect anyone who likes
you and doesn't even know you? If people hate you for your skin
or uniform colour, it's of course more painful than if they *love*
you for the same reason, but the scenario is similarly stupid.

There were lots of decent fans of course. Appreciators of the
game. Guys who used to play themselves. Mums and dads who
took their kids. The row of folks in their wheelchairs, some with
heads resting over on their shoulders, others done up with team
jackets, waving pennants. There were memorable, funny fans as
well. Here, in Freddie Beach, twenty years ago, he'd forgotten
about her — she was maybe sixty, floppy homemade hat in team
colours, cowbell, tartan blanket on the lap, and most of all the
big whisky-voice. She would pick quiet spots, ring her bell twice,
and the fans would fall quieter still to hear her yell her weird
stuff. *Hey, Seven. Yer mother still stink?* Another one he remembered, *Hey, Ref, that a banana?* Years later in a bar in Dayton the
subject of this fan had come up and Bonaduce was surprised that
other guys had all assumed that she was a weird old *he*. Anyway,
lots of fans used the game to get their ya-yas out. Ripping shirts
off and jumping up against the glass, leading cheers, picking
fights, grenading the visitors' bench with cups of beer, whatever. In the Des Moines penalty box, Bonaduce had taken an
empty mickey bottle off the helmet. His team went into the stands
after the guy while he rested for a bit with his head between his
knees.

In the lounge Bonaduce had nodded to Jan after her traitor-
ous quip and said, "Yeah, me grow up." Then refilled his coffee
and started down to the ice house. It was as close to a fight as he
was going to get. He would be only nice. To Jan, to Kirsten, to

Phil. To Toby and Leah and everybody. You get too tired for anything else.

He drove home with a kink in his neck after an awkward snooze in the library reading room. The chairs there were designed for sitting up; a guy should complain. Downtown at an intersection he found himself staring at a pack of kids. It took him five seconds to register that they were dressed as a witch, a Darth Vader, a what might have been Robin Hood. Jesus, Hallowe'en.

He pulled into a convenience store and spent far too much money on their whole stock of Mars bars. Screw the bags of little Hallowe'en-size bars, it was one night you could be a hero for not a lot of money. A real bar falling heavy from your hand, surprised muffled shout through the monster mask: *Wow, thanks*.

Marg and her sister and Toby were home, Marg and her sister on their way to a costume party. It was also a Friday night. In her white robe and pants, black belt and headband, Marg was a karate person, while her sister was a Bad Santa — your basic Santa outfit but with stitches on the face, toting a machine gun, bottle of whisky sticking out the pocket. Toby, slumped in the living room starting a bottle of wine, and who Bonaduce realized was a sort of natural Bad Santa, wasn't going anywhere.

"Wanna come, Robert?" Marg asked, martial artist forcing down a quick beer at the kitchen counter.

"Don't think so, thanks. I don't have a costume."

At this Toby snorted, and Marg shot him a look, the exchange making Bonaduce see his creased pants and tight haircut. Not bad, Toby lad.

The invitation was tempting, especially as he'd be here alone with Toby otherwise. But he wouldn't know anyone, and Marg's voice in asking hadn't been enthusiastic. He found an old salad bowl in a kitchen cupboard, dumped the bars in it and came back to the living room with that and an empty glass. Because Toby would offer him some wine, he would accept, and Toby would say, Well, go get yourself a glass then. Bringing the glass in advance risked looking presumptuous and might lose him his offer of wine, which would be fine. He set the bowl of bars on the floor by the front door and switched on the porch light. He found the Yahtzee score sheet and the dice, one still lost. He hated playing with four, you had to reroll one die and remember too much. He did like solo Yahtzee, however. It gave you a feel for averages, and the duration of luck, which felt less like stamina than grace.

"No kids'll come," said Toby matter-of-factly, in the act of rising to fill Bonaduce's glass.

"Why not?"

A car crunched into the drive, Marg and her sister banged beer bottles on the counter and rushed out the back door, calling goodbyes.

Toby answered as though Bonaduce were a kid himself.

"It's the Trans-Canada Highway, there's no streetlights, there's a house only every hundred yards. The people around here are poor and they drive their kids to the rich suburbs."

Well shit. Bonaduce eyed the bowl of Mars bars. As he did so the doorbell rang. He opened the door onto a two-and-a-half foot devil, a three-foot grim reaper and their Satanic mom. Ooo, Toby would hate him for this. He dropped a chocolate bar in their bags, empty so far, and in a childlike voice their mother sang a thank-you on her children's behalf.

"Maybe if," Bonaduce said, closing the door, "you know, maybe if the porch light's on, they'll come."

"Well there's going to be a *few*."

In the ensuing hour he was ready to concede this round to Toby, because only one more kid had come, and he was alone, tall enough to be fourteen, and under the tossed-on costume you could see quick hot eyes that looked less intent on candy than on vandalism.

Bonaduce picked up the empty wine bottle to take to the kitchen to rinse while Toby went down for another. Some CD of Toby's by a band called Dead Can Dance was on in honour of the night, though the music sounded basically Middle Eastern, a quarter-tone-wailing female singer backed by spacey ambient organ. As he washed out the bottle, he noticed the homemade label said "Mountain Frog '99," and he got a chuckle from it.

In the bathroom he found a garish red lipstick Marg's sister had used for her face blood. He smiled as he applied it to his nose. He liked Hallowe'en. He almost never got to enjoy one, there always seemed to be a game scheduled, the arena full of clowns and witches and team-colour harlequins, an extra buzz in the air. The nose began with just a small dot on the tip and then, what the hell, the whole schnozz, bright red. What was he? Maybe a wino.

He used to like those houses back in Winnipeg where instead of just dumping some candy in your bag they'd make you come inside and do something: sing, or a joke. Often they were European, or foreign-sounding at least, and they'd be dressed up too. Ten-year-old Bonaduce stumbling to get a song or a joke out, his buddies nervous or pissed off beside him. At one of these houses in his neighbourhood lived a boy — maybe he was twelve, maybe much older — in a wheelchair, and he'd sit there smiling like crazy, his head sort of flopped over and his fat hands palm up and unmoving on his thighs. Hallowe'en was the only time in the year you'd see him. Rumour had it his name was Jordy. Then one year Jordy wasn't there. In any case — Bonaduce finished the nose, even going up into the nostrils a tad — these people who invited the ghosts and goblins inside and made them come alive for their candy seemed to know something more about Hallowe'en than the rest did. Because, otherwise, these big-eyed four-year-olds upon whose heads parents had slammed a hat and mask, these little first-timers must be thinking, Holy, alls I do is go up there with this bag and they throw candy in it, why haven't we been doing this every night?

Toby snorted a kind of approval at Bonaduce's nose when he looked up from his display of bottle uncorking. Bonaduce lumbered over to read the label and this one was an Earth Spit '53. He laughed aloud at this and commented to Toby that his friend was pretty funny, to which Toby shrugged, noncommittal. The music got cranked up so that conversation was made difficult, and Toby wasn't pleased when the doorbell rang again and Bonaduce invited a Zorro (a Zorro! They must have a big ol' attic) and a princess inside. With a pretty good Irish wino accent, he demanded a joke or song of them, their teenaged sister or babysitter looking on nervously. They sang a quavering Row, Row, Row Your Boat, got three full-sized Mars bars each, and that was it for trick-or-treaters that night. Though Bonaduce himself hung in there till one a.m., the radio turned to what twenty-year-olds might be listening to at this moment, eating bars and sipping intermittently from a bottle of "Tidal Flats '02." No, he wasn't sipping, he caught himself gulping.

He put his hand over his mug, as if it was someone else offering to pour, then laughed, took his hand off.

This morning he'd been reading a book by Ven Begamudré, a male Asian Canadian writer writing about being a female soldier/gourmet in Scotland. It was decent writing, but for some reason he'd grown cold and he couldn't get warm. He had been cold a lot lately. He saw how the bit of wine at night had helped warm him and smooth things. Beer was good after games with the boys, get the grin on, but wine was good alone, in the night. Mornings he felt gritty and more tired for it, even after two glasses. Last night he'd had a bucket-full. How soothing was alcohol, how thick the bandage, but then the bandage gets ripped off in the morning, how clear and hurtful this part was. His body felt beaten and shocked. So, no more drinking. It was just boredom. He shouldn't be drinking at all, he was in training, and he was, he was possibly — it just wasn't good for him right now. But no worry about making it a habit, he was too poor. Nor could he afford to keep stealing Toby's.

Nor was he all that worried he'd tossed last night's last swallow of wine against his wall.

This room, this bed, had become his place. His nasty little niche. Jesus, look at it. My, how he'd come down in the world. You get used to anything. Tired all the time, of company in general and Toby in particular, he read here, strummed here, laptopped here, sipped wine here.

Paced here. He stopped himself. A three-step pace is ridiculous anyway. And it was a sham, an act — you can pretend all you want that you're a martyr and a prisoner but you're not and you know it.

He lay on his bed. Eyes can pace too. He pictured himself as a wolf in his forest den, a wolf who has eaten and is lying on his stomach, head on his paws. His eyes are open and looking, and his ears twitch at this sound or another, but the wolf is otherwise quite calm. Apparently waiting for something. But, being a dumb animal, he doesn't have a clue what it is.

He remembered last night deciding that his room was green. Years faded, it was one of those industrial almost-colours. Depending on the light, it was grey, or yellow, or even blue. But it was green, barely green. Last night he'd added the splash of red wine, a sudden impulse to see if wine would sink in, or drip down. It did both, a blob sinking in and the rest running down, an octopus body with skinny legs dangling to the floor.

If the ways of your own damn heart are hard to know, what dumb grin of red-lipped stupidity leads you to think you can know the heartways of anybody else?

How much of their anger is just anger at the past?

He ached picturing Jason's face. In the concrete corridor, in wet underwear, the steaming body. He'd seen clear as life that something of the father had created the boy and swelled in the boy's flesh ...

Arrogant to assume this, and infantile to need it.

He lay back on his bed and closed his eyes. With the light off, his room was so dim that closing his eyes gave him perfect darkness. Which, if you cared to see things a certain way, could be a desirable and perfect thing. No comet, dreamcatcher, wine octopus. No stage.

. . .

OSCAR.

Leah rose and quickly stepped into her clothes. Mornings it was her wont to linger here, choosing blouses, hair clasps, trying things in the mirror. Turning away from him — modestly? unconsciously? coyly? — when she removed underwear. Either not caring that he watched — because she did know he liked to watch — or perhaps understanding that a committed relationship legitimized his brand of voyeurism, if that is what it was called. Then she would stand at her writing desk and consult her day planner, review the human disasters on her schedule this week. After which she liked to lean on the windowsill, take in their view of the river over to the north side, gazing out, perhaps contemplating human suffering and the potential for freedom from it. It occurred to him this morning that maybe it was because Bob Bonaduce was over there on the north side that lately she hadn't been doing this.

This was simply not good. She was so knotted about Bob's being here and she could not talk about it. It was not good keeping such things inside. With prodding, Leah usually opened up. It didn't appear that Bob Bonaduce was going to take a hint and leave town. Or even well enough alone. Jason was knotted as well. Though it was harder to tell with him, due to Jason's knottiness in general. That was a horrible pun. It was like something a Bobby Bonaduce would say.

Wafts of coffee drifted up the stairs, his wake-up call. The timed coffee-maker one of the century's underappreciated inventions. Leah descended to pour herself her half-cup, which she would top with hot water, the coward.

He leapt up and peeked at her day planner, saw she likely wouldn't be heading out for an hour. She sometimes came back up with her coffee, so he quickly put on his robe and sweat pants. He no longer liked to be caught undressed. He realized he had

become content to just cover up the ten pounds he seemed incapable of losing. Maybe it was fifteen pounds now. Maybe this
year he would dust off the NordicTrack ski machine, or the stair-
stepper.

Leah arrived back in their room. He felt the slightest hurt
that she hadn't brought him up a cup of coffee. Not that she
wouldn't happily do so if he was to ask. Would she just as happily doff her clothes if he were to ask?

"Leah?"

She raised her eyebrows for him while continuing to jot notes
in her planner.

"I really think you should make amends with him."

Leah put her pen down flat and lifted her gaze out the window, across the river.

"What exactly does that mean? 'Make amends.'"

"Well, air it out. Talk. Make peace." He came upon a smart
idea. "You know, instead of popping his balloon, you could help
him pop it himself."

"He makes me see what a teenager I was."

What?

"Well, maybe that's not a bad thing."

Leah didn't respond. Uneasy, he was tempted to make a joke
about Bobby Bonaduce the fountain of youth, but humour didn't
seem right, didn't seem to enter into her current relationship
with her ex. Her mood also prevented him from telling her what
he'd planned to tell her, which was what an odd duck he'd decided Bob was during his last visit. After putting the strange gift
of Dutch cheese in the fridge, he'd returned as she and Bob
were blurting at each other about Gordie Howe. What he'd seen
was Bonaduce as an Eighties man, being out of touch with everything dire about the Nineties. But then he seemed more Seventies, because he was so impractically naïve. On third thought,
make that Sixties — the fellow was absurdly idealistic. No, wrong
again, he was Fifties, just look at him. Okay, let's keep this going: the post-war simplicity of the Forties supplied the best description yet. Simplicity, or simplistic? He envisioned the pictures

of sailors docking, getting off their ship, the certain looks on their faces, soon to be genuinely happy with wife and job and new barbecue.

Watching Leah and Bob hard at their argument, he'd still considered Bonaduce a good man, and maybe in the right, but he'd also understood that, twenty years ago, Leah had been intellectually slumming.

"Leah, I think you should call him."

"Why."

"For Jason. Even though he's twenty" — Oscar found himself voicing what he'd formulated — "and even though he never did have the man around as his father, the psychology of broken homes is complex, and gluey, and so maybe for Jason's sake you might consider, I don't know, normalizing diplomatic relations."

Leah stood gazing at the north side of the river.

"I will act as your ambassador if you like."

Leah staring across.

"Call the man. I can't stand your, your *mood* any more."

§

Sitting cross-legged on the bed, he glanced out his window, at the leafless trees through to the river. Knees sticking stiffly way up, he cradled a notepad over his crotch. Time to write something serious. Beside the bed a first cup of coffee steamed on a table he'd banged together out of two-by-fours and a serving tray he'd plucked from roadside garbage two houses down.

After a couple of sips and some staring into space, he wrote:

> The leafless trees looking black against the
> morning's frost.

He reached for his coffee, took a sip. It was a decent observation. Where it would go, who could tell, but those trees looked extremely black this morning even though you knew they were brown. Leafless? He crossed out "leafless." Jan's rule number one said that every word had to count. If there was frost, readers would assume leafless, wouldn't they? Unless they were evergreens. Hey, that-there frost was so white, even the *ever*greens looked black.

He changed it to:

The treetrunks looked black against the snow.

Because the idea, the effect, was snow, rather than frost. Then he crossed out "looked." Why did you need it? They *were* black against the snow. Though without the "looked" you might think the trees were in fact black, whereas "looked" suggested the optical illusion. Well, but, so what was the sentence about — the blackness, or the illusion of blackness? What *should* the sentence be about? Well, what should *any* fucking sentence be about. Settle down. Maybe once the paragraph got going he'd know. Maybe you shouldn't dwell too long on any particular—

"*Hey Marg.*" He heard Marg stop walking up the staircase.

"Yes?"

"*Get in here.*"

She came in smiling at his yell, she was a buddy. He had no shirt on, but he sensed this was okay, though some women weren't enamoured of body hair. And his, from the belt to the tops of his cheeks, didn't give your eye much of a break.

"What colour are those trees out there?"

"*Wow* this room is small."

"Welcome to my coffin."

"You hardly fit."

"Tell me what colour those trees are."

"That's a nice place for it." Margaret was looking at the dreamcatcher hanging low in the window. "Though if you hung it higher it'd, you know, be more up in the sky. Framed by the sky."

"No, there I can look right through it from bed."

"Why do you look through it?"

"So what colour are the trees?"

"Those?"

"What colour."

"I dunno. Brown?"

"No, I mean right now. Sitting against that white frost like that."

"Grey? The frost is almost gone."

"Shit. No, c'mon."

"How should *I* know. Charcoal? Charcoal. No, don't cross out what you had. What are you writing?"

"My novel. Until you ruined it."

"I just—"

"Marg. I'm kidding you."

Some people, when they go serious, it's like all their skin suddenly falls off and everything hurts. And they aren't so great to be with. He would've liked to tell Marg this, but she was serious at the moment.


## BOBO DOES THE TREES

BoBo Bombsaway was right tuckered after cuttin seven cord a hardwood usin only a ax. Choppin all them trees into finnicky eighteen inch chunks. But the wife Marg liked hers eighteen inches, heh heh. Though she yelled at him, why'd ya fuckin cut all them trees down? Cause they was too fuckin BLACK! he yelled back. An buy me a new chainsaw, woman! BoBo kicked at the old one, lyin there on the bed. These saws, once their teeth are mostly broke off, all they're good for is fixin cars.

. . .

MARGARET.

Robert opened her door and poked his head in like he knew she was awake. It was past midnight, maybe close to one. She'd heard him downstairs playing Yahtzee by himself, which he did a lot lately, head down and immersed sometimes for a couple of hours. Like he said, killing time. But she hadn't heard him climb the stairs, maybe she'd fallen asleep after all. She'd been lying in bed trying to decide whether or not to move out. Lately she'd gotten very tired of the general slovenliness of the place. Her sister was not around much, and Joyce was not around ever, and these bastards were trying to leave the cleaning to her, screw them. Jesus H, there was still deepcorner grunge from the tenants before them. And the aura of depression here lately, or was it just aimlessness? It had changed from what she first took to be a cool, healthy, open quality, a letting things fall as they may. A "don't worry be happy" house mood. No TV, and that uniquely open gesture of Toby's when he unpinned his bedroom door and stashed it in the basement. But gradually this good house *mañana* had fallen to a lazy and wheedling "So I wonder what's to eat and who might get around to cooking it?" The guys, Robert too, would too easily tip into dinosaur ways and let themselves get waited on hand and foot and not even notice it was happening. Robert you might expect this of, and you might forgive it. Robert was kind, he would make it up in little ways he had. He would get all concerned, for instance, about how you talked — gently joking about how you, like, talked — and he would sincerely try to help you. Corny bugger.

Food smells too. She suspected she was allergic to the food smells of this house, they actually seemed to plug her up. When one of them did cook, it was all onions and grease smell for hours after. It went into the curtains, it smelled like years of grease in those curtains. Lately Robert had gotten into a habit of midnight popcorn. She could smell it again tonight.

And tension. Toby and Robert at each other, who knows why. They were quite a pair. Boys, play nice.

Toby was the last straw. She had slept with him three times now, and he was beginning to make demands and have expectations, though they'd promised well before the clothes were off that this would not happen. Rejection was such a hideous monster to him. Which was to be expected. But it would be impossible ever to tell him the truth, that his arm bothered her less than his drinking, or his being two inches shorter than her. He would still blame it on his arm. You could see how he used it as a magnifying glass, all hurts coming through it and burning him. Life was probably simpler that way.

As life would be simpler if she moved.

But then Robert's knock on the door, Robert poking his head into her plans. Her first thought was that he was going to read some of his novel to her. The second was that he'd discovered she'd slept with Toby and felt a little lonely because of it. The third was that they were going to talk about his illness.

He sat not at the foot of the bed this time but in the middle, and when she sat up, his arms opened and he was hugging her. All heavy and serious, his heart and body both. He felt even bigger than he looked. She had never felt a man like this. Hard as wood. Solid as ground. But denser, the moving blood in him somehow making him seem denser still.

Her breasts moulded to his shape, and she could feel his awareness of them. She pulled back a little and kissed him on the neck, small and soft, not at all clear what she wanted. There was something so passive about him and, despite the heaviness, so ready to change. To be led away like a dog.

He answered with his own identical little kiss on her neck. He removed his hand from her shoulder. What was he going to do with it? So softly she could hardly feel it, the hand was on her hair. Then it was pressing, huge and sad and gentle, spanning the back of her head, cupping it ear to ear. She resisted falling against the hand, trusting it fully, the way it cupped her head, holding all the thoughts she might ever have.

Then he sighed, long and low. The release of something deep. At its sound she knew nothing more would come of this night, nothing physical. But neither did he speak. He squeezed her head again, and once more kissed her neck. She pecked his neck back, identically, almost as a joke, but one he didn't get, because he sighed again sadly. It was all quite dramatic, really, as he got up in a hurry then and stood watching her in the darkness, and then went to the door and watched her some more, then left. Alone once more, she felt herself glad it had happened, whatever it was.

Still she thought of moving. Where to go. Jesus H, after this house, where. Alone?

The image of Robert and her sharing a place scared her. Not because it was a naturally bad idea, but because of how the image grew, and flipped. First it was them at home, a phantom living room, smiling together over a glass of wine that wasn't Toby's, the Yahtzee dice on an elegant table. Then it was her standing behind him, able to see only the back of his head, which wobbled with the movement. She was pushing his wheelchair.

§

Bespectacled Patrick talking, talking. After these couple of months, Bonaduce understood half of it. Bits and pieces he caught himself actually enjoying. Getting the hang of it was no small source of pride. You spend time with this stuff, you witness yourself falling into word-mode too. In class on occasion he even caught himself clucking and taking ironic offence, a regulation grad student.

Normally shy Patrick had worked himself into a fever of confidence. Speaking, he looked over people's heads lest errant eye contact dam his stream of words.

"Ideologically embodied in object." That mean "symbolic," Patrick? A Marxist hidden inside every shovel? A dope in every hockey stick?

"Sub-meta-fictional." Patrick, c'mon Patrick, that translates as "under above the story."

Presentation finished, fielding questions, Patrick fell to nervous defence. He stuttered into sentences that began "I didn't mean to imply," which was like tossing blood bags to sharks. Phil slouched diagonally in his chair, radiating boredom, eyes taking in the shape of the room, as in: This discussion occupies not a lot of my brain. The posture worked. The others, Patrick too, were as hungry for Phil's approval as they were for Gail Smith's. In hockey as well you saw the one or two guys who worked the attitude and got to be daddy, backing it up not with words, but with goals or violence.

It was still mostly bullshit. The circle of wristwatches ticked, and Bonaduce sat occasionally in awe, generally asleep, other times nodding as if he agreed, but hating these long dips into fakery. He was intimate with everyone's jewellery, hair-habits, moles. (Phil had a hefty wart on his temple, at which he pictured himself pointing and laughing if things ever got rough between them.) He let himself x-ray Kirsten's limp sweater, arriving at a likely sense of her pair, and shame when this image stirred the nether zone. Sometimes he winced with the wasted time — What was Jason doing right now? Where was, where was his fucking Utica *money?* — but stayed willing to encounter language at its best, hearing new groups of words and feeling little wafts of oxygen coming off his understandings. He'd begun jotting down phrases, and words to look up. You never knew what you might use writing a novel, even one about hockey. But mostly he suffered a drifting mind, one which was repeatedly elbowed in the snout by fear. Once he woke hearing someone quote, "as he waited for his cataracts to develop so he could have the operation," and he decided that this described the sensation of sitting in this room with these people.

"Disfunction of the male–female." This from Doctor Gail, summing up. Disfunction at Gender Junction. Almost an old blues line there, What's the function, of the junction? Hey, what's better, Gail, "Disfunction of the male–female" or "Smash-up at the hairy-ugly"? C'mon, Gail.

Look up:

> nascent
> concomitant (sp?)
> self-reflexive (sounds kinky)
> quotidian

Neat Phrases:

> delicate with parody
> gently hyperbolized diction
> rife with serious play

It was UNB's third or fourth home game. Dalhousie in town to do battle. Bonaduce lined up like a loner to buy a single ticket. Not looking right or left. Checking out his shoe tops.

He sat surrounded by empty seats in the thirtieth row, feeling foolish, collar turned up, flinching into himself whenever Jason skated back to the bench. Averting his own eyes as if this would hide him from his son's.

He still hadn't tried calling him, not since outside the dressing room. The longer he left it, the more foolish he felt and the harder it got — it was one of those.

Doubtful that in the heat of the game the boy would catch

sight of him. And Jason's back was almost always turned — he wasn't getting off the bench much. Jesus, the fourth line. Number 19. *BONADUCE* in red letters.

This arena could seat four thousand, and tonight there were maybe three hundred, clustered at ice level behind the benches. A few scattered, like Bonaduce. He knew the players could feel it too: like a lone rider on a bus, like a BB in a boxcar. Sounds echoed, haunted. Most of the crowd were students who wanted to cheer and party, but what should have been a crowd's roar was thin and tinny and worse than nothing, a reminder of what it wasn't. It made everything you did on the ice feel a little apologetic.

Fourth line and killed penalties. Here was a guy with pro ambitions, a nobody in a league not bothered much by scouts to begin with. Though you never knew. He did have the size and speed. And guys did suddenly "get good," as if their bodies found some dormant grace or oomph that clicks in like it had been there all along. But for now Jason was likely on the fourth line for a reason.

There was Whetter, pacing behind the bench in his cheap suit and tie, as nervous and frustrated as any coach anywhere. Bonaduce hadn't called him either. Had Whetter bothered to pursue the matter of his eligibility, or had his disappearance been a relief? Maybe he would saunter down after the game, have a chat. Maybe he wouldn't. Some avenues of life here were embarrassing to walk.

By the third period he understood. Jason was a right-winger, and the three right-wingers ahead of him were maybe the three best guys on the team. Jesus, luck of the draw. All Jason needed was somebody to get injured. Then step in, pop a few goals, make the newly healed guy work to dislodge you. It could happen. The first-line right-winger, guy named Harrington, Bonaduce hated from the getgo. A bony, haughty guy, wouldn't go near a corner, and both times after both his goals he cruised to centre ice doing a white man's try at a touchdown dance before letting the other guys high-five with him. Harrington was the kind of guy who could break an arm and no one on the team would mind.

The Reds won six-four. For a close game it was boring. Dalhousie was a bunch of small skill-guys in yellow uniforms. The refs let the bigger Reds get away with lots of clutch-and-grab. Jason would have been effective in a game like this. If he focused on defence he could be a small Bob Gainey, a guy so unflashy yet so bothersome he was noticed only by the other team.

Bonaduce rose from his seat ready for a beer. But, wait, he hadn't earned it, he hadn't played. Smiling, he saw he was nothing but a dog, salivating at a buzzer at the end of a game.


OSCAR.

Bonaduce called just as Peter Mansbridge announced the top stories on the ten o'clock News. Bob had a knack for putting a wedge in a man's routine, which, while theoretically not a bad thing, could be irritating. Phone to his ear, Oscar tried to watch the News as well.

"So how're things there, Oscar old man?"

"... Great ..." Kosovo had proved a shameful mess. Another mass grave with all fingers pointing to—

"Sorry for that bit of kerfuffle with Leah the other day. Last week, whenever."

"Not a problem ..." He should tell him it was Leah who had felt badly about it. Leah should be apologizing to you. The look on her face, the staring-at-nothing for ten minutes. It had given him a jealous pang.

"How was the cheese?"

"Absolutely fantastic. Thank you."

"Oscar, I was wondering. I really have to get in shape here before playing with UNB and I was wondering if you knew of any oldtimers' teams. I need a contact. You know, our age, guys who play, friends of yours—"

Oscar sighed and muted the TV.

"—someone I could call to see if I could get on a team. My eligibility's still up in the air, but if I don't get on the ice soon, well ..."

There was loud laughing and banging in the background, and he noticed now that Bonaduce had been close to shouting all of this.

"Where are you?"

"At the arena. Aitken Centre. Jason just had a game."

"Oh! Right, right!" He probably should be going to these games but he was fairly certain Jason didn't want him to. And Leah wouldn't go near the place. He could go with Bonaduce, of course. Join the mess.

"Did he win?"

"You know it."

His attempt, last week, to talk with Jason about this mess had been a parody of concerned parent interrogating mute youth. "So your father's in town!" "Yeah." "Quite a surprise?" "I guess." "And I understand he's going to be playing on your team?" "I dunno." "Well, how do you feel about that?" Jason at the fridge gulping milk from the carton and, to complete the sitcom scene, shrugging. Impatient, Oscar had repeated himself. "No, how do you *feel* about it?" Equally impatient, Jason met his eye and said, "I don't *know*." And Oscar felt stupid. As if knowing how you felt was a simple thing, and Jason hadn't been accurate the first time.

"And Jace had a few good shifts. They're playing him on sort of a checking line. And penalty-killing. I guess he's your basic digger."

Oscar could tell from the man's voice that he and Jason still hadn't spoken. Bonaduce was slurring, it sounded like. Not good. You could imagine the fellow in the bleachers sipping rum from a flask. He had the compassionate urge to tell Bob he shouldn't take Jason's silences personally because his son was as a rule quiet and, on top of that, simply shy, emotion not being one of the lad's skills. But Oscar couldn't locate the delicate way to tell a father something so elementary about his own child.

"Well, that's right, he's certainly always been eager about the game." He felt awkward having nothing more technical to offer. He also would've liked to add that Jason was especially shy around other men. But this might imply the equation of Jason having grown up with the role model *in absentia*. There was so much you couldn't say.

Jason had smiled and shrugged again for him as he put back the milk, shut the fridge and left the kitchen. There'd been something of the father in this and other gestures — Oscar could see this now. Traces of Bonaduce in the latent power of Jason's legs and arms, and in his almost musical striding away. Jason "carried himself well." As in Bonaduce dancing. In such synchronization one could sense invisible, internal juggling, bowling pins kept effortlessly in the air. There are those who can walk and chew gum at the same time.

In any case, in the kitchen, watching Jason move, Oscar had suddenly felt a more solid presence of Bob Bonaduce in town.

"I do know a couple of oldtimers players. Not friends exactly. I don't know if their teams are filled up or whatever, or how that might work, but there's this fellow at the office, Andrew Frenette. Andy Frenette."

"Great."

"You want his number?"

"Please." A pause. "Actually, I don't have a pen or anything."

Oscar suggested that he'd get Andy to call him. Bob sounded doubtful, indeed he pulled away to ask passersby for pens, but in the end he let himself be assured that Frenette would call.

"From the sounds of it" — Oscar heard himself chuckle raucously into the phone — "they have quite a colourful crew. Andy tells me a good many of them are rural lads, as he calls them, and the little trips they take for tournaments and what have you tend to the, shall we say, wild-and-crazy."

"Sounds good."

"One fellow, in fact, according to Andy, one fellow, a tough character, was convicted, along with his uncle — this was some years back, but — convicted for raising fighting dogs. Outside of Moncton. Dogs for dogfights, gambling. Can you imagine?"

"Well you probably wouldn't want to tangle with a lad like that."

"I should say you wouldn't." Not that "tangle" was something Oscar imagined doing with any lad at all.

"Oscar? I should go. But hey, we should do it again some night soon. Whatever it was we did the last time. Rockin Rodeo."

"Some night soon, Bob." Actually, why not? Beer, music, discussions never remotely crucial. Though why was it that talking to this man made him feel lonelier, more friendless, than ever?

"Oscar? Sounds good."

§

Everyone was asleep when Bonaduce got home. In the arena parking lot, his car hadn't started and he'd fiddled under the hood with it and ended up wearing down the battery. He'd had to collar someone for a jump. He'd cut his finger on the cable. He was tired, gritty and cold.

He washed his hands at the kitchen sink, eyeing the bottle of wine on the counter. White wine, a rare thing, labelled "Beard Filtered '72." He left the wine and took the half-bowl of cold popcorn into the living room. Marg's laptop was there.

story about a guy, in the kitchen cuts his finger to the bone and washing it sees his bone is made of what turns out to be pure diamond. After some thought he amputates it, sells the diamond-bone, gets enough to buy a house, etc. Gets used to the house of course, cuts off and sells another finger. Lives high for a year, nice car, sea cruise. Sells off a little toe, another finger, etc., gets to the point where he weighs lifestyle against healthy body, ends up with one arm and legless in a motorized wheelchair, but has private jet, tropical island, servants, women. Maybe end it with him waggling his lower jaw in the mirror, wondering if he needs it. Use gently hyperbolized diction.

He woke earlier than usual, senses already attuned to — what? Maybe it was the muffled highway traffic. Maybe it was the soft light coming through the window frost, the grey prism-shadows on the ceiling.

No, it was out his window. He got up to an elbow and looked. It was snow. The first real snow. Wonderful, a wonderful sight. As always. Didn't matter where you were, what your life was like. Look at that. Winter wonderland, get the toboggan, the skates, the hot chocolate.

Pause first, settle the kid-in-you. Look at the world turned white. It felt like everyone's good fortune. You could almost smell it through the window.

This wasn't much more than an inch or two. It was only early November. You could still see the spikes of cut hay. But nice all the same. He wanted to wake somebody up, get Marg up and tell her. It was still snowing lightly, they might get a proper dump after all.

What was that red blotch? Who'd spilled paint in the middle of— There was blood out there in the field. Blood is what it had to be. He dressed quickly, plugged in the kettle on his way through the kitchen, pulled on his leather coat. He had no gloves or scarf or boots yet. He went round back, past the pile of beer cases, now with snow on it, the cardboard would shmush when it melted, a nightmare taking them back — he'd get on that today. He'd claim the money for gas for all the trips to town.

Through sneakers you could feel the snow's cold. He approached the red, a two-foot splotch that faded to pink at the edges. It was some animal's smeared meal. He stood over it. He wouldn't have seen it without the background of snow. Canvas for an intense little painting. Bits of fur, anonymous brown. One thin clean bone, curved, a rib. Just beyond the smear a furry foot. He found a twig and stooped to prod what might be the foot of a rabbit? gopher? cat? He decided rabbit. It must have happened recently, no more than an hour ago, judging from the way this lightly falling snow was covering it up. Bonaduce thought he could remember hearing, in his dawn dreaming, the faint ragged growls, the piping screams. It had happened under the fuzzy cartoon comet.

He stood and surveyed the surrounding fields. For what, he didn't know. Cold, he tucked himself deeper into his coat and walked back for his coffee. Maybe this happened all the time, you just needed snow to see the blood, it was a battlefield out here, a charnel ground. Almost funny: this was the first wildlife he'd seen from his window.

He considered going back with a baggie for the foot. Let it dry, hang it from his rearview all stained and beaten up, and kind of intense for that. Though what would such a thing have to do with luck?

Ideas:

> she looked at him with eyes that were two
> tunnels to the sun. (tunnels to hell?) (tunnels to
> nothing?)

> A man stroking a rabbit's foot with a vigour unknown to the sane

> You're safe only when you're in the middle. Because when you're inside it, it's not inside you.

. . .

The night of the big grad party he started out shaky but got calmer with time. The shakiness came from two phone calls. The second call, right before the party, was Oscar's buddy Andy Frenette calling about oldtimer hockey. According to Frenette, not only his team but all the oldtimer teams in town were to his knowledge full, too full in fact. Guys paid to play and were protective of their icetime. Bonaduce asking, You sure? and finally as a last resort sliding in how he'd played pro, so maybe some team would ... But this guy Frenette says, No, no, I heard about ya, Oscar told me, thing is we got some pretty good fellas too, and winning ain't all that important in this league here, just a good time. Bonaduce is now gutfrozen with shame. Hanging up, he heard his Tiny Tim words to himself: Nobody, not even old hackers, wants me on their team.

He shrugged that call off and showered, and got Marg going, and the party turned out well enough. Nice just to relax in wealthy digs for an evening. The solid comfy chairs, the sinky cream carpet. Grad students' eyes going big at such finger food: shrimp, fancy cheese, the see-through ham with the Italian name, toothpicked to green melon. Everything tasteful. On the stereo a medium jazz no one could argue with.

Marg didn't say much, maybe she was intimidated. Maybe in their midst she could hear herself and how often she said "like" and "I mean." Marg working on that wouldn't be a bad thing. She'd earn more respect, people would see past the valley girl to someone most likely smarter than they were. In any case, despite her looking at him a bit too close for his comfort these days, she seemed okay being left pretty much on her own while he nibbled, and sipped his limit of two beers, and listened in on conversations more than added to them. He had nothing much to say. And he couldn't quite get over the morning's phone call, Leah.

She had called him, finally. Her voice warm, soft. It followed him now to the fridge as he hunted more shrimp. It followed him to the bathroom, her voice was in the mirror behind his face as he washed his hands. Leah apologizing. Admitting to her confusion about him being here in general. Suggesting they meet. Somewhere where they wouldn't be seen and interrupted and nudged off the matter at hand. She named a motel restaurant off the highway, twenty minutes out of town.

The party rolled along fine, any nastiness being confined to the professors, of which there were eight. The main participants of one duke-up were none other than his own Gail Smith and Big Jan Dionne. The spat — all smiles and edge — was about creative writing versus literary criticism, which Bonaduce considered apples and bananas but didn't say so, and good old Jan stated the obvious, that without the creative there'd be nothing to crit, but she said it in the properly deluxe way. Apropos of something else, Jan got off another one, something that made him reconsider the books he was up to his eyeballs not reading. She said, "If what you read doesn't change you for the better, why read it?" Bonaduce and a few gathered others gave this rhetorical grape some silence and a nod. But Gail Smith turned it into a raisin by asking how one could possibly know what might change one until one's read it? She looked Jan Dionne in the eye and shook her head. Eager nods now, a snicker. For the *coup de grâce* Smith turned to the nut dish and said, "Plato died, get over it," and walked away.

Bonaduce found other sparring matches worth attending. He almost liked this world. They had guts and a willingness to scuffle. The party was at Doctor Professor Daniel Kirk's house, and another prof — a Professor Tillmann, Classics — arrived wearing no less than a black cape. He entered, took in the furnishings and then host Kirk, and announced in a fey, ballsy way, "A retentive, at play!" You could see Kirk's tight humour had no room for this, or maybe they knew each other's secrets and the remark was a get-back. Kirk mumbled something about the phantom of the opera, but it was clear that Tillmann was the type who loved anyone saying anything about him.

Other than Smith, no professors talked to Big Jan, or maybe it was the other way around. In any case she was surrounded by students, and seemed part and parcel with them, though cerebrally taller perhaps, something of Socrates-in-the-grove about her, except that she laughed too much, too eager with the young jokes. Once, on her way to the bathroom, Bonaduce grabbed her and pulled her into the dining room to dance to a dumb old Dr. Hook song. She was game enough, though disturbed by the question of sex — them so close in age, of course it's going to be in the air. He had no way of reassuring her that his intentions were only fun, that she was nice but — but she could in no way compete with Leah, whose soft voice wasn't leaving him tonight, whose body he—

Where was his head, what was he thinking? It had only been a phone call. As if it meant anything. Someone treats you like a human and you respond like a dog. And what about Oscar?

But a decent party. He even had a word with Phuckphace Phil, Bonaduce first humbling himself by plunking down on the couch and asking him outright, "What the hell does *deconstruction* mean, Phil?" In this world such a gesture was the animal equivalent of approaching with underbelly exposed. Bonaduce sort of knew the answer, but Phil enjoyed the chance to say, "If we liken any given piece of text to a sphere, around which one visits its context, historical and current, as well as the reader's pre- and misconceptions," and so on. When Bonaduce, friendly hockey guy, asked near the end if this meant keeping an eye peeled to just who's doing the reading and the writing, Phil paused and thought and nodded in tentative agreement. When Bonaduce asked if Phil'd mind getting him a Moosehead, because his leg had for some reason gone all wobbly, Phil did so in good humour, and Bonaduce knew he had maybe an odd friend in the making, one who would in any case laugh when asked if he'd sell him an essay.

Otherwise he enjoyed his second beer and came downstairs with the guitar he found. It surprised everyone all to hell, like they'd never seen a guitar or heard Jerry Lee Lewis before. He had a way of doing a guitar like Jerry Lee did a piano, the machine-gun thing and, despite each of them having an old dusty book up their ass, since this was the Maritimes they eventually did get into it.

MARGARET.

He was boyish asking her and had to joke about it. Pointing to where it said "Mr. Bonaduce and Friend" on the xerox sheet, he said if he went Friendless it would be a waste of free booze and food, and she was looking frail these days, which they both knew was so not true. He said she didn't have to see it as "a date" if she didn't want to, him using that word at all showing their ages again. She told him, "Robert, I am definitely seeing this as a *date.*" He seemed embarrassed enough, asking at all. She wondered what it meant, though, the difference between date and non. A corsage? A smooch goodnight at her bedroom door? He was acting as though the other night in her bedroom had never happened.

Robert explained that this was a yearly event, the profs hosting the students. A prof supplied a house, the English Department supplied supplies. On the drive over, more than once he asked himself aloud why he was even going. He liked no one, he didn't fit in. He did want her to meet his creative writing prof, Jan, who he described as "a regular guy." He looked serious saying this. Knowing she still played with the idea of grad school, he added that this was a chance to see for herself how boring that world was, how amazingly neurotically boring. A real spectacle, the rest of the world wouldn't believe it, especially how they talked, it was like a Monty Python parody. Archaeology might be different — it was bones, not words — but he bet it was the same. This rant seemed to get Robert excited about going.

She'd planned to use the drive over to get into the illness

question. And the wife question. And their long and serious hugging too. But watching him jolly at the wheel, joking himself out of his nervousness about this bad-party and their non-date, she decided to wait till the drive back. She hadn't told him about his friend Fournier's call, it had been weeks now and she'd left it too long. But she'd been watching him closely, how he moved and spoke. When she'd proposed to Fournier that maybe he was getting better, Fournier had paused and at least considered this. He told her his girlfriend, Kim, said MS could go into remission but it never went away. Mostly Fournier emphasized, actually raising his voice at her, that "if you're a friend, Bonaduce has to fucking look after himself, okay?"

These words had stayed with her as she watched Robert and his late nights, his obvious bouts with Toby's wine, and now through the party. Late in the evening she heard him drop a beer bottle in the kitchen — Was that him drunk or sick or an honest mistake? He was never not holding a beer. He laughed, he was confident, he'd either drunk away his nervousness with these people or he knew how to hide it. He and his professor, Jan, were the only ones who had the guts to dance, and he was stumbling as he twirled her. He had to be pretty drunk to go right into a bedroom upstairs and come down with a guitar. He started to sing, and everyone was embarrassed for him, and then a guy named Phil started to sing along mockingly and now she hated these people. She started to sing too, but seriously. She wasn't good at it, but hell she was on a *date* here and this was her fella, and ten minutes later everyone but the most shy were bellowing away and it got uncool *not* to sing. Good for him.

The last to leave, they drove home at three, trying to see Hale-Bopp through the dirty windshield. Robert was funny, declaring astronomers had the best jobs in the world, "teams of mountaintop nerds and throb-heads" up in their observatories, where they invented liqueurs and named things Dog Star and Hale-Bopp and Johnson's Worm Hole, which they claimed *sucks in everything, including light and time*; giggling, their eyes swimming behind lenses like plums in milk, they put out press releases saying that that comet out there, let's see, what should we tell them? yeah, it's made of *dirt and ice*, yeah, but that's only what we can *see* — inside, we suspect there's this giant magic *surprise*, something that should, if our predictions are right, make cults in California castrate then shoot themselves.

When they finally clattered into the kitchen she was an inch away from joking to him that he partied pretty hard for a *married man*. Or even venturing, Care to come up for another *hug*? But Robert's velocity through the door kept him going down the hall and lurching off to bed. He did look suddenly exhausted, as if all evening he'd kept his body propped up to perform, and at last he could relax. He slurred a goodnight, and when he slowed up to look back over his shoulder and smile at her, he was staggering.

§

Saturday night, UNB versus St. Mary's. Jason had one shift in the first period and none in the second, after which the game was tied at three. Close games you don't play your weaker players.

If UNB lost, he'd go down and talk to Whetter. If they won, he wouldn't.

The Reds lost six to three. Jason got on near the end, only to take a cheap shot in the face and leave the game with a towel pressed to his mouth. At the buzzer the guys clomped mad down the tunnel to the dressing room while Whetter lingered at the bench to argue a bad call with the ref, who listened patiently, eyeing his tunnel across the ice, looking like he wanted a beer. Whetter finished with a friendly enough "I dunno, Dave." He turned away and found Bonaduce there waiting with his hand out.

"Hiya. Too bad there's a third period sometimes."

"God, yes." Whetter shook his hand and stared angrily at the wet rubber floor. "But it'll come. It'll come."

"It will. I was wondering if you looked into that matter of my—"

"Only two games left."

Bonaduce nodded as if he knew what this meant.

"February fourteen, you're free. We phoned around. You left a sinking ship there in Utica, eh?"

"Sure did."

"Since you didn't play from mid-February, it seems by then you'll have sat out your year in effect. You were still under contract of sorts, but it's a technicality I think we'd survive."

"Hey. Good stuff." Only by feeling good news flood his body did he realize how rare good news had been.

"Not that it'll be an issue."

"No?"

"Because by then we only have two games left in the season."

"But, and the playoffs."

"We need more of your kind of optimism." Whetter smiled and looked up at him for the first time.

"I'll be there."

"Well, hang on. Thing is, you still can't practise. Not officially. So no way you'll be in game shape. Two games won't give you that either."

"I'll get on with an oldtimers team, skate my butt off."

"Maybe. Sure." Whetter hesitated. "What I really wanted to ask is a favour. After we talked, it hit me. But no one had your phone number. Not even Jason." A brief but questioning look from the younger man. "He said you were here incognito."

"I've been hittin' the books, eh?" Bonaduce smiled so as to let Whetter know he'd also been having himself some fun. It was suddenly strange, the two of them talking here, tiny in the bottom of this immense building shaped like a funnel, surrounded on all sides by empty seats. Two men in blue uniforms with brooms were way up top, beginning with the highest row. When they knocked over an empty Coke cup, you could hear it.

Jason could have got his number from all sorts of places.

"Anyway, the obvious thing was to ask you to be an assistant coach. The defence coach. Ever thought of coaching?"

They turned and started through the mouth of the tunnel. Bonaduce lagging behind, wanting to hear this but not wanting to go all the way to the dressing-room door.

"Thought of it." Thought he'd hate it. Telling the guys what to do, shoved you right out of the loop. Guys, management. "Sounds good."

"And that way you could get some ice. Practise without really practising. Scrimmage even, who's gonna know."

"Sounds good."

"So maybe you get in shape and maybe we use you."

"Sounds great."

"Puts Jason in a position, the boys might poke a bit of fun, but he wouldn't mind that, I don't think."

"No problem there."

"He's a good lad."

"Hey."

"Took a good one on the mouth tonight."

"Happens."

"And he'll get his chance to play."

"Good stuff."

"Whoops, gotcha—" Whetter had him by the arm.

"Tripped on a piece of mat there."

Bonaduce stamped his foot on the culprit. He'd tripped, sending Jason in alone with the perfect pass, Jace tucks it upstairs to win the game and send them into the playoffs, he circles back to whack Assistant Playing Coach Dad on the ass like a buddy.

Set a guy up, no matter how much he hates you he has to come and whack you on the ass.

· · ·

Ideas:

Castrated men shed their containers to chase the
holy comet. We see them as the silly-dead.

Ball of ice, keeping its distance from the sun. Snow-
ball in hell.

these words become a line
that turns into a poem I need
for Big J to give me an A
so I will be allowed to stay
and play
wiff the boy I wuv

"Whatever happened to subtlety?" Toby says, chewing, the blank
face of the professional passive-aggressive.

Sometimes you know you've been insulted. Toby, man. He
could get to you.

You cash your little teaching cheque, you make a choice between the used snow tires you're going to need any day now and
a Mexican take-out spree for the house. To celebrate your new,
secret, unpaid job of assistant coach — and also Frenette calling
you last night after all and you going out with his team, a weird
experience despite scoring your first official oldtimer goal. To
celebrate all this you arrive with a double box of beer and four
bags of Mexican, spiced extra hot. The start of a good night for
the house: Marg, Beth, Rod, even Joyce was home to sit down
for this. A hissing of beer tops and clinking of bottles, and everyone's just fine, except Toby, who suddenly hates spicy. He in-
forms his housemates that its only purpose is to hide the taste of
bad meat in poor hot countries and bullshit like this, pure
Tobyness to knock in one fell swoop not only you for buying his
dinner, but also any country, from Thailand to Togo, for enjoying

a bit of pepper in the mouth and sweat on the brow. Then, Whatever happened to subtlety? Looking right at you as you shovel the rellenos in. You can now not brag, as you'd been gearing up to, about how in Tulsa you would chop jalapeños right into your scrambled eggs and could even gobble one of the buggers straight. Sure, macho sneer at boredom perhaps is all it was, but why not give the mouth a little hip-hop.

You had to hand it to Toby. It's a rare spice-wimp with the pills to turn the tables on everyone else. Almost made you stop chewing and feel your numb tongue, almost made you feel like a tasteless beast because it was true, you could in fact no longer taste the refried beans. Which almost made you say something very unsubtle to the one-armed bastard. But there he was, opening up another of his bottles of wine for everyone. Then going to his cupboard and coming back with a big bag of ketchup potato chips to eat.

He watched Toby eat his junk, his two-buck bag of treasure wedged in his lap, not offering any. Greasy shitty red-coloured crispies. You could see the link between food and body. It wasn't hard to connect Toby's shit-food with his shit-spirit. It wasn't farfetched. You are what you stuff down the hatch.

In Rochester, briefly, there'd been Yoshi, that Japanese winger. Purportedly a huge star in Japan, the best there ever. He had NHL speed, for sure, but aside from speed he had nothing. Too scared to relax into the flow, too used to stardom to recognize his new status as average guy, and therefore unable to adapt and learn. But the main thing was his undeniable foreignness — which Bonaduce put down to food. You could see it. The way he skated wasn't meat, it was fish. You could see seaweed in the way he sat inscrutably in the dressing room. Noodles in the attitude, tofu in the shyness. You knew you couldn't really see anything so exact as that, but Yoshi was definitely marked by a general dietary weirdness. Same with the Russians. Wooden bread, tough bad meat. They spoke like they ate.

Toby sitting here with his rancid, pinched, cellophane thoughts.

. . .

Fuel
—by Robert Bonafide

Whether dogfood or spice, food is a window on the soul, so on roadtrips, in restaurant after restaurant, it's impossible not to get to know your teammates in this way. Tommy, your defense partner, with his taboo about any vegetable — amazing he stayed alive let alone so nimble and bashing. There was Ray, who loved pizza, but only without the tomato sauce, said he couldn't stomach it (no matter how many times he got yelled at for contradicting himself by *eating the tomatoes in his fucking salad*). A lot of pizza goes down in motels after games, but with Ray around you couldn't just say "large works" into the phone, you had to explain twice to some guy with a heavy accent. Or you'd be in a real city and want to hit a sushi place and two thirds of the guys won't even bother responding to the suggestion, won't even try the word out in their brain, even after you explain how they can get teriyaki there, which they'll love, it's barbecue. But the unstated thing looms about hanging together as a team, and once more you have to forgo sushi for the steak joint, all dark and done up like a gold chain in black chest hair.

Guys who never eat breakfast, guys who only eat breakfast. Some guys, enormous cheapskates, banking their per diem while they order nothing and eat the table's basket of buns and breadsticks and butter, and then half your fries. Some guys with what might be actual allergies, JD with a bad one for anything wheat, maybe it was even Crohn's, he did eventually have an operation after getting traded to Phoenix — no matter, he was hated for being a pain to find a restaurant with. Some guys eating ugly with their mouths open. Some prim with little knives and forks in big hammy hands. Some eating at private tables — coaches, management. Some dumping ketchup without caring what it landed on. Some don't talk while they eat, some can't shut up. A few have a butt going in the ashtray while they stab at six a.m. eggs — though you don't see this much any more. Nor do you see as much carefree guzzling after games.

It seems the younger guys have learned about food, what it does. You hear words like "amino acids." "Complex carbohydrates." Last year, last road trip in my playing career perhaps, enough guys expressed interest in hitting a health-food store on the way out of Wheeling that they actually got the bus driver to stop. I watched the old coach sitting waiting for them, brow knit and staring, like his guys were in there looking at porno or astrophysics or something equally out of his league.

He was exhausted, he should sleep. Leah tomorrow. Leah, roadside motel.

He closed the laptop, thinking: Recipes. He should put in some recipes, these days every novel had them. So put some in, put in some genuine hockey player recipes: Mac 'n' Cheese With Big Chunks of Meat. Spagetty With Tomato Sauce On It. Potatoes Cut in the Middle With Butter In There. Ham Samwidge With Two Slices of Ham.

Probably shouldn't have stolen the bottle. Why steal wine that costs two bucks? Because you spent all your money on the guy's dinner and he took you down, that's why. And because it was impossible to out-and-out ask him for it. Better to steal the guy's wine than say something truly hurtful, like challenging him to an arm wrestle. He'd sipped his two glasses of it, then had to pour the rest out, hide the evidence.

He could hear Toby upstairs now, bumping around the bathroom. It was maybe three. You could somehow tell it was Toby. And Toby was probably aware of him down here typing. Toby didn't seem to sleep much either.

Leah. It really was not the best time for this. He'd hardly slept. He didn't feel good about much. Tired, gritty in the eyes, unsteady top to bottom. Thoughts didn't come clear. His inner ugliness showed. Whenever he'd pictured today, he'd looked his best.

But why? *What* are your intentions?

He showered and shaved. Somehow he was late. It was cold, the coldest day yet, the bleak time of year, with the leaves long down but no snow. He felt thankful for his leather coat.

One of the chest buttons popped when he got into his car, and this made him sit and stare out the window, shaking his head. He cupped the big black button in his hand, examining it. He checked where it had come off, the circle of darker, shinier leather, the four pinholes and ragged broken thread.

And he had been somehow prepared for his car not to start. He ran his battery down trying, then faced the choice of hitching or calling a taxi. He'd be late either way. Maybe he shouldn't go. He shouldn't go.

And felt cheap as hell taking his sixty cents change from the ten. Sixty cents is sixty cents. He said, Sorry, I need it, but the taxi driver said nothing and wouldn't look at him, a mopey martyr for sixty cents, something to gripe about with the boys at the stand.

Bonaduce stood in the parking lot. This was like out of a movie. It certainly wasn't real, in any case. Roadside motel, and fronting the row of rooms her red car, its little ass pointing up. There in the big window of the café, Leah sat alone in a black-leatherette booth. Thinking hard at something as she sipped through a straw. Seeing him approach, looking quickly down, then looking up again and smiling.

The booths even had those private chrome jukeboxes on the wall, and when he sat across from her he had to resist the urge to search the titles, maybe find something corny for them to hear, something she'd recognize and they'd laugh.

"You're limping."

"No I'm not."

"I thought you were."

"Well I've been working out a bit."

Her lips, you couldn't tell if she had something on them or not. Wasn't that exactly the point, the art— But what was he thinking here? And what about Oscar.

He'd promised himself he wouldn't read anything into her idea of meeting at, well, at a motel. But here they were, together at a motel. Her suggestion. Back in those days, their days, when beds *meant* sex, motels meant beds. Look at her. Shy? Sad? Her silence thick with what? Jeans and a fuzzy sweater again, like at her party, his favourite, he might have told her this once and she might have remembered.

*Was* Oscar a buddy?

"So. Hi, Bobby."

Apology in her smile. A sad summing-up.

"Hiya." Look at her. "So, how's work? How're those guys down in that church?" He felt twenty again with her, inarticulate. He didn't mind this.

"They're still 'down in that church.' They might be there a year. But they're safe. Donations have been good and they have a nice little apartment set up. We even had to turn down a new living-room suite from Wal-Mart."

"Hey, I'll take it."

Leah smiled. "It gets so complicated. Wal-Mart is American, and its investment portfolio includes, you know, 'the usual.'"

His look prompted her to say more.

"Well, Juan admits to his involvement in a group that pamphlets against the monoculture — bananas — that's destroying all other agriculture there, and the whole pesticide health issue, and it's all American-owned, all Chiquita and a couple of others, so his real fight was against the U.S. So, Wal-Mart? Sorry."

"Maybe Wal-Mart's trying to make it up to him?"

"Right." Leah smiled with him.

She'd used *pamphlets* as a verb. She was a professional, and he no longer was. He shook his head at twenty years.

"What?"

"I dunno. A year in a basement. Holy."

A waitress came for their order. Leah ordered a sandwich and tea. He asked for a glass of icewater. He was desperate for a coffee because the cupboard had been bare and he'd done without, but coffee was eighty cents plus tax. You couldn't borrow a quarter from her. If you want a relationship with her son, you could not be a destitute bum.

And maybe you want more than a relationship with the son.

"Half a year easily. Ottawa's sitting on it. If they get in, the rednecks argue everyone'll get in. As if we can't tell the heroin smugglers from the— Juan has *scars* on his back. The kids saw their *uncle* killed."

"Who put the scars on his back?" He resisted a Wal-Mart joke.

"It's complicated."

The last thing you want to do is blow this. She hates you enough already, even if for a while there back in history she was your home. The last thing you want to do is misread the situation, come on to her just when she's got herself ready to talk and treat you like a human. You could blow it by looking at her wrong, by raising one cool sexy eyebrow, don't forget how well she knows you. Blow it when you don't even know what you want yourself, you can't put your finger on your intentions long enough to see whether your need is to get the mother in your camp so she'll get the son to come too, or whether this mixed-up welling of sadness and tears and breathing at the sight of her has to do with her alone or with you not being with a woman in God knows how long and needing, Christ, maybe just needing to be touched like this on the arm by someone.

"What's wrong?" Leah leaning in with tilted head. "Bobby? You crying?"

"Ah, hey, you know. No." He felt her eyes still on him, though no one spoke.

"Well, Bob. Jason ... he lost a tooth. The other night."

"Really?" He looked up. She didn't look like she was blaming him for it.

"Did you know? A front tooth?"

"I didn't know. He okay?"

"At least it wasn't from a fight."

Didn't *look* like she blamed him. Fighting. The subject had been heavy in her silences, her distant look when it was celebrated in the bar with the guys and their wives after the game. If he'd studied her more closely that first season, he would have learned sooner that the few times she was not in the mood coincided with the few times she'd seen him fight. And here he'd been feeling jealous whenever Jim Murphy got into one and from behind the bench his Cindy would yell *C'mon, Murph, C'mon, Murph*, the good warrior's-wife. He imagined a Cindy more eager that night in bed, her black-and-blue knight gallant on top of her. He'd joked once to Leah something about how you'd figure a gal who fanged into the Alpo wouldn't be opposed to a small display of brute force from her man. But Leah had no use for it, and it was not one of her secrets. She smiled politely when he dismissed fighting as two tempers in a teapot. Or when he shrugged and said simply, "Consenting adults." Sure there were loose screws out there, guys who might try for an eye. In general, fighting was a war-in-a-box where no one got hurt. Black eyes, the odd nose or helmet-broken finger. And how many times did you see guys who'd fought that night clink glasses later in the bar?

It wasn't until he'd left Fredericton that he realized she may have been afraid. Not for him. Of him.

Well, hell. He wanted so much to tell her how that just wasn't in his makeup. Also how he suspected that hockey players in general were less likely to get violent with their women. It only made sense. At home on the couch the guy had no reason to be anything but a pacifist: hockey his outlet for whatever violent streak he had. He was happy to be home and at rest, a gentle sigh at the wife's ministrations.

Bonaduce had since dropped this theory, and not just because of all the athletes in the news for domestic stuff. Things had changed. The pressure. The frustrations at not making it. These days, to play in the minors was seen as nothing but failure. Fighting was more calculated now, a career tool, a spectacle, no real honour left in it. And steroids. He could imagine women in the awful privacy of their homes getting whacked because of that shit. Jesus, but he'd seen some young guys on the 'roid rage, flailing away, 220-pound tantrum, anger unheld as a child's, all teeth and paranoia, guy's face with its spread of telltale pimples oozing bad hormones and grease.

"Shit, a front tooth. But he's okay?"

"If he wasn't okay, he wouldn't have told me."

"Well, are *you* okay?"

Leah looked down, nodded. When she looked up again he could tell the subject had changed. She had dismissed their son, she had not invited him here just to talk about Jason. Her eyes were deep and clear, and rich with what she had become in the last twenty years. She was checking his eyes for what he had become during that time too, and it was hard not to look away.

Now it seemed that she might cry.

"Bobby, let's — let's not be in a hurry."

The words gave him an instant erection, though her eyes showed nothing but openness and sincerity. Her sandwich came, and his water. When her coffee arrived he said it smelled so good, could he have a sip? and he drank some, and when she took it back and drank some too, he saw how her lips touched the same spot.

He stood in his driveway, her car getting smaller, his hand still up in a wave. When he'd gotten out, neither of them had smiled.

His dead car with its hood open. In his hurry to the cab he'd forgotten to put the damn thing down. What did Leah think, seeing this yard, this house, this car with its hood up. White trash. In class Kirsten had given Phil shit for using that term, saying it implied that expected trash was black.

The keys were still in the ignition. Another picture of Bonaduce in a hurry. He decided against trying to start it, and closed the hood. None of what happened would have, had this car not died. Should he thank it or pound on it with a hammer? He would go in and have a bath, let it all percolate.

They'd ended up in her little car, Leah about to give him a simple ride home. They had talked and talked, Bonaduce ordering his fill of coffee, having decided to play the dufuss who'd forgotten his wallet. He'd come expecting a business-like discussion about Jason and for that alone he would have been grateful. But she had met him this morning to make a connection. They talked like ordinary people, they talked more about her work and he talked about his school, and she laughed at the stories of his fumblings. They talked about Oscar and Jason, but not in the sense that there was anything to *do* about either of them, and Bonaduce had only the slightest pang at the news that Jason's sights were set on Law. It was them simply catching up, enjoying each other's company, though of course they both knew that underneath it all was the *bloodbeast* that erupted in Leah's car. It was a tiny car and he was a clumsy hulk climbing in. He couldn't remember whose fault it was that their knees touched, and then he simply patted it, her knee, safe there in her jeans, and he thanked her.

"Leah? Thanks for this," he'd said, and meant it. Both for the ride, but also more. And it worked because she looked up at him and he down at her and their faces were so close that the kiss was both their faults. At first neither of them betrayed anything other than a friendly kiss, a smack with the eyes open. But the kiss continued, and deepened, and got gently wild and down to business. Leah pulled away and, alone with herself for a moment, swore and slapped the steering wheel. Then she laughed, they both laughed. They kissed small again, then got right into it this time, and they were almost out of control there in the parking lot.

He did feel the dumb dufuss while she paid for the room. When they walked in, he wondered if she'd envisioned — maybe even planned for — this moment, too, this thrill, the delicious doom of the door locking shut behind them, then the brief relapse into shyness, their eyes falling on anything but the bed.

It was the best possible time. Right now. With his fingers on her neck and cheeks, the skin so soft he could hardly feel it through his own roughness. With her breasts and her legs teasing him with its clothing. With her head falling back under the full weight of this moment, with her fingers finding his belt loops, gently taking hold and drawing him to her.

III

At first light, the old men upright and drooling.
—Cormac McCarthy, *Suttree*

He was consumed by doubts as to his own identity, as to the
nature of his body and the cast of his countenance.
In what manner did he relieve these doubts?
By the sensory perception of his ten fingers.
—Flann O'Brien, *At Swim-Two-Birds*

December 1, Bonaduce bought a Christmas tree. It was early, he knew he was pushing things, but there they were as he drove by. You could smell the shaggy stack from the street through his open window, reek of pine after-life. If he wasn't supposed to buy one, they wouldn't be there. That it was the same gas station where he'd bought his only other Fredericton tree twenty years ago clinched it.

He interrupted an old guy who was just finishing the job of unloading the trees from the flatbed. He was skinny, unshaven, and permanently asquint from the smoke of the cigarette dangling in his mouth, surprising he could move one tree, let alone a stack. Anywhere but a jobsite he'd be taken for a derelict.

"You're the first." He gave Bonaduce a congratulatory nod and pocketed the twenty. He may have chuckled as he watched Bonaduce wrestle the tree onto his station wagon.

"Got some rust, eh?" the man added, indicating with his chin and cigarette the bottom of the driver's door.

"I guess."

Bonaduce groped in the back-seat mess for the bungees. What do you say to such things? You're wearing clothes, eh? You have yellow eyebrows, eh?

"Well, get 'er in some water quick."

It took a moment to realize he meant the tree, not the rust. He tried to picture what kind of tree stand might be scroungeable back at the house. A big bucket, full of stones, bricks. Maybe he'd have to buy a proper rig.

But the car wouldn't start. He tried and tried, then got out. He didn't open the hood, because it wasn't flooded. The old guy standing beside him, he stared at his station wagon sitting there mulishly stubborn, as if it didn't like its burden of the tree.

"There's a good one right in there." The old man jerked his head back toward the garage. A sign read: Mechanic On Duty.

What money he might have had for tree rigs was now gone. Only because he was at a gas station to begin with did he decide to spring for a proper job. The old guy helped him and the mechanic push his car into the bay. If it was something major, kiss the car goodbye, he'd have to walk away from it. And the tree.

Well, but. He'd been trying not to think about it, the American Express card in the back of his wallet. He'd maxed it out before coming north. What sort of trouble could you get in for just trying it? Oops, silly me, wrong card, jeez I thought I'd lost that. And what about these guys you read about who, in debt to six maxed-out cards, declare bankruptcy and in a month receive invites for new cards? What if his card worked, what if he had three thousand U.S. to spend? Hey and while you're at it, throw in all those doughnuts, and that case of pop. And that bin of ice scrapers, please, I go through them.

It was a strange sight, his wagon rising on the hoist, Christmas tree on top. Two worlds strapped together, one fresh and green, the other stinking of oil and rust. Both in their way half-alive. Or half-dead, depending on your mood.

He walked and ran all the way home, adjusting his pace to the waves of fatigue as they rose. You could get on them, surf them. It was not unpleasant to slow life down, letting the cars *whoosh* on past. The noises, the smells. This was fine. It all depended on your mood. Moods were upon you, no choice in the matter. Sometimes you could stick-handle your way out of a bad one, sometimes you couldn't.

That Christmas in Tulsa, with Fournier. Christmas, never a good time for Bonaduce, was this year awful for Fournier, whose mother was sick. How sick, Fournier didn't know, and this was the crux. He hadn't made it back the previous year, and once again their game schedule was rotten. A travel agent helped him calculate that, with Christmas congestion and changing planes, he'd have a total of minus five hours to spend in Chicoutimi with his mother. So Fournier was down in the dumps. Sitting in a chair in the middle of the kitchen, he told Bonaduce with great gravity that Christmas in Tulsa was hell on earth.

Misery secretly loving company, Bonaduce went out and bought four bottles of champagne. Well, bubbly white. He'd once seen Fournier get near silly on the stuff. He also bought a funny Christmas card. In the background was the lower part of the tree and spread of presents. In the foreground, a guy's feet dangled in the air. It took you a second to see he'd hanged himself.

The card worked and Fournier got near silly on the wine. They gathered at a teammate's with eight or ten others who were suffering Christmas in Tulsa. A couple of them snickered but, unlike Fournier, they thought the card was sick.

A mile to go, along the Trans-Canada. Freezing rain was falling now and Bonaduce had to stop and turn his face away when a semi roared by. Some guys just didn't get black humour, had no talent for fire-with-fire. They didn't understand that sometimes you could slap a mood in the face and win.


The Birth of Hockey


Because it is dark and smoky inside. Because Granddad drinks and after he wakes from his sour moanings his mood is prickly and his eyes follow you, looking for reasons to shout. Because outside it is bright and clean, and the pond gives you magical speed, and the faster you go the bigger the thrill, till it scares you. Because inside, the smell of a cooked onion takes all day to leave the house. Because Grandma gets sour herself when Granddad doesn't talk all through supper. Because it's only December and already she's hanging on for spring. Outside, your friends escape their hot houses and drift by with plans. Because you are too young to hunt and there's no money for bullets in any case, but there is the pond. Because inside, you can't read the Bible any more for it reminds you of inside and winter, of where you were, yet there is no other book. The catalogue is five years old and ripped, and the dreams it gives are tired. Because outside the rules are clear, to the point that if McIlhargy busts your shins again with the club he calls a stick you will fight him. Because inside, you cannot play another game of cards beside the flickering candle, tobacco smoke smarting your eyes and stinking so bad your nose can no longer smell it. Because outside you make sure your little sister played, and that the teams are even because it's more fun that way. Because sometimes, as the sun goes down, you find yourself hugging each other and cheering: McIlhargy falls, but not before the puck slides between his legs and through the holy posts, to nudge up against the backing snow.

On the phone. Out of the blue.
"Hello?"
"Hi. I was just wondering—"
*Jason.*
"Jason, hi."
"—if you wanted to go see Bob Dylan."
"Bob Dylan?"
"He's on the fifteenth. I've got these—"
"Bob Dylan's coming to Fredericton?"

"It's in two weeks, so—"

"That's incredible. Bob Dylan. This is the real Bob Dylan?"

"Yeah, do you want to go?" A trace of impatience. Things to do, fast twenty-year-old life.

"Hey, well yeah! Sure I do. Thanks. And I'll grab the tickets — so where do I—"

"Well, I sort of already got them."

"Hey. Okay. Great. Wow. Bob Dylan." Jason, Jason taking him to Bob Dylan, in Fredericton.

"Okay, see ya."

His boy hung up. No small talk, no further arrangements. No apology for the time in the corridor. All of which was fine. What Jason had just done had been hard for him, what he had just done was a great thing. From his voice you know it had been hard. Good lad.

And Bob Dylan. He sort of liked him, certainly had never loved him. The folky extraordinaire. The kind of guy if you went to high school with would be too arty and distant to like. But you couldn't deny he'd changed the world. He'd been reduced to Fredericton? A superstar demoted to the minors. But it would be great. Bob Dylan. It would be like seeing the *Mona Lisa*. The mummified body of Lenin. He'd get Jason over for a beer before the show and tell him what Bob Dylan meant to the world.

A world full of messages today. He'd just put the phone down, his ear full of Jason's echoes, hungry to replay them, when Marg was handing him a box, its surface colourful with U.S. stamps and Customs stickers.

"There was like a note for you from the post office that something was, you know, there for you. But, I mean, I was in town anyway so I just picked it up."

Why the nervous concern?

"No, I'm glad! Thank you. Great. Thanks."

He plucked the rusty hunting knife from the junk drawer and took it and the box to his room.

On his bed, looking at the window, he tried to hear and feel Jason's voice, but felt nothing more than a jittery stomach. He'd see him on the ice tomorrow night in any case. It was great the boy had called, the timing perfect. Fearing another disaster, Coach Bonaduce had been thinking of not showing up.

He hacked carefully at the parcel, half its top covered in stars-and-stripes stampage. Like he was opening a box containing his past twenty years. Amarica. His fellow Amaricans. Three months here had shown him how he'd become used to them. Their way of talking, proclaiming. Even their hesitations had a showy certainty. They were brave, it was true. Bashers on the biggest rink. Cradling this box, he realized in a mostly physical way that the America he'd left behind contained a neat two decades, a career, a game.

Why dwell on it? What was there to figure out? Over. Finished. Buzzer's gone. What of those past twenty years was even useful to think about? That this box was small seemed appropriate. You could pop it into a closet. You could flick it, *flick* it, out the window.

He put the knife to it. Inside was a health book about yeast infections, a letter from Fournier and a stern note of instructions from the girlfriend. Six bottles, vitamins looking like foliage crushed and capsuled. The two-page typed instructions said first you did the kidney cleanse, then the liver cleanse, then you started the main— You drank this at eight, that at noon, then you took— After the two-week juice fast you started the brown rice, introducing one different steamed vegetable every—

Fournier's note made no mention of their possible last paycheque except to say, "Wharton he's fucking unbelievable." Referring no doubt to continuing dirty legal manoeuvres. Fournier had finished his real-estate course and was about to start his new profession. "I wonder if buyers will trust a handsome Frenchman." Bonaduce pictured Fournier in a suit trying to sell something. Fournier would look good in a suit. If he relaxed and didn't smile all the time. Fournier could do the little charismatic eye-glint if he slowed down and didn't want something out of a situation.

Bonaduce restuffed the box. He placed it on the floor and, without looking, heeled it under his bed. What sounded like a vitamin bottle fell out and rolled to a stop somewhere. He didn't have a yeast infection. In fact he was feeling pretty damn good. Yesterday from the garage he'd more or less trotted all the way back here. It had to be four miles. He'd walked maybe only a mile of it and today his legs felt okay. Appropriately stiff and achy. In his general soul it did feel something like a flu rising, but he hadn't had a cold in a while so he was due. He was fine. Tomorrow was the start of his playing-coach career. Things were picking up, the towering gears of the universe were clunking more harmoniously of late. Though you couldn't deny the logic of it all: You sleep with the mother and, bang, the son calls, asking, Hey Dad, wanna go to a show? Had Leah spoken to him, put in a good word? Well, why the hell wouldn't she. She sleeps with you it means she at least likes you. Something about you.

Hey Dad, wanna go to a show? Hear some music? Just like it should be. He smiled, shaking his head. Life was a running stumble in the dark forest, truly wild. Bear pits, trip roots, cannibals. Sometimes you got a berry patch, a surprise waterfall, a sunlit clearing.

Bonaduce had to laugh, taking in his tiny bed and tiny room. He reached out like Jesus on the cross, and his hands almost touched both walls at once. Fournier had ended his letter saying that he and his girlfriend were thinking of driving up, pay a visit, could he put them up at his place, was there room?

Did Fournier think that when he'd left Utica he'd been called up to the bigs or something?

God he was tired. Time for a long nap, stay in bed all day, happy enough, but hope for no more boxes or messages.

. . .

The time he played in the NHL. "The Show" the kids called it now, copying baseball. His third season he was called up from Rochester to join Toronto on the road, meeting them in Philadelphia to play the Flyers that night. He would always remember the limo from the airport. Him with skates and overnight bag. That it was a plane at all was a taste of the bigs. He would always remember walking into the Leaf dressing room, the scattered greetings from guys who remembered him from training camp. There were three trainers, instead of one, taping ankles, giving rubdowns. Everything a bit newer, the gear better, lighter, cleaner, no thought of budget. Towels thicker, everything laid out, a choice of shampoos. There was Sittler; there was Lanny, who, when he said hi through that moustache, you couldn't see his lips move; and there was Tiger Williams, not as dumb as he came across on TV. They were as pale and bruised and mortal as the guys you left in Rochester. Same habits, same morals or lack thereof. As funny, and as limited in their speech. But there was something different in their eyes — a loftiness, a genuine knowing. Which posed a question you needed to answer for your own professional future: Was this confidence their reward, or was it what got them here in the first place?

From the bench Bonaduce watched his teammates get beaten by Philly, six-one. Clarke was fierce, and television didn't show how fast Leach could fly. But Bonaduce saw he could play in this league, these guys weren't all great, there were grinders like him. He was put on for the hell of it with two minutes to go. His shift lasted forty, fifty seconds and he didn't touch the puck. After the game he was informed of more travel arrangements. He had to hustle in and out of the shower and leave the dressing room just as the guys, sitting in their steaming gear, started to shake off the loss and joke around a bit. He was put on a smoky overnight train to rejoin his real team. And in the years that followed, whenever anyone asked if he'd ever played in the NHL, if he'd ever been called up, he simply said not yet. Because it hadn't really happened, not in the way it was going to.

He wouldn't know whether to remember it as life's treat or

life's tease, this feast he'd been allowed only to smell. It was, as they say, a learning experience. The curt impersonality taught him that no one cared. Getting traded that second time — rupturing whatever family feel the team had given him — taught him he was alone.

Last night a dream about going with Jason to Dylan. Though in the dream it became the Harlem Globetrotters, as Dylan's warm-up act. Jason was thirty and paunchy, unshaven and surly. He smoked. And, damn, Bonaduce realized it was the kind of event you brought far younger sons to. The girl took their tickets. Father and son navigated the crowd, checking their stubs against the numbers over the tunnels. They passed a group of midgets, and Jason laughed at them cruelly and openly. This father–son thing, who said it would be easy? Bonaduce asked, "Ever seen these guys?" and Jason's answer, "Can't remember," irritated him. To say the Globetrotters could make so little impression that maybe he'd seen them, maybe he hadn't, was rude. He'd said it with a slackness of face that was ruder still. But he was being honest, they were beyond fake politeness at least. And they had the great seats. Couldn't help but love the Globetrotters, look at them warm up, shooting casual hoops, God they were loose, all high-five and whoop-up. How could you not love a seven-foot guy leaving the floor at full speed, faking a shot and cruising mid-air beneath the basket to come out from under and spin in a no-looker? You didn't see big guys like this in Canada. Sitting beside them suddenly, a tiny black man, the team clown, birthed a full-sized wet basketball from his hinged, snake-like mouth and Bonaduce knew this was a dream. He turned to Jason to tell him, and Jason was a huge fat older guy, stuffing a hotdog in his frowning maw, his belly resting on his thighs, one big repulsive bad mood. It was all funny now, just a dream, none of it true.

. . .

In the morning he arrived humming in the kitchen. It was incredible but his lack of a car and a ride to give seemed to be sparking resentment in his housemates. Toby's deadpan, Well, what the hell else ya good for? was dangerous but funny, and Bonaduce shot him an approving wink. They leafed through the junk-drawer paper for a bus schedule they doubted they'd ever had. They grumbled about pooling their dimes for a taxi. No one was at all enthused by his smiling invitation to join him in his jog-and-walk to campus. He knew they found him idiotic in his sweatpants as he bolted his coffee and did his stretches hanging on to the counter edge. Even Marg was disturbed with him. Her asking, So what was in the box from the States? arose with a clunk out of some strained need to make conversation, and his reply, "Yeast infection," didn't put the kind of smirk on her face it normally would have. Maybe she took it as sexist sass, and not a decent non sequitur. Maybe he shouldn't have had that tender moment with her up in her room.

He sometimes shortcut through fields and leapt ditches, feet crashing in brittle leaves, their crisp and perfect December sound. His steady breathing was the sound of health itself. The smell of smoke and pleasant garden-rot wafted over from what looked like a cauliflower farm, lots of unpicked white–brown bodies. Pungent smell of gravel kicked up by his feet. Soon all would go into the deepfreeze, this could be the last day of the sun warm on the face. Crows yelled at him from nearby trees and chickadees made him smile with their mournful, *geee*zer. If you're going to go schiz and let the world start talking to you, let's hope at least some of the voices are funny.

Things were coming together. The son. The son's mother. Even the hockey. Maybe even the school, why not. Next week, the last week of classes before the Christmas break, his stuff was being done in Big Jan's workshop, and then he would present *The English Patient* at Gail Smith's. He'd whined successfully to get both delayed and now time was up. He'd done only peripheral work on either, but pressure was his middle name, in the playoffs just drop the puck and turn the Bonaduce loose.

He was jogging first to the garage to pick up his car. If it wasn't ready today he'd jog in again tomorrow. It could only be good to fight through this tiredness. Put some teenage back in the legs. Things were moving and things were okay, everything pretty much as he'd wished, pretty much as he'd foreseen.

Luck, often you don't know you've had it till it's gone, but sometimes, like today, you can feel the blossoming, and you can feel that it's way bigger than you. That time, a solid month in 'Mazoo, when the goals just started coming, first a bunch of flukes and deflections, and then he actually started trying to score, turned into a bit of a rushing defenceman, and they kept coming. Basher turned offensive threat. He anticipated a call from on high. Call they did, but only to suggest that he stick to his game, not try to do too much. At which point he started to doubt himself, just enough to knock him off his edge and put a stop to the goals. Doubt can kill luck all by itself.

Jogging, he discovered he was whistling. It was a phony whistle. Trying to distract himself.

He made a quick trespass over the highway, to the river-edge where a stand of cattails promised entertainment. Holding his hands up like a boxer, he took left-handed swipes at the brown cigars, *whap*, he'd read the Natives used to eat these things, *whap*, made a kind of flour, *whap*. There were frogs down there in the muddy roots, *whap*, didn't they freeze, *whap*, solid?

Shit, why is it, *whap*, in middle age, *whap*, even the good times, *whap-whap*, are only iffy?

Right, damn, so let's have a look. Why the doubt. I'm jogging along, happy as a fast clam, yet here's doubt and here it had been all along. Doubt making the breath sound only hopeful. Doubt rising up deep from muscle and bone. Here was the sun full on the face — why the dark and the chill?

Because of the look on Leah's face.

Because of the sound in Jason's voice.

Because doubt has brought up the one and only question: Why jog, why do anything, when you're only going to die.

It's like there comes a time when, if you haven't been honest with yourself about certain questions, they get fed up and stand and shout at you all by themselves.

At Leah's insistence, communicated only through her hands, which moved as though caught in a graceful trance, the clothes had come off slowly. They did each other's, tugging at foreign buttons and clasps. In the delicious pace and clumsiness of this, he could feel all the more the hunger of twenty years. Slower, her hands said. I want to remember this — her mouth explained slowly into his ear — because it's going to be the only time.

While her saying this didn't dent his ardour, if there was darkness about their coming together, her words darkened things further. It was her right. She had the partner. Bonaduce was only free.

They stood in their underwear lightly embracing, pulling back a little in the semi-dark to take each other in, coming together to kiss and squeeze and almost lose control again because it was too much. If time had drained and scuffed their bodies, it wasn't noticeable in this light, and time hadn't hurt their urge at all. Leah was shaking. As for him, he was almost there from just the hard hugging, which would be a shame, a waste of this. She was smiling down at his underwear and what it could hardly contain. The straining thing in its ridiculous push, Leah looking a bit proud of herself.

She took further control, which again was fine and for the same reason. Shakily she whispered that if they didn't "literally" make love she could maybe live with herself. She had them retreat to separate beds. She pulled off her underwear, he pulled off his. Looking at him from across the two-foot chasm she played with herself. He did the same, though carefully, intermittently, because it was still almost over. He forced his thoughts to wander.

He'd noticed that above both beds hung what appeared to be identical pictures of lake-and-distant-snowy-mountains. He checked now and they were in fact identical. What was the thinking.

"What's that?"

"What?" He stopped his hand and looked at her. Leah was pointing at his inner thigh.

"That."

"Oh. Bruise." From the oldtimer game. It was purple as a birthmark, fresh as a stamp, the size of a saucer and growing. Maybe it was age but he'd never had one quite like it, its centre almost black. He wished she hadn't seen it. Hockey was so much of the reason they had stopped—

But Leah could no longer stand it. She pulled her hair, she screamed, she laughed, and then she was in his bed. She had him promise that they wouldn't actually, *actually*— He said "fuck" for her but felt tainted for it, though it was a word they'd once used in play. Oh but now the deep taste of her, her soft and helpless moans, he could feel both in the pit of himself. The rules of their touch were further circumscribed when he lifted back his head and warned her not to, not to do *that*, stop, he was too close. It's been a while since the last time, he said, which she took as a joke, meaning since them.

In sweet frustration they continued what they allowed each other and neither could stand it for long. After a look from her and a look from him, in a blur of greased decision and a groaning roll they were on the floor between beds, furiously coupled, rocking now in the heartblood root of each other, and even as they both came she was already hissing, *Oh shit, shit.*

She was quick dressing. She had to meet a lawyer and with him drive a Chilean woman to Nackawic. The woman had all her belongings, there was a question of whether they could do it in just one trip. Leah tried to be cheerful, but couldn't quite pull it off, couldn't look at him squarely. The guilt on her face was plain and, Chilean woman or not, her hurry had more to do with getting away from him and what they had just done.

. . .

"... for this reason one can see the text as an interrogation of the *pretence* of romantic ritual rather than as an interrogation of the ritual *per se*."

Kirsten's sneer dropped like a theatre curtain as she ended her introductory sentence. Bonaduce had read the novel and liked it but had seen no interrogation of romantic rituals, never mind their pretence. It was basically about some East Indian guy in Canada landing only grub work and walking around moony-eyed but too shy to get laid, too shy for the rituals to ever happen. Kirsten's sneer opened on her second sentence and the words "If we consider that" and the next two hours loomed large. The sun was bright outside the window and Bonaduce felt close to panic that life was racing by with him stuck here, a bug pinned writhing, impaled by words so empty they felt evil. Leah was out there cruising highways, alone, passing churches and motels, her ass restless on a car seat.

What was real was his headache. He never got headaches, but now he had a doozy. It was maybe the result of his run to the garage, sometimes a good workout will hock up the toxins. Of which no doubt he had plenty. Toby's wine. He hadn't been eating well. He felt akin to a sink strainer after the week's dishes were done, a carrier of oily rinds and pallid blasted fat.

"... clearly the point is that the rites of matrimony in the old country had become, here in Canada, mere farce. But he believed in the farce and she didn't ..."

Or the headache came from the American Express card. He'd been helpless. The car was ready. Sitting out there in the lot, Christmas tree on top, in fine running order. The mechanic smiling at a job well done, praising the vehicle and all the miles left on her. Bonaduce staring at his car, still seriously puffing from the run. Apparently by signing the work order he'd okayed any necessary work. So they'd planed his warped head, changed the gasket, flushed the rad and replaced all fluids. Sure, he nodded, reading the smudged work order, Sure, I guess it had to be done. When the mechanic said, "I'm surprised it was still running," Bonaduce had to peer at him to see if this was a joke, because, well, the reason the car was there was because it hadn't been. The mechanic assured him that five hundred was a deal and looked ready to get angry if Bonaduce had a question about this.

He slid the credit card from his wallet with what he hoped resembled bored efficiency, handed it over between two fingers like a habit, like a cigarette, jeez I've used this thing five times today. He signed his name with delicate pressure, hoping a too-faint carbon imprint might save him. His stomach went empty and his sweating felt colder, less healthy than it had jogging. The mechanic punched some buttons and inserted the card. The intolerable wait — Bonaduce pictured a severe woman in Washington, D.C., scowling at a beeping computer screen — ended with his card being handed back along with a receipt. Both were smudged with grease, it was that ordinary. The mechanic had already turned away when Bonaduce called him back, holding his card out again and saying, I forgot to ask you how much those snow tires are. And could you fill it up?

"... what could possibly be wrong with her expectation of equal and consensual sex? Well, as we see at this point in the text, *both* cultures find plenty wrong with it, and though her crime was, at most, *naïveté*, the world will extract from her the penalties ritual demands ..."

Leaving the garage lot, car shod for winter, he waved to the old Christmas-tree guy, who stabbed a finger at his roof rack and yelled, parental concern in his raspy voice, Get 'er in some water! Late for his seminar, he risked a ticket by parking in the professors' lot, right up against the building. Who cared about a parking ticket when you were on the Most Wanted list? That's his car, sheriff, the rusty one tied to that Christmas tree.

He'd gotten good at checking his watch without moving either wrist or head. Ten minutes had passed. Next week was his turn, and he would begin it with this: "*The English Patient* is a masterful, poetic work about the tragedies of war and love, and it poses this difficult moral question: Does love excuse a traitor?" After that he had no idea. Other than to say, Well, of *course* love excuses a traitor. Somewhere along the line he would slide in a coy "All's fair in love and war, eh?" But could he talk about nothing real for two hours? He began to sweat again, for the third time today. He realized he could smell himself. This smell was real too. Moronic to dress in track gear and run five miles before sitting shoulder-to-shoulder in a cramped room with this bunch of lily-whites. Some of whom probably wore a nosegay while pooping. Maybe next week if he smelled this bad nobody would notice what he was saying. He'd eat garlic wings and drink heavily the night before, sleep in his clothes, then run five miles and sit right next to Doctor Gail. And oh shit, there she is now, glaring, thinking yet again that he was smirking at today's presenter, not at the presenter to come.

Do you call her? He lolled like a big old morose teenager on his bed, the new phone on the floor beside him by virtue of the thirty-foot extension cord, both of which he'd charged at Radio Shack. His face felt puffy from lying around so much. Might as well lie around in here as slump around out there.

He'd also bought a little cassette player, and *Simon and Garfunkel's Greatest* was on softly, good old-fashioned candy.

Do you call? The signs — not eating, not sleeping too well — probably meant a teenager was supposed to do something.

She'd whispered, *This is the only time*. Nothing more had been said about the possible shape of their future together.

He pictured her after their beautiful fury was done, piecing herself back together, the static crackling of clothes hurriedly pulled on, Leah all too soon a social worker again. Him reclined on the bed, far from sated, but shy now like Adam, the sheet

pulled over. He could still smell her in the bed, which was both
a balm and a stimulant, and she was getting away. At the door,
drawing on her long coat, rifling her purse for keys, about to
leave the room's darkness. Then — like she didn't want to but
felt she should — she looked back at him and smiled. The smile
was worried and therefore false, and you could see her eyes were
already focused on problems to come. The door closed behind
her. Then opened again.

"How you getting home?"

Looking after him like he was a boy. He'd tried waving her
away but she sternly told him to hurry, don't be silly, and so she
drove him home. Sitting quietly beside her as she worked her
car out of the parking lot onto the highway, he could feel how
his letting her drive him cancelled whatever power he may have
gained, and that she knew this too. They drove in silence, except for a few small jokes, as when they passed the bright pink
car, and when nearing his house he stuck out his hand and introduced himself as Ray and she introduced herself back as Suzy
Wong. They'd always had the little jokes.

So do you call her? Bonaduce flopped onto his stomach, his
chin deep into the pillow and its strong smell of his hair. He
really should start washing things, really shouldn't live like this,
the student life should not mean disintegration. Do you risk
ruining her trust that you understand her need for distance right
now? Or is that just your imagination, the paranoid sore of lying
bug-eyed in bed for too long. Look out the window at the flac-
cidly falling snow. Could easily be she wants you to call. Even if
she doesn't know she wants it. Oscar's "There was an early affair." Maybe it was all no big deal, maybe she screwed around all
the time. Could even be she feels fucked and forgotten, she's
waiting by the phone like the other half of this teenage cartoon,
staring off, curling a finger in her greasy neglected hair, which
she will wash, grinning, after you two speak, after you get off
your ass and call her.

No, she doesn't want you to call. Some things you know.

He cocked his left leg, touching his knee to his ear, and bent his head forward to his groin as far as his grabby old spine would allow, not so far these years, to check out the Bruise. There it was, its rainbow of bruise-hues, but blacker, and yellower, and still growing. He'd started thinking of the Bruise as having a capital B because he'd never had one quite like it. And he'd had bruises everywhere. He'd had bruises *on* bruises. He'd never had a week during the season without one. Simple impact crushing and killing a tiny chunk of your body. Dead blood gone black, days to flush. He'd had bruises you couldn't see — the kidney, an eyeball, esophagus. Testicle. Never his penis though. Maybe his unit was his only virgin bit left, all safe there behind the tinny. Dumb little contraption, the balls hanging a bit below it, dangling this huge pain potential. The time, it was first-, second-year junior, when he took a shot full on the rig and it caught an edge of unprotected balls. There was the second or two of de-layed hell, during which time he fell off the ice onto the aisle beside the bench and spent the next minute trying not to vomit, the pain simply ridiculous, no reason for it at all, but the funny part was the erection. Instant, surprising. Why sprout a hard-on at such a time? What was the possible point? Was it linked to whatever sick biology it was that caused hanged guys to spring one as they drop through the trapdoor and ejaculate at the stop? What was *that*? Either an extremely positive preview they may have just had of the afterlife, or maybe more likely their body's pathetically feeble last attempt to replant itself. Jesus.

Enough to make you shudder in the warmth of your teenage bed. Body's attempts to replant itself and what it makes you do.

Absently fondling his Bruise, now Bonaduce pushed it, pushed two fingers hard into the deepness of dead blood until he gasped with the hurt and shot into a wakefulness. He pic-tured a blood clot dislodged and rushing to his brain. He waited.

C'mon Leah, you did feel it. Pretty little angel eyes. Angel eyes, what a perfect two-word description of love, love that went both ways.

There were only two people, two friends, he could ask ad-vice of. The first, Marg, still carried this apparent torch and her advice would be bent wonky. The second friend was Oscar, which was even funnier.

That evening at practice he began his career as a coach. The on-ice part was fine, almost fun. The players showed him friendly respect, though whether it was due to a pro background or a position of power was hard to say. The defencemen in particular acted like a word from Bonaduce might get them on the powerplay or benched, though he himself didn't know if this was the case. He and Whetter hadn't really talked. But it was fun taking shots on the goalies and laying down passes during drills, great to get some puck-work in a non-pressure situation, get the timing going, the small muscles tuned. Fun even to pick up the pylons and crack the odd joke and generally be useful.

He wore nylon warm-ups instead of full gear. Helmetless and unburdened, he felt the wind in his hair, and on a few glides he got the baggy pants to snapping behind the knees, could imagine little pennants trailing. He felt faster than he likely was, because he had no real oomph and one leg was playing a little dumb. Jason he treated like one of the guys, and Jason treated him like one of the coaches, a distance which in this situation was perfectly right.

His favourite time was giving the defencemen pointers about nullifying the enemy in front of the net. He said, "Okay, I've watched you in games and some of you don't know this stuff, or if you do know it you don't do it," to get them listening. He showed them the skate-nudge, then the back-of-the-pants thing, where a two-inch down-thrust with your stick buckles their knees without toppling them, resulting in them fighting to keep their feet but not in you getting a penalty. The guys seemed to appreciate it and laughed when, demonstrating, he went quickly guy-to-guy and sent each of them into helpless little flails.

In the dressing room it was harder. Protocol. Did a "playing coach" dress in the coach's room or out here with the players?

He hadn't done the full workout, so did he shower or not? The more frightening protocol was the father–son kind, of course, though Jason was pretty adept at ignoring him. Which was fine, probably the way of any coach's son in any dressing room. When Bonaduce had first arrived he and Jason had acknowledged each other with a nod and Bonaduce offered a quick "So, the fifteenth, huh?" and Jason had looked richly blank. He supplied the missing information, mouthing "Dylan," and Jason tossed his head back and said, "Right, right." At which point Bonaduce thought it best to leave well enough alone.

Maybe, Bonaduce decided — unlacing his skates in the players' room but on the bench closest to the coach's room, in this way straddling worlds — maybe it was all any parent could expect from any child, this sort of minimal attention. Why should the young pay attention to the older? Much more exciting were lives yet unlived. The young instinctively knew this. As a parent there was much for him to learn. Another utterly basic idea he had to keep in mind was something Marg had told him just last night — that all children are different. Bonaduce had been amazed that such an obvious truth could catch him off guard. At some level, sure, he knew all kids were different, but he hadn't been operating like he did. No, he'd been asking himself what nineteen-year-old boys did at ten o'clock Tuesdays nights instead of asking what it is Jason might do. "I mean," Marg had added, adding obvious onto obvious and making him feel stupider still, "they're, like, just like you and me." She pointed back and forth at each of their chests, their basic differences, and Bonaduce sat smiling and shaking his head, at his own stupidity but also at the proximity of her two "likes," and wondering if she'd ever stick two right together. I really, like, like you.

He decided he would shower, show these punks a body twice their age, expose them to the hideous consequences of playing this game. His groin bruise had flowered in grand new directions, its basic colour settling down to mauve while taking on an encircling yellow aura that wrapped his entire thigh. Naked, he thought he could feel his son's furtive eyes on him, checking him out, it was only natural. He was trying not to do the same with Jason. Lined up waiting for a free nozzle, he chatted with Tommy, a centreman, and Mike, the spare goalie, about their chances of making the playoffs. Playing it straight, he asked Mike what was each player's share of playoff money if they went all the way.

He heard Jason's low chuckle. He turned and saw his son naked, in line, laughing not at the Bonaduce quip but at something unrelated, some jibe from around a corner.

Maybe it was Bonaduce feeling only average in this roomful of sizable men and muscles, bodies you might in another situation take time to admire; maybe it was the being naked, everyone simply naked. Because the catchphrase he'd for two hours been breathing to himself, "We're both pretending I'm no one special," now transmuted to the thought *He's not pretending*.

Mike the spare goalie chattering in his ear, sucking up a bit, Bonaduce stared past his son's shoulder into the room's centre, into the pile of sticks and pooled meltwater. Why, how, was he in any way special to Jason? How was he any different from any other rutting deer or porcupine or slug who'd done the deed then empty-headed wandered away? Maybe Jason harboured none of the delusions Dad did. "Dad." Yes, let's put that one in quotes.

Or maybe Jason, who owned a fine scowl and whose expertise at ignoring "Dad" was starting to bug "Dad" a little, maybe since Jason's relationship with Father was still so young, maybe he was only now going through the Freudian phase, the wanting to kill the him and sleep with the her ... It would be so great to be able to joke with the kid about this stuff, run back out to the shower line, grab that naked shoulder and look him in the eye and plead, deadpan, Do what you have to do to me but *please* don't sleep with your mother, son.

You couldn't help suspecting by now that this kind of joking might never happen.

Whetter there watching him, smiling at him staring off.

"You look a little tired."

"Took a beating out there, those pylons, I dunno."
"So you want to work the bench against Acadia Friday night?"
"Sounds good."

This morning he woke out of a truly wild bad dream, heart pounding, hot sweat, everything. He'd been in the campus bookstore, browsing. Suddenly the whole row of novels was by Kirsten, her face on the cover jackets, a different sneer for each. Now there were books by Gail Smith, and everyone he knew, Marg and Toby and Jason, and even a trainer from Dayton he hadn't thought of for ten years. Everyone had written books except him. He sidestepped to the next rack, it was health books. One title was *MS and You*. Another was *Multiple Sclerosis*. The whole rack was on nothing but. One, *SCLEROSIS!*, had letters embossed, backlit and flashing like a cheap marquee. He picked up one, *YOUR SYMPTOMS!*, and tried to open it but — ha ha, very funny — his hands no longer worked. They didn't work and didn't work and still didn't work, flop flop thud, two slabs of dead baloney, he couldn't scream and couldn't scream and couldn't scream.

Marg's fucking dreamcatcher was turning out to be some kind of comedy machine.

"Your dreamcatcher's turning out to be some kind of comedy machine."

He said this to her big behind as she stooped to sweep under the kitchen table. As soon as he said it, he realized he'd have to avoid some details. Though he had his suspicions now about what Fournier may have blabbed to her. He was just basically trying to engage her in conversation, for it felt like they hadn't been talking much lately. He'd been in his room a lot. He hated the feeling of fading friendship.

"How so." Marg was breathing hard, arms working away. Toby, at the table finishing his scrambled eggs, lifted his legs for her to sweep there. A rustle and scrape of wrappers and beer-bottle caps.

"I had a wild dream. You were in it."

"What was I doing."

"You were an author."

"That's comedy? Thanks."

"No — everyone I knew was a famous author, except me."

Marg was putting the broom away in the closet. She turned her head and smiled for him.

"'S not funny," Toby said, leaning back, mouth full of egg and toast, "'s pathetic."

It is funny *because* I am aware just how pathetic it *is*, you mean and gimpy twerp. Marg was wrapping a lunch sandwich in wax paper. Bonaduce, hungrily aware that his cupboard was bare, said in singsong: Make me a samwidge an' I'll drive you to school?

In the car she stared out at the riverside underbrush. Looking for winter birds. Some time ago she'd told him how birds bored her except in winter, when she loved seeing those that stayed.

Whatever she saw out that window was keeping her quiet. She commented neither when he slapped his forehead for always forgetting to take the damned tree off the roof, nor when he complained about how noisy his new snow tires were.

"But I guess they'll plough through anything winter can throw at them."

She turned to him with a no-nonsense look.

"Are you bothered by me and Toby?"

"Sorry?"

"No, please just say if you are. Are you bothered by me and Toby."

"Well, I'm sure as hell bothered by Toby."

Not missing a beat, Marg said in identical tones, "Well he's sure as hell bothered by you stealing his wine."

Ooo. Yikes. Damn. An embarrassment best left alone. How

did he know? He didn't seem the type to keep count. Bonaduce leaned down to snap the radio on and fiddle for a station.

"You know Toby has lupus, and he had a stroke when he was sixteen? Can you please maybe see why he's a little bit bitter?"

"Well hell. I didn't know that." He was prepared to feel like an asshole, and indeed sat prepared for the feeling to dawn. But he felt fine. He saw that, at the mere mention of lupus, he had instantly decided there were others with lupus who weren't mean.

"So it doesn't bug you that he and I sleep together."

Then snapped the radio off. Marg and Toby? Was he supposed to know this? *Did* he know this? He didn't think so.

"You're both adults. No, it doesn't bug me." Did it? He didn't think it did.

"That's good. I'm glad."

She didn't seem it.

"Well, sure, yes it does bug me — that it's Toby. I mean, it's only natural for me to want you to be with someone I liked. Someone who's good for you."

Marg met this, his decent declaration of friendship, with more of the same severity. Only when he bent forward to threaten turning on the radio again did she speak.

"I mean like, you've been awfully distant lately."

"I guess."

"Sitting there in that room."

"How do you know I've just been, you know, 'sitting'?" He winked, but no humour in the lady today.

"Marg, I'm in a phase. It's a strange time of life for me." Try her again. "I like to think of my room as, you know, a cocoon. And out of cocoons come, you know ..." She wasn't budging.

"I want you to talk to me, okay?" It was as if she hadn't heard him. Her voice descended into warmth as she said this, and her hand slid across the fabric of the seat and took his right hand, which had been at rest on his thigh.

"Hey. What ya wanna know?" He smirked for her but his hand and senses were afire, the hair on the back of his neck bristling. Young people could scare the hell out of you with their directness. Your own words could get stunned in the surprise and glare.

"Your friend Fournier says you're really sick."

"*Oh* hell. Hey. Fournier's all over the map. Don't listen to Fournier. He's French. He's a goalie."

"He thinks you're not taking care of yourself. And, Robert, *I* think—"

"You can't play university varsity fucking hockey if you have a serious fucking disease."

"I didn't know you were playing."

"I'm about to start."

"Maybe if you just looked after yourself a tiny bit better, and waited to—"

"There's nothing wrong with me."

"There is and I worry about you. Fatigue? Fatigue and depression are two first big symptoms, and all the time you spend in your room?"

"I've been writing."

It felt like punishment the way she withdrew her hand.

"Even if I did have it, which I don't, there's nothing you can do. So I'm not going to get myself in a knot about it."

"Well, I mean, that's not true. There is stuff you can do."

"Think positively. Swing a rooster over your head."

"All your joking," she said softly, making him sit up a little straighter, "all your humour is gallows humour."

Oh, she wanted morbid, did she? Well, he could help her there. In his sweaty little cocoon with the octopus-stained walls, he'd become a grad student of morbid.

"Marg? Where we're all going? *All* humour is gallows humour."

It was his turn to shut her out, some of her own medicine. They were at a red light. A gust of wind hit the back of the car, and a scatter of Christmas tree needles rained on the windshield.

"You know, like, I'm moving out?"

Marg all softness again. Bonaduce nodded for her.

"Well, and sometimes I've wanted to ask you if you want to get a place together."

Bonaduce became very aware of his driving.

"And sometimes I don't. I mean we've become good friends but I guess if we lived together I'd want to be able to talk about stuff that matters."

"That only makes sense."

He didn't enjoy Marg like this. Like she had completely lost control of herself. Her seriousness bugging out all over the place, staring at him. Nor did he like what was expected of him in this conversation. They were nearing the campus. He would either drive her to her building first, or she would tell him to go park and she would walk in with him.

"Living together might, you know, be 'dangerous,'" he said, giving in. "Just the two of us?"

"I know. I don't care." Her voice husky and fatalistic and unsurprising.

"There's all sorts of stuff you don't know about me."

"I know. I don't care." Repeating this, she smiled, more a smirk, the Marg he liked. She started chewing some gum they both knew wasn't there. "Like what?"

He almost said, Like I'm in love with someone.

Stopped at a crosswalk while a string of students Marg's age filed in front, he played with the sound of this soap-opera sentence. He checked out the feel of its main word. He couldn't tell if it was true. He hadn't used the word in a while. What a word it had turned out to be, it, too, growing so complicated with age. All the guys and their wives who'd had counselling to help them find it or get it back, who learned the words for love's fool's gold: obsession, dependency, habit. These days, on bus trips you could actually hear such words murmured through the drone, guys with fat lips, black eyes, earrings.

Marg nervous beside him as he pretended to be frustrated by all these pedestrians. He would love to ask Marg where good old lust fit in. He would love to describe to her what he could

still clearly picture, he and Leah lying in the motel bed not knowing what to do with their eyes. Each time they met eyes, twenty
years was giddily flown right over, gaining a version of each other
that was up-to-date and surprising and too too full, a potency
forcing them to look away, except for a brief few times when
they made themselves hold it. One time he told her it felt like
looking in a mirror. However corny it sounded, he felt it was
true, and her angel eyes staring deeply back he took to be her
agreement.

"Wanna just park? I'll walk in with you."

They walked through the lots, past student housing, and
damned if he wasn't limping again but worse, like the hip joint
had lost its little brain. Marg seemed lighter in mood, but she
still wanted to hear about how dangerous living together would
be. Bonaduce didn't announce his soap-opera sentence less out
of fear of hurting her than of having to talk about it. Best talk to
himself about it first.

As to living with Marg, the notion felt undeniably cozy. He
could see, as though it were already happening, the pots of spicy
pasta, the games of Yahtzee, the endless talk. Bohemian friends
dropping by. He liked the idea of looking for used furniture with
her, joking about each other's bad taste. He could be buddies
with her, with a woman. Why not? He could be a Nineties guy.
Apparently all the kids were doing it. Boys and girls playing together. Who needs sex, we're friends. If you believed what you
saw on TV, it was like the war was over.

He pictured Jason coming by, checking out his place and
thinking Dad a pretty cool dude.

"But like, definitely we'd get a two-bedroom place."

"—Whoops! Ouch. Fuck *off.*"

He shouted at the foot that was still on the other side of the
snowbank, it having refused to take part in his little leap over.
He'd caught his fall with his hands, scraping his palms on the
sanded sidewalk ice; it looked like he was doing a spread-eagle
push-up. When they got going again, good old Marg took his
arm in a nursy way, as if supporting him. They both smirked at

this, but she left her hand there, and he went on the alert again, feeling through her mitt and its soft squeeze the expectations that must be smoothed away before moving in together could be an option. It wouldn't be fair for anybody.

"Well, hey, let's definitely talk about it."

Nurse Marg squeezed his arm.

"But do me a favour and leave Toby where he is. We don't want to be living with Toby again."

Damn, it had been a joke, a simple "I don't like the guy." Not at all a "I want you to break up with him." But through her mitt you could feel all the way up to her head, thoughts shifting into high rev over it.

## ROMANCE
### —by Lady Bonaduce

You might not think it, but what a soap opera the minors are. Consider the mix: you have a pack of young men whose only goal is to be somewhere else and who, if in their third or fourth year in the minors, are staring a life's failure full in the face. You have women who, while not exactly groupies, are attracted to these men mostly for their bodies and the fact that you have to pay to watch them. You have road trips and bars and more not-exactly-groupies, and young, tireless men-in-motels glad for the team's code of secrecy. You wouldn't say that many minor-league romances begin on a firm foundation, unless you're talking about the quality of the bed.

Soap opera. You see some good scenes before road trips outside the arena as the bus idles impatient diesel fumes, its cargo doors open. Shouting matches, public demands, mascara-blasted eyes. A guy stowing his gear in silence, the girlfriend conspicuously not there, the whispered rumors. There are the usual couples who milk a crisis to get things up, but most of the displays are painfully real. But the bus has to leave, and as it reaches the outskirts of town, you can look back at the rows of guys in their seats, a whole smack of them just staring into space, maybe shaking their heads in awe of what soap operas their lives had become. Jesus H, they were just down here to play till they got called, hadn't planned on meeting *her*, hadn't wanted these questions of loyalty. But soon enough the cards come out, or if it looked like a guy was ready for a laugh Bombsaway might haul out the guitar and do a hurtin' song. Soon begins the quiet talk about tonight's team, which asshole to watch for in the corners, and the new nightclub two blocks from the hotel where you can get two, three quick ones in before curfew, and hey isn't Toledo where they have that little place with the lasagna? Mother Tucker's? with that waitress? she still there? what, traded to a Pizza Hut in Des Moines? Bullshit a relief from the jagged sourness left behind. Later that night on the ice, sometimes you find a good heartache fuels your game, and sometimes you find it drains you.

Someone up cooking bacon. Out his window, a frigid morning like so many back on the prairies, sunny, windy and hard-assed. The term "freeze-dried" came to mind.

He considered his wardrobe hanging on its hooks, the choices available to him. He recalled Whetter behind the bench in the standard sports coat and tie. Okay, did an assistant coach wear a tie. Or did he go casual like a trainer. Would the guys respect him more, or less. Would they even notice. Would Jason. Did any of this in the slightest way matter.

Clothes. He used to like clothes, what they did.

Noon he paid a visit to the English Department office to drop off the stuff to be xeroxed for the writing workshop — a manila folder of his collected observations and aborted beginnings to novels, most of them silly. In the mailbox he found a memo from the registrar informing him of his revised status, from full-time to part-time student. It showed him listed only in Gail Smith's and Big Jan's, meaning Kirk had officially pulled the plug. The note asked him to confirm this status or inform them if an error had been made. If he was in fact part-time, said the note, "overpayment of tuition monies might be owed and subsequently reimbursed."

Wearing a dress shirt under his leather coat, and a tie rolled tight in his pocket, Bonaduce frowned at the piece of paper in his hand, seeing right through it to the clear horns of his dilemma. He would love to be owed and subsequently reimbursed. Otherwise, unless he tried his credit card again, he would not eat today or all weekend. This horn was already goring his stomach. The second horn was more fuzzy: if he confirmed his part-time status, he would officially not be allowed to play for the Varsity Reds.

He ripped, balled and tossed the memo. Deny he'd seen it. He'd knock around in academic limbo a while longer. Limbo could last a long time, being the one thing bureaucracy excelled at.

There's no thrill in coaching. You stand behind the defencemen. They're yours, you oversee their changes and pairings. You can feel what a masochist's game coaching is. If the team won, who takes credit? It's the guys out there with the blades who take the hit, feather the pass. If the team lost — well, why didn't the coach have a system that worked?

It was a tight game, they were up two-one early in the third period, hanging on. Acadia was small, fast, gutsy. Anything could happen. Coach Bonaduce did catch himself growing excited. But it was nothing like being out there working your guts out to be the hero, working even harder not to be the goat.

When the guys were filing through the corridor on their way to begin the game, Coach Bonaduce had shouted, "Lean and mean, guys, lean and mean!" and he hadn't felt out of place doing it. (He hadn't eaten and it was how he felt.) But he saw he wasn't one of them. At the edge of the tunnel he stopped and let them pass by, into the arena light and scant cheers. Red and white warriors, tall and anonymous in their helmets and face cages, clomping the rubber with their contrived steel feet. They yipped, hollered and punched each other's shoulders, a nervous herd urging itself to become something carnivorous.

The few shifts Jason got, Bonaduce found himself so intent on the boy he forgot his coaching duties, but so what. At ice level you got a better feel for the play, and Jason was fast, very fast, he could play in this league, maybe a bit beyond, who knows. What he needed was a break. The asshole right-winger Harrington stood in his way. You tried not to hope for an injury to anyone, but. Your heart lifts when the Reds score to make it three-one, then you understand it was Harrington who tipped it in and you wish it was still two-one. Jason just needed a chance. And — Bonaduce's gut sank for an instant — Whetter might be the kind of coach who feared showing favouritism to the point that he might play Jason *less* now that Dad was coaching. Jesus, maybe Jason saw this too.

During the game he spoke to Jason once — a simple "Go hard, Jace" as he jumped on for a shift. And touched him once. His general yell, "*C'mon guys!*," followed by his cupped palm — *whop, whop* — onto the shoulder pad of someone who just happened to be Jason, though Bonaduce had sort of known this out of the corner of his eye. Jason answered with the half-fierce nod of a player who hasn't been on for a while and might not get on again and whose disappointment is battling his team spirit. Had he known whose hand it was on his shoulder? Of course.

What struck Bonaduce a second later — he couldn't tell if it was pathetic or funny, where was Toby when you needed him — what struck him was how, while clopping his son on the shoulder, he'd had his nose wide open wanting a smell of the boy.

Hanging alone by the red line, Harrington picked up a loose puck and scored an empty-netter to clinch the deal.

. . .

He got home late, having gone for beers with three of the Reds, who apparently didn't hang together as a team. This was a known and significant liability and he'd have a cautionary word with Whetter about it. He'd heard Jason beg off in the shower, a cold coming on, gotta watch it, exams coming. (Coach Bonaduce raised his eyebrows at the boy's priorities: the worry about exams, not next week's games.)

On his arrival home, as soon as his tired body landed on the bed, too swirly in the head to account for two draft beer, a fight broke out upstairs, Marg and Toby going at it. Marg yelled a few times and you could hear Toby's monotone scorn. You couldn't quite make out the words, though he did think he heard his name. Beth's softer voice began moderating. Eventually Marg's door slammed, right overhead.

You couldn't hear her crying but you knew she was.

Coming suddenly out of all that noise, silence. The absence of noise had its own weird force, a rising steadiness. Bonaduce perked up. Out his window the night felt wide and deep. He looked and the stars were brighter because there was no moon at all. Having fun, aiming his gaze through the dreamcatcher, he studied the sky long enough to make sure the comet was gone. Taken its cold warm-and-fuzziness elsewhere.

There's a feeling you get for disintegration, how it sometimes feels right. Or at least inevitable, which was maybe the same thing. The house felt that way now. Though no one knew it at the time, they'd enjoyed a modest golden age, then a falling, now a falling apart.

Someday soon they'd all be in different bedrooms and circumstances, new loyalties, feeling all right. It all had a rhythm to it, as predictable as a song.

. . .

Leah, I want to do it again. I just want to do it again. There's nothing I want to do more. I can now admit this to myself.

And maybe I want more than just it. And maybe Oscar should be told. And maybe Jason should be told. Leah should definitely be told.

He found himself punching her phone number, hearing its coyly flat music. Don't think. Take the puck and go with it.

Oscar answered, a friendly singing hello.

"Oscar, buddy. It's Bonaduce. How's it goin'?"

"Great! How are things with you?"

"Great! Leah around by any chance?"

"Well I'll just go and locate her."

The teasing airiness again, but could you not hear something nervous in it, maybe an anger? Had she dropped the bomb on him?

"Bobby?"

Oh, there's the proof, when her voice alone can get you half-way there.

"Leah — why are we still married?"

She was long to answer. He couldn't hear if she was smiling or not.

"Well, Bobby, you tell me."

"Maybe I will, another time. I have my version. Maybe we, maybe we should talk about it." His chest swelling with romance.

"When I didn't get them back, I just figured, I don't know, I figured that—"

"What back?"

"Silence, and then slow, incredulous laughter, not completely friendly.

"Didn't you get them?"

"Get what?"

Leah explained. Her business-like manner no doubt had to

do with Oscar being in earshot. She explained how she'd mailed divorce papers long ago. She'd assumed, when her lawyer didn't get Bonaduce's signature back, that he didn't want to.

"Leah, I didn't get any papers. So I thought the same thing. That you didn't want to." He forced a little chuckle.

Leah laughed lightly. "Imagine. All these years."

"Imagine." How, how lightly entertaining.

"So, well, I'm getting dinner ready here, but what do you want to do?"

"I want to sleep with you as soon as possible."

Her silence was dense and unreadable, but as five seconds became six he could hear a direction in it.

"Don't hang up, Leah."

"It's — not really the best time to get into these sorts of details," she said, instantly relieving and arousing him. Oscar, within earshot, wasn't the one getting the truth here.

"When's a good time? To get into every detail we can."

More silence, through which Bonaduce didn't breathe.

"No, I really don't see it coming to that. I don't think, I don't think they would be that ridiculous."

He could hear Oscar's muffled enquiry. Leah pulled away from the phone and said, "Bob never did get the divorce papers, and now someone's, they seem to be after him about marital status or some such at the university, something about tuition." More muffled Oscar words, and then Leah's "Here, you talk to him."

Leah, you bastard. He had to stop himself from hanging up. This wasn't fun. The phone being passed to Oscar. I love her, Bob.

"Bob? Legal difficulties? Here, I'll just turn my meter on."

"Oscar, yeah. But not really. Just, well, there's this form, when I signed up here, registered, it said 'marital status,' and I left it, you know, left it blank" — several coils of phone cord had at some point gotten wrapped tightly around his elbow and he saw his forearm was swelling up — "not knowing *what* the hell status I was, right? And they sent it back, and there's, there's—"

"Why would they send it back?"

"Well, who knows."

"That kind of thing doesn't matter much these days. None of their business. Legally or otherwise. Unless it's for benefits, or taxes. Spousal deductions. Curious."

Oh, Oscar knows. The sly dog knows.

"Well I did apply for a loan. And stuff. Good old bureaucracy, eh? Go figure."

"I'll look into the divorce status if you want."

"Nah — like you say, it doesn't matter."

"It's no problem, really. I'm having a half-price sale."

"Right. No, it's okay."

"It probably is. Well, hey. I hear you're going with Jason to see Bob Dylan."

"Sure are."

"Well, let's get together some time soon. You and me."

"Sounds good."

"No. I mean it."


Dylan was upon them and he'd heard nothing from Jason about arrangements. Where, when to meet, at what bohemian café, I'll be the one wearing the beret. He had a tape for him too, a *Dylan's Greatest Hits* he'd bought new and in the meantime scuffed up the cover, as with new running shoes, no sense embarrassing the boy with expensive gifts.

He forced himself to call.

"Jason. Hi. It's—"

"Hi."

Interrupting quick, hearing the father's wondering how exactly to identify himself. He'd been toying with "It's your dad," but feared Jason's possible anger there. "It's me" assumed intimacy. "Hi, it's Bob" made him queasy.

"It's your assistant coach here."

"Yeah. Hi."

"Anyway, couple of, couple of things." He stumbled, he was a teenager asking someone to a dance. "I was wondering if you wanted to borrow some Dylan music. You know, before going to hear him. I've got this tape you can have."

"Nah, thanks. I don't have a player."

His son's voice was deep, deep as his. Children did not have voices so deep. So resonant through the plastic, vibrating the bone of your head.

"No stereo at all? I mean, I could lend you the same thing in a CD."

"Nope. I'm music-less. Doesn't matter. Thanks."

"Okay." He'd told himself to not be instructive, yet here he was, launching in. "Maybe it's better that way, you won't be disappointed if he isn't as good as on record."

Jason agreed with his logic. They arranged to meet at eight, outside the main doors.

"You gonna wear full gear, or just your helmet?"

Bonaduce had had his two glasses of Toby-wine, and this had just come out. Jason chuckled, politely or not. Maybe their senses of humour weren't that far off.

"Another thing, Jace. A hockey thing."

"Yeah?"

"Now, *as your coach*," he said in a good deep comic voice, though there was no answering chuckle this time. "No, but really, I've been wondering about how much ice time you're getting, and it's the shits, eh?"

"Well, sure. But that's the way—"

"No. Bullshit. You deserve more. And I'm not saying this just because I'm, you know, on your side."

Nothing from Jason.

"Anyway, so I was thinking of saying something to Whetter about how if you're moved up to the third line, even the second, it would add your punch in the corners, you could dish it out to the fancy guys in front and in no way would it—"

"Jesus, no. Don't."

"No?"

"No way. C'mon. Thanks, but no."

"Yeah, you're probably right."

Why, why had he gone with a ploy he'd all along known was pathetic, the worst?

"Okay then. I guess I'll see you, you know, when I see you."

"Okay."

"See ya buddy."

"Yup."

See ya buddy. He felt barely tolerated, indulged. Some things you know you'll be cringing about in darker moments to come.

He rifled the medicine cabinet for aspirin. Nothing but a bottle of Midol, which he'd heard of guys using.

The hole in the wall beside the toilet was even more embarrassing on these frigid days when the exposed boards grew a white sheet of frost and you could feel the cold as you sat on the throne. He could imagine the girls cursing him, feeling like white trash as they suffered their icy morning pee.

He rattled under the sink, knocking Marg's and Beth's bottles this way and that. A clue to love here, him under this sink. How you felt about a female's cache of stuff was definitely linked to how you felt about her. The creams the scents the soaps the brushes — was it vain clutter or was it sexy mystery?

If you're in love, it doesn't even matter if she's clean.

He hadn't lived with anyone before Leah, and her discreet lotions and bath oils (pre-Bonaduce gifts, from who knows) and makeup; even her styling combs and hair dryer and, God, even her tampons, had been a surprising source of shy joy and horniness. That he was living with someone who used this stuff was proof of their difference, the difference that fuelled the fire. Under the sink this junky palette of Marg's and Beth's and maybe earlier tenants' was only irritating. There was nothing for him except the Midol, two tablets of which he pocketed in case the pounding got worse. Dylan tonight, but before that the workshop of his stuff, his "novel," no two pages of which fit together. Three hours of Bonaduce roasted. His brain's balls kicked and forked apart.

He closed the cabinet with a foot. What he really needed was some amphetamine. He was starving, and about to go into the kitchen to steal someone else's food. He'd lost weight and his lousy diet had been making him tired, he could feel it. *Jesus* it would be nice to bring home a few bags of groceries. He eyed the gaping wall, the frost, the roll of toilet paper sitting stuck in the ice on a two-by-four.

Had he ever gone grocery shopping with Leah? He couldn't remember ever doing that together. There was always practice, or road trips. It would have been nice. Choosing a lettuce, cuts of meat, aren't we out of dish soap? How would you know? she'd quip. He'd be coy in the pet-food aisle. Bring a huge load of food home and over the days put it all in their mouths. How basic and sexy can you get?

He realized that he would love nothing better, save having sex with her, than to go with Leah to a drugstore and watch her buy lipstick, watch her try it on, wipe it off, another colour, that one, choosing the colour of his lust.

"Marg. G'mornin'." He spoke to her baby-blue-bath-robed back, elbows going up as she lifted bacon out of the pan.

"Morning."

"Any spare crusts of bread for a fella to catch the drippings?"


Before the workshop Big Jan found him in the lounge, having a nervous coffee. A bunch of writers were about to discuss his writing. He knew it wasn't spectacular. It sure could have been better. But he did care about it so he should have sat down and put way more effort in.

He looked up, Jan standing right over him. He grimaced for her and made as if biting his nails. Jan didn't crack a smile back. Which wasn't like her. Maybe on the day you were being roasted you got treated with nothing but professional—

"Come out in the hall. We need a word." Unsmiling, in fact shaking her head, she turned and left the lounge. He took another sip of coffee and glanced at Phil, who shrugged.

Out in the hall, a glaring Jan Dionne met him. She shook her head again, this time baring her teeth. Before she spoke she stopped to glare again.

"I was going through Manuel Diaz's new collection yesterday, Robert." She stared him in the eye, waiting.

Nothing occurred to him, save the tiniest seed of panic at the guy's name, Diaz. Diaz.

"A poem called 'Eye of the Cross.'"

His memory churned, caught, then blasted apart in panic. He'd forgotten it, all those poems he'd borrowed to get in here.

"I mean listen, fuck you, Robert, you didn't even spell the title right."

"Well, I think I was trying to fix it. '*On* the Cross' gave it two mean—"

"I don't need this. I could easily, *easily*, have you kicked out. Out of the whole program."

"Jan? What it was, was me having no time to get enough of my own stuff together."

"Last night I felt betrayed, Robert. But right now I don't feel anything."

How clear his own feeling was. He cared less about getting kicked out than he did about being hated by the one person in school he liked. And yet in the back of his mind a childish voice was telling him, Doesn't matter, I'm going to Dylan with Jason tonight.

"Jan, I know saying sorry won't do it, I know that. Do what you have to do."

"Don't worry. I will."

"I guess, I guess if I could ask a favour, it would be that you look at my real work, the work I've done for the class, and let it rest on that. I swear *that's* my work."

"Robert? I know *that's* your work because it's not very good. If I do you this favour your chances aren't much better."

He didn't say touché. He knew she liked his work better than that. She was a hard one, staring at him not out of teacherly anger but something worse, an emotionless, clear-eyed dismissal, the kind that rings so true you take it home with you on your skin. And avoid mirrors for a while.

This was the shits, because he still liked her. He could probably still talk to her.

"Hey, buy you a dinner some night?"

He'd meant it as a joke, he was pretty sure of this, though things were blurring. Jan wasn't up to humour right then and, after her disbelieving look, she turned and walked.

The arena, where a few nights previous he'd helped coach the Reds to a sloppy victory under bright lights amidst scattered fans, was now crammed full, dark, and rowdy with expectations. Jason's tickets were great. They were sitting off to the side a few rows up, overlooking the ice surface, which had been tarped and floored. On it sat perhaps a thousand. Up and down the aisles people moved, a bemused ambling. Lots of little kids running and pushing through. It was a hidden side of Fredericton, all these old Jerry Garcia, Gandalf, Che Guevara guys, their kids or maybe even grandkids wearing similar gear. And womenfolk in ankle-length gingham, unbelievable. Lots of ten-year-old girls with hippy bandanas around their heads. Probably lots of these older guys had come from the woods, back-to-the-landers trucking here in amazement that the Man had chosen Fredericton.

But there were also lots of regular sorts, even hockey-jacket types like him and Jason. Holy moly, him and Jason at Dylan. Who would've—

"See anybody selling Cokes?"

Bonaduce craned around, searching the aisles.

"Doesn't look like the vendors are out tonight. Probably have to hit the concessions."

Jason got up without a word and squeezed past people's knees.

The pressure off for a moment, Bonaduce sighed and stretched and looked around. This was fun, Jason or not. The steady deep buzz, the happy rumble, you could actually hear the smile in it, it was the noise of several thousand people who thought themselves lucky. You could smell marijuana — it wasn't hard to spot people passing joints. He hadn't seen this since Pink Floyd in Boston about a hundred years ago. He tapped his inner pocket, feeling the outline of the lighter and Rod's two joints in there, and the nauseating tickle of illegality. The stuff did make music stand out more brightly. Those times after a toke with Fournier, Fournier would go off and read and he'd lay back with the headphones and welcome a new take on songs he'd heard plenty of times before. He remembered one time listening stoned to Los Lobos and thinking he was able to distinguish, just through the way they played, not only their personalities, but also who were best friends and why. But dope could sure take the ambition out of a fellah. And playing your own guitar while high was too, somehow, complicated, a brain busy watching itself watch how fast those fingers—

"Coke?" Jason was handing him down a drink. Jason, decent, respectful son.

They sat sipping for a while, taking in the scene.

"Hey, aren't these great seats?" Off to the side like this they were actually too near the stage for good sound. But they'd be able to see faces, and who played what. They'd see Dylan squinting, they'd see his cheeks hollow to suck his harmonica.

Jason nodded and said, "Yeah, not bad," and seemed to look around for the first time. He even glanced up at the ceiling.

"And thanks again, eh? It must have cost a bit. You sure?" He started going for his wallet, the twenty in it he'd borrowed from Marg.

"No. Oscar bought them."

"Ah. Good man. Oscar."

This was fine. Of course it was. They were together, who cares how. Oscar, good man.

"So how's the school going?"

"Okay."

"You switched to Forestry, right?"

"Second-year Forestry."

"So, so is it mostly about the business? Or, you know, the biology. The way they teach Forestry. What they prepare you for."

Jason tilted his head and appeared to consider something he hadn't before.

"Well, it's lots of stuff. You have to have Chemistry, and Statistics, lots of different stuff."

"So it's not just bigger guys with bigger axes."

"I just hope there's jobs still out in B.C. when I'm out," Jason said, shaking his head wistfully, not hearing the little joke.

Jobs, foremost in Jason's mind. Well, you did have to think about jobs. Though what about that last letter, Jason communicating some kind of desire to play pro? Maybe his time on the bench this year had snuffed that. Which wasn't fair. That asshole right-winger Harrington. A selfish one-way game, scores a few goals. Fans don't see through that, and apparently some coaches don't either.

Because they'd started talking, this pause was painful. They shouldn't be sitting in this clumsy hell.

"B.C.?"

"I guess."

"Why B.C.? Seems to me they have quite the tree infestation right here."

Jason was studying a hash pipe as it moved right below them, cloying in the nose. He didn't seem at all shocked. The smell, for some reason, made Bonaduce think of Jethro Tull, Montreal, the prancing Brit with the codpiece and flute. A decent show, though.

He reached into his pocket not knowing if there was a good way to broach this. It definitely straddled parent and buddy territory. You didn't want to come off like you were trying to be cool.

He nudged his son and pointed down to the guys passing the peace pipe.

"Ever smoke any of that stuff?"

Jason shrugged. "Nah. Parties maybe."

"Yeah, me neither. But, hell, I figured, Hey, it's Mr. Dylan. Spirit of the occasion. I brought some."

Jason frowned and nodded in a way that could have meant yes, so Bonaduce slid the joint out of his leather like a sliver out of a wound. In the little ritual of lighting it and inhaling semi-fiercely he realized he looked too practised. My dad, he didn't make the NHL probably because of his drug problem.

It tasted strong and went right to his head. He held it out to Jason.

"Tokahontas?"

Jason considered the smouldering thing for a second before shrugging and saying "Nah."

Well, hell, bad idea, and what to do with it now. He took another drag, then sat with it. The guy to his left was his age and had a ponytail, so he nudged him and offered it. The guy took it but didn't smoke any. Instead he passed it further along, and Bonaduce watched Rod's joint go hand-to-hand a few more times before anyone took a puff. And then it kept right on going.

"So I wonder when they're going to start this party."

"Dunno," mumbled Jason, staring straight ahead.

"So, you very familiar with, with, you know, his music?"

"A little. Not much."

"Well, what do you think, do you *like* it?"

"It's okay."

Laconic little bastard. If there was one word that perfectly didn't describe Bob Dylan's music, it was "okay." This boy of his had taken bad lessons in Clint Eastwood. The one question was, was Jason always like this? Was this Jason, or was this Jason being angry? Was this his normal cool, or was this him punishing a wayward father? More to the crux of the matter, was this shitty silence a call for the same distance from him, or a demand that amends be made?

Bonaduce was on the verge, but felt that a gushing apology, here and now, would be ridiculous. But maybe not. Maybe one good sentence. One perfect phrase. Jason, let's. Jason, why don't we. This silence was ripe, was torture. God this dope was strong.

"Jason—"

His son turned to him, they met eyes. But the lights fell, and the crowd roared. Bonaduce felt the relief whoosh forth in his huge exhaled breath. Those *eyes*. He'd never seen into them before, and why was it that he was so surprised to see himself? And Leah, but mostly himself. But the boredom in them, the aggressive neutrality, it felt— It ripped your—

The band walked on, a bunch of young guys in T-shirts. Then on stepped the Man. No warm-up act, no announcer even, just him. Casual, classy. You want Dylan, you get Dylan. His band could have been his children, age-wise. Two were black. Bonaduce had forgotten how he'd wanted to joke with Jason about what he'd read in the paper that morning, the description of Dylan's voice as sounding like a bee in a jam jar, which was pretty good. Then the gossip about how the band members were under instructions never to look Dylan in the eye. Yikes, what did that say about him? Either major paranoia or some kind of insane regal—

They started playing: bass riff, drum walking itself in, organ noodling over top, rhythm guitar comes chunking along in back, ooo this was nice. Bonaduce leaned over, whapped Jason's shoulder and yelled.

"*This is nice, eh?*"

Woops. The music stopped. It was only a tune-up.

"Only a tune-up I guess. But it sounded good, eh? I think this is going to be good."

"Sounded good."

"Isn't it funny how music, how music can, you know, 're-solve itself'? You know, how sounds can sort of ask a kind of question, and then come up with an answer? and we can *hear* that? I mean, in *noise*? The art of noise."

Jason nodding, staring at the stage, a little smile. Don't get paranoid yourself. But slow down.

What might have been the stub of Rod's joint was being passed hand-to-hand in the aisle below him.

Finally they did start, a song he didn't recognize. You couldn't hear the lyrics, the sound system was not great. Which was, c'mon, this was awful, the guy was basically a poet, his words his strength, and you couldn't make them out. Why hadn't they— Or maybe it was his voice itself, that nasal whining, it was hardly human, maybe no microphone could translate it, maybe with Dylan distortion was automatic. Man this dope was strong, but man this man was bad. Bee in a jam jar — guy who wrote *that* was the best poet in the English language.

Whoops, was that a little stagger? Dylan addled, to boot. Who knows what the guy's done to himself, booze and drugs fit for a king. Probably a travelling good doctor with him, keep him alive and tuned. Quick, yells the doc, get me my bag, the drummer just looked at Bobby, he needs a sedative, he has a booboo on his spirit.

After two songs Dylan took a short break, it looked like to replace a guitar string and fiddle with the sound mix. It was a laid-back show, no sense of hurry or trying to keep the crowd happy. Well, with the Man no one was going anywhere. People looked as attentive to how he sipped from his cup as they were to his music.

Bonaduce made a loud gush noise sucking his own cup dry. It sounded better than Dylan. This was fun, he was definitely having fun. Not even Big Jan could steal his fun right now. Though why was he on her case, it wasn't her fault. But it wasn't his fault either, Jesus Christ. He wouldn't be here having fun if he hadn't lied his way in. The workshop had gone okay, considering. He hadn't been keen on continuing after what had come to pass with Jan, but you sign on the line, you pay the fine. As expected, Jan was not too praising, and the others picked up on this and followed like the righteous lemmings they were; though

Phil, good old Phil, had laughed and liked his stuff, liked that it wasn't connected, called it a "revealing pastiche." Next term, if there was a next term, he would prove to them that he could write up a big fine piece of—

A woman, a wild-bodied Asian beauty, was bouncing up the steps, all eyes on her. He nudged Jason with an elbow, feeling instantly foolish for it. Well, will you look at her. She was in stylish rather than idealistic hippy gear and in full body-stocking flaunt. He turned to Jason and Jason smiled and nodded and facetiously waggled his eyebrows, and Bonaduce had to tell himself not to feel insulted and stupid. God this kid of his was a quiet bugger. The thought that he might be gay struck him. It felt suddenly possible. He'd never heard mention of a girlfriend, and come to think of it he hadn't been part of any dressing-room sex banter Bonaduce had heard. Well. He knew he was entering a stoned tangent now as he interpreted all of Jason's silences to be akin to shame. Don't get close to Father because then Father will find out. This was all nonsense, of course. Jason was too — what? — too boring to be gay, gays had a spark. Though what if he was? It would be fine with him. You wouldn't *choose* it for your son, but hell he wouldn't hesitate marching in a Pride parade with him, why not? hell, he'd wear his team sweater to bug the guys — maybe a goalie mask too, stay hidden, ha ha — but you wouldn't choose it, I mean why subject your kid to the roll of the dice when it comes to AIDS, and you don't want him to suffer the social thing, the life of paranoia about what people think. Then that switching over to snark and hate, you couldn't blame gay guys for hating everything that wasn't gay. Come to think of it, maybe life was easier that way, something to focus on, and anger for fuel. This dope is extremely strong. It's fun. And the *main* reason you don't want Jason to be gay is because — there she's heading back down the stairs and the horny little bugger is stealing glances at her — is because then Jason wouldn't grow up and have children and have *this same joy inside, this joy of having a son of his very own!*

"What's so funny?" Jason staring, smiling at the dad's end-less laughter.

Bonaduce was about to try to explain, that is, lie, when the band began again. A huge relief, moving the load from inside the head to outside. And it sounded beautiful, it truly did, until the Man stopped sipping whatever was in that cup and got up off a chair and began to play along. Bonaduce noticed some-thing else when Dylan began to play. The band had been having a great time, but as soon as Dylan wanged out a couple of bars they went sober and rigid and watched him — actually turned as a group to face him so they could see his guitar work, and not because it was good. It was bad and unpredictable and they were on the lookout for accidents. Bonaduce saw it actually happen, Dylan springing out of sequence and the guys having to stutter with their fingers to compensate. A few times Dylan was simply unfollowable and the song had streaks of chaos. Luckily the speakers were cranked up to fuzzy. You had music more pol-ished than this at any bar in town.

Between songs Jason leaned over. "That one was one of his radio hits wasn't it?"

"Yeah."

He'd been unsure what song he'd been listening to. But— Jason, asking. It might be a first. Cherish this. It's beginning. He sat back in his seat and watched Jason from the side of his face. Watched him nodding to the beat, took in the bobbing nose, the blinking, the parted lips, the jaw working the gum. Jason knew he was being watched and seemed to accept it, naturally the long-lost dad's going to check him out. Maybe he liked be-ing checked out. Maybe he had the Bonaduce ego. What's in a DNAme? This was great, this concert was great. Thanks, Os-car. What was the question? Radio hit.

"I think it was one of those he had right around his stupid Christian—"

The song erupted in what became an embarrassing barrage of what turned into the Man playing a five-minute lead. Acting out senile old dreams of Clapton grandeur. *This* was Spinal Tap. The guy had been playing guitar for decades and hadn't learned how. He'd love to get Jason back to the house and play for him, a few tricky ones, maybe even sing a bit — could he sing to Jason? Might be a bit queasy for both of them, a crooning dad. Dylan was blowing notes now and, c'mon, even his harmonica-playing — it was his trademark and his trademark was bad playing. The guy was maybe a great songwriter but that was all. People had mistaken eccentric delivery for great performance. This was also the guy who put deep meaning into rock and roll and in doing so took out the humour. After Dylan everyone had to be a philosopher, you couldn't rock around the clock any more. Guy takes some nice old Woody Guthrie stuff and lays the oblique snark to it and sings it like a hornet in a bean can and gets studied in English classes across the land. People forget this was a guy who had himself baptised in Pat Boone's white-shoe swimming pool. Not that you wanted consistency, and maybe for Dylan it was a huge tipsy wisecrack, but here he was playing lead guitar like an emperor wearing not one stitch of—

Jason was leaning into him, yelling.

*"Guy rocks, eh?"*

He dropped Jason off after Jason declined the offer of a beer back at his place, which was fine, it was late, the boy had a cold and had to study.

"See ya later. Thanks for the ride."

"See ya Jace. See ya on the ice."

Jason wanged the door shut, and a dump of needles hit the windshield, the strong bugger.

He watched Jason's lope on the snowy walk, pleased with the notion that after Christmas he'd be playing an actual game with the boy, let's not forget why he was here. Jason turned and waved in the glass door of the shabby three-storey building, not unlike the place Leah and himself had occupied when they first met, where Jason had been planted.

He had had enough family for one night, truth be told. However nice it had been, however nice a start.

Back home, no way he could sleep. He walked the house lightly, aimlessly, ears still droning full. He checked Marg's room and she was out. Lots to tell her, where was she?

Well, damn, the dad also had to study. Time to put some major thought into Friday morning's presentation. In two days he'd have his ass up in the air in Doctor Gail's class. Here he was all dope-addled and tomorrow he'd be mud. In the living room — no more little coffin bedroom for him — he set up his Ondaatje notes and opened the special-occasion Heineken, one of the six he'd picked up in case Jason had come back. A beer to counteract the high, hopefully downshift to the pace of words on a page. It would've been so much more fun Friday to be a Bob Dylan critic than an Ondaatje critic. If Jason were here he could have practised, lobbing grenades into the Dylan myth, converting Jason with precision, rigour, the new academic Bonaduce tongue. Sad the boy didn't have a feel for music, but then neither did Leah, there'd been a sense of her putting up with rather than enjoying his record collection.

Another Heineken in Jason's honour. Then a third — take the night off — in honour of not worrying about Ondaatje. He'd read the book twice, how prepared can you get. He had the notes, the major points to make. He would have to fill in blanks, wing the bulk of it, but that was the nature of discourse, it wasn't a speech. He even had a way to get in the word *postmodern:* this book is not postmodern, but good old-fashioned storytelling. So there.

In the spirit of winging it, he lit up the other joint, because it helped words fly in his head. He'd stick a butterfly net up there and bring some down, get some insights pinned to the page. Friday he'd have a fighting chance.

He put on some of their snark music, not too loud, and stole another of Toby's bottles too, but came to his senses and cut himself off after one glass, remembering that not only was he not in shape, but that Christmas layoff would put a further dent in what shape he had. Tomorrow night was the last practice until the New Year. Actually it was a game, something called the annual Red–White Fight, where they divvied the guys in two, and the losers bought the winners pizza and beer. A little tradition, sounded good.

After tomorrow night, and Friday's presentation, it was two weeks off, no hockey no school. Then he'd have plenty of time for. He could do whatever he damn well.

He slouched deeply into the couch. His foot accidentally nudged Ondaatje off the coffee table. A Fredericton band, Modabo, was on. Nice harmonies. You could tell they were good guys. A clue about Fredericton, what it engendered in its sons, what kind of spirit. Despite his many sins, he'd left Jason in a decent nest.

He was glad he'd come back.

He caught himself sitting motionless, smiling, staring slightly up at nothing. A gleaming swirl in the gut was flooding up the neck, taking leaps into his face. Sometimes you cannot deny your happiness, there's a big happy fish looping in your stomach, you're on the verge of an idiot guffaw.

He had to move his body, something. He dove to the floor for push-ups. He counted. He did either fifty-six or sixty-five.

Still high, still happy, he brought his box of tapes from his room. He settled back with a homemade compilation of oldies. "Little Latin Lupe Lu" made him laugh, did these guys know how funny they were? Demanding sex, *shouting* for it, wailing, then a wheedling plea, pure pure jungle need. All in five-bar simple. Then "Stay," another pleading classic, hard-penis falsetto, some black Italian guy from New York City. Next a Woody Guthrie, his ultimate get-back song, "Little Black Train," about death, all of us being in the same boat, the train's a-comin' fer ya. Here, rich folks, you kin fight mah politics but you cain't argue this'n. Next was something Fournier had insisted he throw on the tape, some hot new poet type, Beck. One of these guys, like Cher, had only the one name, really cheap parents. Beck proved pretty negative, a Toby with a song to sing. But decent lyrics, "toxins won't kill your day job." Maybe a double negative makes a positive, who knows. But at my funeral, play "Pretty Little Angel Eyes" please.

No sleep yet. In deference to Oscar he tried some *Best of Pink Floyd*. It was okay; sure, they were good at ominous. But their druggy calculations told him they weren't playing from their balls, they really weren't. This thing Oscar had for Brits was a fundamental wall between them, it was worth calling the guy on, it would be a good argument over a beer. British was head, American was heart. You can't get much more apart than that. Earth and sky. Though Lennon's "Well Well Well" could scrape your guts out and cure your indigestion.

Coming out of a dream of what would've been the world's greatest song, Slim Whitman singing a cameo on Pink Floyd's "Money," he realized he was head-lollingly tired. He tilted the wine bottle for more but it was empty. He remembered having lots of insights, some about Ondaatje, but he couldn't remember what they were. He hadn't liked Dylan and Jason had. Unless he was being polite, wanting the both of them to be having a good time, a thought which took Bonaduce back up to glad.

This — Jason wanting them both to have a good time — was the closest he'd come to what Jason's love might be like. A fearsome thought, and enough for tonight.

He whistled — he never whistled — on his way to the bathroom. He almost went down, grabbed at a wall without looking. He liked it here, he knew this house's bones and didn't really want to leave it. Marg was bailing early. Kick Toby out, it'd be a decent place to live.

Howling, now he was howling. He heard Rod or someone yell *Shut-up* but he couldn't stop laughing. Because he'd found himself standing at the toilet, pointing the wrong way. Busy thinking of Marg moving, of life without Marg, he'd unzipped and taken his dick out, then half-asleep wondered if maybe he didn't have to do the other, so he'd pivoted, but still with his pants up and dick out, but now pointed at the bathtub, then he awoke to the situation and howled.

He turned to successfully pee. He'd once had a girlfriend who he'd *twice* found sitting backwards on the toilet, peeing. Elbows on the porcelain reservoir, hands in her hair, calmly deranged. He suspected a serious drug or alcohol problem and gently ditched her.

Still whistling, but sincerely bound for his room, he found himself stopping at the phone. It couldn't be all that far past midnight, maybe it was one or two. The idea was to thank Oscar for the tickets, for the idea to begin with, maybe give him shit about Pink Floyd. Good man like Oscar wouldn't be asleep yet. He pressed the buttons which his hands knew by heart, and wouldn't you know it but at the other end after some fumbling with the receiver it was her who picked up the phone tonight.

"Hello?"

"Hi, it's me."

That's all he said and all he planned to say, but her voice, all cozy and warm in the way she said hi back, the lovely sleepiness and the sweet concern, made Bonaduce simply lose his mind.

"I have to be with you."

Silence, a shuffling, then, "Hello?" From Oscar.

Bonaduce hung up, heart racing. Had Oscar heard? Had she passed the phone? Had Oscar grabbed it? What had just happened? Did Oscar know?

Did he want Oscar to know?

Why, damn, why did he have to call? What kind of guy are you, anyway? You don't do that to people.

Why do you want it *all*?

Right now, as he was finding a kitchen chair with his hand and Oscar was going upstairs to her, to ask about the call, who would she be truthful to? Neither answer made him feel good. What had he done?

The happy fish looping in the gut was gone. So was sleep.

• • •

Lat e

What am I good for, what am I good at, what's the point of m.

Can't help but wondering. Been wondering twenty years. The thing with playing in the minors, youre always wreslting mediocrity. As a description of yoursel. Worse because when a kid you were the best on your team etc. You grow up assuming youll always be that. Suddenly you arent, and there's a whole other league up there that wont even look at you.

To make it, you have to be the best, the very best, at one thing. Just one. In the minors its guys like me, jack of all, master of nothign.

Famous people are all like that, they have the one big thing. Can Bob Dylan skate? Who cares — he had the best words to put the tunes to. Could Ghandhi do anything else? Could he cook? Tell a decent joke? No but he was the best at taking punches without ever punching back.

Could the Buddha drive a jeep.

For a couple of years in Kalamazooo I was the best at being an asshole in front of the net. Was called The Zookeeper. I was a master. It was an act. Almsot worked though. Almsot got me called up. I was almsot a famous asshole.

So whats Jackofalltrades Bonaduce the best at. It isnt hockey. It isnt literature or writing. It isnt women. It definitely isnt fatherhood. Friendship has come under serious doubt, too.

No — how could I have missed it? Its right in front of my face. It made me phone her. Im the best in the world at staying up all night feeling sorry for myself. So, quit it. And typing is getttting

. . .

Panic.

It had taken him hours of steady breathing, of hard focus, to get this far. The meanest work he'd ever done, meaner than push-ups this getting out of bed, getting enough clothes on, getting to the bathroom after asking God to let you please just not piss on your floor. Fighting panic the whole while. Finally making it to the kitchen table. Easy to flip back into panic at any moment here. Pick up that fork.

Steady breaths. Normal life. Hold your fork. Dead hand on the lap under the table. Marg is watching.

"Tomorrow night, Regent Mall, eight-thirty?" she asked from the door. Wearing a big absurd beaver hat, the RCMP kind he hadn't seen since Winnipeg. It was apparently freezing outside. She had the earflaps down and the ribbon tied under her chin.

"Regent Mall. Eight-thirty," he repeated, softly, because even his tongue was gone this morning and eight-thirty was *ay-thiry*. He was trying to eat the eggs she had made him, hoping she wouldn't notice he was using his left hand.

It was almost noon. He had stayed in bed as long as possible, wishing it wasn't true. So deadbody tired that even lying down felt like a strain, so tired that staying alive took effort.

"I think it'll be four, five places at most. We can do it in an hour." She was talking louder with her earflaps down. "And I mean, thanks, eh?"

"Hey. For nothing." She'd lined up appointments to view apartments, and he was driving her around to them.

"Taxi's here. 'Bye."

It was her first day of a Christmas-rush job in the mall bookstore, the same bookstore he'd had his bad dream about. Here he was with a floppy right hand, what a humorous meshing of worlds.

"Two of them aren't two-bedrooms," she was saying, pausing

in the open kitchen door, frosty air billowing in. Her eyes were impish, fun-filled, at her best. "Just in case you wanna, you know, tie the knot."

He worked up a smile. Said something approximating "We'll bring along the preacherman."

It was the kind of deeply frozen world he hadn't walked into in many years. It was a childhood morning, a prairie morning, arctic. Your face burned and, in a minute, ached. Well, today only half the face: ha ha, the hidden rewards. He saw the tree on his car roof and looked away because it seemed only dead. Too scant of needle to consider any more. Last night, Jason hadn't mentioned the tree on his roof.

The mucous in his nose had instantly frozen and his eyes were tearing and blinding him. He went back in, found someone's mauve scarf, came out again with it awkward and ugly around his face and head, a bad wrapping job, done with more awareness of a dangling right arm than of the left clumsily working, self-pity rising out of panic to erupt in a sob. He sobbed just the once and stopped it. Poor me. Feeling sorry for yourself — it felt like warm soup, you saw guys fall into it and never get out, you could see them wearing it on the face for all to see.

The idea was to walk it off.

Limping mummy, a slit in the thick bandage for his ancient sick eyes. Muted grunting at every right footfall. Why not drool through the scarf, scare some kids.

He worked his way along the highway, bypassing the snow for a while, heading for a distant field he'd seen all along from his window but had never visited. In this cold even the truck noise was thinner, muffled. Tires sounding hard as plastic on the cold concrete, you could feel the crisp sound right in your nerves. Jesus, what did the truckers think of him, hobbling maniac out on the road, heading east. He thought of his occasionally entertaining bus window, its flashing frame of car wrecks, grass fires, chicken yards, barefoot kids and gawking trashy idiots, roadside tragedies like himself.

There wasn't much traffic. The quiet was nearly peace if he could keep from thinking. He lurched up onto the snow. You could see the tree and its cluster.

As he approached, it sounded electric. It crackled, rice crispies freshly in milk. It soon grew louder than his crunching steps, louder even than his fear. When a pause and tremor appeared to rifle through them *en masse*, he stopped. He was a hundred feet away. The tree's branches were full and heavy with them, weighted down. He could see now what he'd suspected, that they were all one species of bird. All noisily eating, clusters of orange berries. The words *mountain ash* came to mind. You made hockey sticks from ash.

He took smaller steps, trying for a harmless-looking rhythm. His right mitt he tried to keep from smushing dumbly against his thigh. Hundreds of birds eating, frenzy in the extreme cold. Massed crackle of their plucking, beaking, biting. Closer, looking hard, he saw he didn't know what they were. Crested head like a cardinal, with what looked like yellow over the eye, and their bodies were a nice, a subtle, an almost unnatural kind of tan.

Like a child's view of things. In one black tree identical birds eat orange berries. On the snow a man with a scarf around his face watches, arms held out because it's so cold.

He'd probably gotten as close as he could anyway, but at his faltering half-step they all leapt away, making him jump. A sudden flapping *whoosh*, the whole instantly apart in so many pieces, birds exploding away in all directions.

The full moon up there, frozen pearl bouncing at his shoulder.

He stabbed three times before hitting the doorbell, with his right hand. All day it had improved to the point where now a doorbell was possible.

From the street he'd seen their Christmas tree in the window, all lit up and heartbreaking. Wonderful, now he was invading their home. He could see in the door window many coats hung, boots on cardboard stretching well into the hallway. A gathering of some sort. Maybe an office party. Great, he was bashing and crashing a party on top of things. He just wanted to take her aside and— He didn't know what he wanted.

"Bob! Just in time."

"Oscar buddy." His tongue was back. He slowly unwrapped his scarf.

"Our little festival-of-nations party. Come right on in."

Oscar was good at not showing surprise, at showing nothing at all. Maybe he greeted criminal clients like this. Polite to murderers, thieves, adulterers.

"I just came by to—"

"Come on, come in, it's cold. Everyone's here. Jason's here. I hear it was a fantastic concert."

"Sure was. The Man. Thanks for that."

Oscar waved away the thanks and took his leather coat, didn't seem to notice that it was a while coming off. There was no friendliness, no eye-to-eye before he rushed away toward the kitchen, yelling behind his back to make yourself at home.

He stood in the entranceway. Everyone's here. He hadn't wanted Jason in on this. Whatever this was. But maybe it was okay. Maybe Jason was a buddy now. Maybe it was best, in fact. Had to happen sometime.

About twenty men, women and children sat around, the majority of them Latino. Many had gifts unwrapped and sitting in their laps. Cutlery sets looked like the popular item, that and ceramic teapots. Board games for the children. They kept their gifts cradled in the wrapping paper. They looked too tropical for either the gifts or the Christmas tree, which swelled in the corner with bright ornaments and smell, that essence sharp in the nose always reminding Bonaduce of snow.

You thought "Mexican," but of course, being refugees, they were probably anything but. The women tended to favour lots of makeup, like TV women from the Fifties. Soon enough you could see the range of nationality, or race. Long faces, round faces, darker, lighter, some looked Indian, some almost Chinese. A few of the young men looked solo, and sad for it. A fair number looked like they felt themselves above this quaint gathering, their eyes bored and condescending. It may have been his nerves but some seemed to be watching him with suspicion. Well, he was the biggest guy in the room. Big tough hairy face. He didn't have the energy to think about this.

He felt like a huge fool and wished he hadn't come. This had nothing to do with him. There would be no talking with Leah here, if that is what he had come for. But how could he just run? At least say hi, Merry Christmas.

He took a seat on a couch beside a plump woman who looked his age. Though when he smiled at her and she smiled back, she looked younger. He noticed a scar on her head, on her temple, that looked like it had once been a hole. You don't come to Canada after a bullet to the temple. It was probably a pox scar, a vaccination scar. Though they don't vaccinate you in the head.

"Bob," he said, nodding. He'd almost put out his right hand, offering the limpest handshake in history. Here in Canada, we are very gentle.

The woman smiled and nodded back.

"Where are you from?"

"I from Chile." *Chee-lay*. Big professional immigrant smile.

"Ah," he said, tilting back his head as if she had explained something.

She added nothing more. He saw how much he didn't know this person, let alone these people. And people are not alike. He'd gotten to know Finns, and they were nothing like Swedes, who were nothing like Russians.

"How long have you been in Canada?"

"I here two day." Her non-stop smile, unfelt.

"That must— You must be in shock. Have you found— Have they found you a place to—"

"I just visiting." She smiled for real now, something of the imp in her, knowing his presumptions.

"Ah."

He should really get going. That clatter in the kitchen might be Leah. He could go in, say his hello, make his apology, go. That's why he was here, to apologize.

"My brother." The woman pointed to a man helping himself at the punch bowl. Oscar was suddenly at the man's side, holding a bottle of vodka. Oscar laughed and made some kind of moaning noise, glugged some into the punch.

Jason appeared bearing a tray of glasses. Was he wearing an ascot? The boy didn't look up, though by now of course he knew his father was here. Instead he went back to the kitchen and reappeared with a plate of something, some pastry Bonaduce didn't recognize. Jason said something to a woman who stood surveying the food, and they both laughed.

Jason had grown up with this, with these people. His son went back to the kitchen.

"He come ten years. Now he wife. Now he kids." She pointed to a Caucasian woman delicately fingering tree ornaments, many of which looked handmade.

"Now he help others come. With the worker Leah."

"Ah." He pictured himself, dumb American tourist, shouting to her, *Leah my wife!*, stabbing his chest with a finger.

Now here was Jason, approaching him with a beer, striding the room self-consciously. He looked nervous. Jason, take your father a beer, will you? Bonaduce gave him a little left-hand wave of greeting. Voices, what sounded like Oscar and Leah, arguing in the kitchen.

"Jace."

"Hi."

"What's with the neck?" He saw it wasn't an ascot but a towel, and Jason's watery eyes.

"I got this lousy cold."

"Looks like some kind of giant weird poultice." The image of ascots as poultices was amusing for some reason, ascots giant poultices for intellectuals, absorb any unworthy, common notions trying to rise to the head.

"No. Just a shitty cold." He either didn't know the word *poultice* or didn't find it funny.

"Jeez. And the Red–White game tonight."

"I'll probably be there."

"Jace, you sign the name, you play the game, eh?"

Hey, Jason, want to see your father try to sign his name?

From the kitchen, Leah definitely said "Bob." Something loud about "Bob."

"But hey, you gotta watch your health, nobody's gonna watch it for you."

"I guess."

"Though I *am* looking forward to you buying me my pizza and beer."

"No way." Jason finally cracking a sleepy smile.

"Way." This was good, this was all right. "Just keep your head up."

"Yeah, right. As if."

This was really okay. Jason, eyes down, but smiling and joking back. Hard not feeling like a loud fool around him but maybe that would be their way, these the roles they would play. It felt good just to have a role.

"Helpin' Mum a bit. Gotta go do some stuff."

"Okay. Go for it. See ya later."

Go for it. Loud fool.

Jason went for it, went to help the mum you could no longer hear arguing. Not a trace of cynicism about helping mum in the kitchen. Jason was a good kid. And if he was a momma's boy, what the hell else could you expect after—

What came next was fast and furious. Jason had no sooner left when Leah was loud again and he was at the party table again with another platter of food. Oscar was at Jason's side with the vodka, pouring. Neither smiled or talked. Bonaduce was startled to see Leah in the hallway, pointing a finger right at him. She turned on her heel, looking nothing but angry. Apparently he was to follow. She looked so pretty, heavily made up like these women she was hosting.

He followed her into the laundry room, limping stupidly past her with his beer as she stood in the door with her hand on the doorknob. She closed the door, locked it. Absurdly, the faintest notion of sex stirred below his belt. Who knows what she and Oscar do, allow, pursue. Ridiculous, because her face was set. She bent down, scooped up two sneakers and a plastic cat-food dish, wrenched open the dryer door, threw them in, slammed the door and hit some buttons on the control panel. The dryer roared into thuds and clatters that shook the walls.

*"What the hell are you trying to do?"*

"I just, *I just wanted to—"*

*"What was last night all about?"*

*"I'm sorry I—"*

*"Are you a complete moron?"*

"Did you, did you tell him?"

"No, thanks, *you* told him."

Ah, man, hated by Oscar. Didn't want that.

*"And now here you are at my party!"*

If sarcasm could kill, he'd be dust. He'd forgotten how good she was at mean. Her eyes cut away the two decades easily, and he saw it again, in her glare the knife that had severed and kept them apart in the first place. He'd forgotten but now could feel it, the truth of her, the truth of him and her. The truth he'd known while leaving Fredericton for Rochester, that this knife had finished off their hearts.

*"I just wanted to thank Oscar for the tickets. For Dylan."*

Leah's eyes incredulous, her head tilted to deal with a moron.

"You mean for *paying Jason to go with you?"*

"Well—"

*"He had to pay Jason fifty dollars before he'd go with you."*

Ah shit.

*"Oh, good, you're drunk."*

Stooping in the foaming beer to pick up the shards of brown

glass, he cut himself, then had to lean back against the washing machine.

"*Don't step in it. Jesus.*"

She moved past him to an open closet where the household brooms and mops were kept, good proper convenient household. He leaned against the washer and breathed. He thought he could smell burning plastic. Burning plastic cat-food dish.

"Okay. I'm sorry. *I'm sorry. I'm sorry for what we did, and I'm—*"

"*Don't worry. So am I.*"

"*—sorry for Oscar. I just want to get to know Jason. I won't bug you any—*"

"*Bobby?*" Smiling, shaking her head, not looking at the drunken moron as she swept up his broken bottle. "*Why do you even think Jason's yours?*"

Falling to all fours, he helped himself up to standing. He didn't look at her. One sock was wet with beer and he limped it past, to the door. He fumbled at the knob, swatting her hand when she shouted *Jesus* and made to help him. Burning plastic making them both cough.

Wet sock on the linoleum, a little counter-slap to the beat of his limping, you could almost smile walking past, in view of the living room. Concerned rising murmurs, they had heard the yelling and now they smelled strange smoke as you smacked by with your beer-sock. From a peg in the entranceway he plucked his coat, didn't want to, but while struggling with it one-handed he looked up and nodded to the swirl of Mexicans, Incas, Mayans. He went for his boots. What do you know. A cat he couldn't feel had been rubbing up against the leg.

The next morning, sitting in his car outside the building supply store, waiting for it to open, he thumped the wallet on his thigh and wondered what a chunk of drywall might cost these days. He also reviewed last night's Red–White game, how it had gone, how the Zookeeper had appeared out of nowhere. Though maybe he'd always known the Zookeeper would arrive, maybe that's why he'd come north to begin with. Can't build bridges, you might as well burn them.

It was storming pretty hard and traffic was slow on the way to campus. Despite the snow he walked quickly in from the parking lot. He could feel the flakes hooking onto the whiskers, he hadn't shaved in a while. The limp was glaring at this pace, no avoiding it, but you didn't want to be late. Didn't want to give them the chance to start talking without you. They'd all read the book, they'd probably read all Ondaatje's books. Someone like Phil would grab the reins and take over, and you don't want to walk in on that. You want to get in the first punches.

Moving through such benevolent big-flaked snow, you could almost feel that things were normal and good. Up all night, he'd slept no more than a fretful two or three hours. The fatigue and the worry that kept him awake was gone now, he was ready for the game. This kind of snow, like the sky is softly falling on your head. Its silence so deep it is a sound, *hush*. An awareness to it all. Snow like this made him think of the words *the baby Jesus*, and — he could see it clearly — a white embossed Christmas card he'd touched with his fingertips as a child. He could remember the card's pasty smell.

Up all night with Ondaatje, he could riff off whole paragraphs if called upon. To back up his points. Take, for instance, when Kip says. Well, this kind of metaphor can also be found in the passage where Hana imagines that.

He can even quote a critic on the book. Last night in the shaky two hours between Leah's delightful Christmas party and his spectacular Red–White game he'd found himself in the library, at the keyboard, searching. *The English Patient* was new enough that there wasn't much on it. Apparently it takes years for academics to work stuff up. But he found a few articles. One by a guy named Bird suited him perfectly, having to do with Ondaatje's good old-fashioned storytelling techniques of withholding information. In the stacks he located the journal and tore Bird out of it, and now in his bookbag on his shoulder Bird felt like the Bible. With Bird as ammo you could start the presentation with something like "It's all very ordinary. Behind the poetry *The English Patient* is a spy story, and a love story, only the whole time James Bond is lying mortally wounded in bed."

He could feel the melting snow as cold ointment against his old dead skin.

It was two minutes before class time when he got to Carleton Hall. As usual they'd all be early. They'd be up there in their strategic chairs, sipping coffee, firing up their synapses, whacking their wit on the ass, flexing their shoulders. But no one will have gotten started on a good sentence quite yet.

So here you were at the annual Red–White game. Here in a room with a bunch of guys, throwing jokes about winning the beer and pizza. You're taking a while with the gear, the trainer tightening your skates for you after your story about dislocating a knuckle shovelling snow, bizarre how these things happen. The guy kneeling at your feet, grunting. Hey, I like this, says the Bonaduce, what else can you do while you're down there? He tells you to fuck off, guys laugh. You look and notice Harrington isn't laughing, in fact he's rolled his eyes and maybe that's what cements it for you. He's wearing red and you ask for a white jersey. You have fuel to burn.

Jason wasn't here. No surprise, and so what.

You step on. Whetter's suited up too, and they've got some guy dressed as Santa to ref. Girlfriends and scattered others in the stands. Though it's fun bullshit it's the closest thing to a game you've played in a year and the butterflies are going a little, despite everything else. Which makes the game of hockey such a wonderful thing.

You warm up, take a few shots. You can move okay, maybe you can hold your own. In any case here you are starting at right defence. A local TV station has sent a camera guy and he softsteps to centre ice to catch the ceremonial face-off. A Moosehead rep, whose company has funded the beer, stands ready to drop the puck. He actually looks a little nervous. In the penalty box is a three-foot dented mock-up Moosehead beer can, the trophy. One centreman is the team captain, a red-haired pepperpot named Sullivan but called Maniac, and the other is Harrington, who's an assistant captain and has no nickname. The puck gets dropped. Sullivan smiles and doesn't budge, while Harrington, whose teeth are gritted, actually slashes for the stupid thing.

No hitting to speak of, an unwritten code. So lots of goals. Bonaduce himself picked up an assist on his second shift, nice little pass over the Red guy's stick, laying down flat for your streaking White buddy to send him in alone. On the bench then, breathing hard, respite from a world where there's no time to think. A world you're a million times more familiar with, though it's always swiftly brand new. Catch your breath, feel your age, heart pounding, sweating freely, watch the game go by, involuntary groan when your guy hits the post. This is great, take a deep catch-up breath. Look down at your white jersey, look at the shiny lights coming off the black helmet beside you, look at the row of guys identically slumped. Just look around.

Third shift, Harrington put it through his legs trying to go around him, trying to suck him out, make a fool of the stumbly old guy enjoying his first game in a year. Wonky as he was it wasn't hard to fall into a curl and get his ass out to submarine the guy, catch his knee just right, you could feel it bend in the wrong direction, hear the second or two of surprise before the scream.

They carried Harrington off. Bonaduce, Whetter kicked off. Little Christmas present for you there Jace. Whoever you are. Gets fifty bucks, buys me a fucking Coke. Which I accepted with the dumb smile and big eyes of a dog. A Coke.

They'd already put Harrington into a car. In the dressing room there was no one to make Tonya Harding jokes to, except for the silent trainer, who actually smirked a bit — this Harrington was simply not well liked — and who was kind enough to help Bonaduce off with his skates. His skates which, after the good hot shower, after dressing and climbing into the heavy leather coat for the storm out there, after a moment's empty-handed consideration in the hall, he went back for. He picked the blades up out of their pool of water on the dressing-room floor, tucked them under his arm and, out in the parking lot, threw them in the back of the wagon.

This morning, inside Carleton Hall, he could feel snow melting on one side of his face, though you had to assume it was melting on both. Between classes, the hallway was crowded. Out of the blue he was bone-deep exhausted, and dizzy in the sudden thudding heat. He paused a moment. Now he was moving sideways, now a wall thankfully against his shoulder. He took a few deep breaths. Something vital was sinking inside. He blinked, closed his eyes, and when he opened them, one eye was almost blind. As if one lid hadn't come up. He touched, and felt eyeball. Blindness was that fast, it was almost as if blinking had done it. Maybe it had.

Grab a little rest here, against the wall. He looked around, pretending to search for some notice announcing some event, a poster on these walls, the ceiling, trying to will his dead eye back. There was the sense of vision close under the surface, not unlike the sense of something huge but somehow forgotten, memory at the tip of the tongue. With the good eye he noted the bland colours, the grey, the beige, the ceiling the colour of nothing but shadow. He shouldn't be standing staring like this. Unshaven Bonaduce, studying walls. Security please, I'd like to report a staring mess loose in the halls of academe.

He'd caught his breath. The eye hadn't come back, but it would. There'd be no more hockey after Harrington, so why was he even doing this, going to talk for three hours about a book? It wasn't the first time he'd asked this question of himself. Well, you sign the name you dah the dah. As you stare into the grey shadows, on the constant verge of teetering because half of you can't see, whispered phrases sweep in and out, grey *English Patient* insights insistent as jingles. Of *course* Caravaggio had claws for hands, the guy *wanted* everything so much ... One vial of morphine equals one chapter of memory ... You can see why writing is appreciated in a grey place like this. Literature wouldn't have a chance anywhere else. You need boredom, you need quiet. Poetry wouldn't survive an arcade. You'd put Ondaatje down, you'd dump your quarters in the slot. The world had turned arcade. He was searching for a silent, beige classroom to talk about something that was rich and sinewy but could only be born in quiet.

The hall was crammed with hurrying bodies, and loud with everyone saying excuse me and brushing his shoulder, which for no reason had come away from the wall. He was late, and Gail Smith would be up there shaking her head, making a display of looking at her watch, and maybe she had already made her head go back, while here he was comically flailing mid-aisle. Before he went down he grabbed a water fountain, managing a graceful dip to take a drink. Keep moving kids, I just wanted a sip here.

There was just no way for those stairs. There might be an elevator somewhere in the building, but could he get to it? And he was already so late, so late, and damn but it felt like the good eye could be dead in another blink. Time to turn back and get gone.

But ah, damn, he had some good stuff to say.

IV

There is something in this more than natural,
if philosophy could find it out.
—*Hamlet*


Maybe we're going a bit too hard on him, he warned. You
can easily give a man a bigger hiding than he can hold.
We're only starting, man, said Shanahan.
—Flann O'Brien, *At Swim-Two-Birds*

OSCAR.

This Margaret had been in the bathroom a long time. It was strange being on a trip with an unknown young woman. Here at the café of a roadside motel barely a half-hour outside of Fredericton. Would anyone see him with her? As if it mattered now, as if it were anything but a bitter joke that such news might get back to Leah.

Why was he doing this?

He only vaguely recalled her as one of the scruffy kids in Bob's driveway looking for the comet, that night he'd driven him home. The sing-along with Bob, the mock-along with Bob.

Maybe she was in the bathroom doing some kind of drug, something for the nerves. If anything, theirs was a nervous mission.

It was a relief to be free of her talking. When he picked her up she'd been shy, but after a few minutes she'd settled down to talk and talk, about Bob of course, Mr. Bonaduce their one thing in common. But how kids communicated these days — I mean, like, y'know, cool. For each word of substance, five fillers, hesitators. Apparently she was in university. Perhaps Jason talked like that with his friends, but one wouldn't imagine so. Though when he'd asked Jason how the Dylan concert went he'd said, "*It ruled*," bobbing his head, genuinely happy about it. Seeing this rare effusiveness, Oscar had been surprised and felt happy for Bonaduce. At the time.

"Sorry."

Margaret slid into the leatherette booth, facing him. Still in the momentum of the slide, she clasped her coffee and brought it to her mouth, slopping some over the rim.

"Not to worry. In fact I ordered us each some apple pie. That okay?"

Margaret shrugged but appeared irritated by something in this. Maybe she was on a diet. Well then, it was good he hadn't ordered the clubhouse sandwiches. She had small eyes in a wide, unreadable face. One of her ears suffered a wild scatter of earrings that was uncomfortable to look at and resisted counting.

"I just thought, who knows when we'll be eating next?"

"Right, so I guess there's no, like, giant hurry."

"No." Woodstock was an hour and a half from Fredericton and they were halfway. It wouldn't take a minute to find the hospital, and as hospitals go it would be extremely—

"I mean like, it's not like he's going anywhere without his toes."

She was sort of smiling, a first. And, like a teenager, chewing away on some gum.

"Doesn't sound like he is, no."

"No but I'm just, I mean, I feel like I'm in a hurry because I have this feeling he's afraid."

This hadn't occurred to him, Bob Bonaduce afraid. Well, there would be the general fear of mortality, certainly, and fear of what sounded like a diabolical disease. But not the kind of fear that was assuaged by two friends showing up. One friend showing up.

"Like, he wakes up in a ditch almost dead, and by now he's been alone for two days."

He realized that this Margaret was giving him subtle shit. His one sign of a dip from reverential concern for Mr. Bonaduce — in the form of a man simply wanting some pie — and her voice takes on the tone of, What kind of friend are you? (Would you like me to explain, Margaret?) Clearly she loved Bonaduce. What other entanglements had Mr. Bonaduce wrought here?

Perchance tupping the white youth. Whom hadn't he tupped?

Hard to know how to feel about this. His guts were, in fact, churning.

It was like his own ambivalence was being held out to him on a platter. The sequence of events had, by turns, found him angry, cruel, impatient. Then selfish, then sad. How could you wish such a thing on anyone? He had at last, and at least, been forced to admit what he and Leah both knew — that it was nothing personal, that Bonaduce could have been anyone, and that his and Leah's problems were their own.

"How well do you know Bob?"

This got her. She stopped and thought, then smiled.

"I don't know."

"I think it's exactly the same with me." He nodded instructively for her.

"No, we were like, thinking of getting a place together." Looking him in the eye. Pie was placed in front of her. "Thank you. But I don't know if it was going to be a platonic place or a non-platonic place."

"Ah, I see."

"That's why I phoned your wife. We were going house-hunting, he was supposed to pick me up, and he didn't."

"I see."

"I mean, when he didn't, I knew something was up." She held a forkful of pie under her mouth, which kept itself open between words, just in case pie was forthcoming. "So, I mean, I know Robert *that* well, anyway. That you can trust him."

"Okay. I see." *Robert*, right.

"Sorry." Margaret put her forkful down and pushed the pie away. "I really don't think I can eat. Can we just go?"

Certainly. Oscar wished he could just give her the car. (And what was this almost superior air about those who hadn't learned to drive?)

Why was he doing this at all? Whatever made him nervous about people in general was further exacerbated by sickness and hospitals.

When he'd first asked Leah, challenged her about the affair, she'd denied it. Only after Bonaduce called her in the middle of the night a week later had she confessed. His rage was simple and he'd threatened to leave. She'd parried with marriage counselling. Oscar, it's happened before, let's fix it so it won't happen again. Him incredulous. *Let's* fix it? As in *us* fix it, as in plural? What was his part in this fixing, go to Canadian Tire and fix her up a chastity belt? But, after some time he came to see that, though hurtful, it was not unwise of her to delegate some blame. These failures did take two.

But he was in no mood for the continuing story, including Jason's worried news of Bonaduce stumbling around drunk at some intersquad game and breaking a player's leg, apparently on purpose. Then Jason smiling and shaking his head in amazement, almost admiration. "Dad's a madman," he'd concluded, shrugging, as uncomplicated a gesture as one of Bonaduce's own.

How does one break a leg on purpose? He'd reached down and felt the dense weight of his own leg bone. Good lord. He imagined Bonaduce attacking that too.

Then the big news. At first he'd been only mad when Leah called to him to the kitchen, where she stood hunched over the phone, wide-eyed and mouth open, her hand covering the receiver. She told him that this was someone named Margaret, a friend of Bob's — Oscar was already enraged at the tears rising in Leah's eyes — and Bobby was in a hospital up in Woodstock, his car had gone off the road. Oscar felt his anger drain as her other words spilled out, multiple sclerosis, hypothermia, coma, amputated toes. He'd been found near the U.S. border in his car, in a ditch, he was there overnight. He's, they think he might be paralyzed.

"I see."

"Margaret wants to know if one of us can go to Woodstock with her. She needs a ride. She'll take a taxi if she has to. But she wants to go now. And I — I shouldn't, Oscar. Not yet. I think he's angry that ..."

She was crying and couldn't finish, and he saw that Leah was already deeply involved in a simple new equation that included him: their relationship was less important than Bonaduce's life.

To his surprise, he'd said, "I'll go."

Jittery with too much coffee, he paid the bill. It was his turn to go to the bathroom. Why he was doing this, he still didn't know. Did he want an apology? Maybe. Or maybe his animal side just didn't want Leah near the man again, though the man was very seriously on his back, and though Leah was going to see him in any case, tomorrow or the next day, depending on Oscar's report. Amazing, though, the jealous animal. Could there be something in him that wanted to see his rival lying there crushed and defeated? One could see now how one could be jealous even of the dead. For he'd been jealous anew even after hearing Bob's condition, when he'd asked Leah how it was that this Margaret knew to call her at all and Leah had told him about her calling Margaret first, the day before, to apologize to Bonaduce for things said at the Christmas party. Leah apologizing to Bonaduce? If there was anyone in morality's jurisdiction who should be apologizing it was Bonaduce and Bonaduce alone. From the sounds of it Bonaduce should be apologizing to everyone with whom he'd come within ten feet.

His question led to other questions.

"You mean Jason isn't even his?"

"Jason's his." Leah couldn't look at him. "I was angry."

"Ah. I see. I think you probably got him with that one."

He snorted derisively — he still had enough upper hand for that. It wasn't until he was alone later that he realized she blamed herself for putting him in that ditch, and that this entanglement wouldn't go away but was about to get deeper in ways no one could predict.

He and Margaret climbed back into Leah's little red Neon. His Jeep was in for a starter transplant. It was freezing today, it was unbelievable, this cold snap. He and Margaret huffed and puffed in the bucket seats while the thing warmed up, their breath frosting the windows, Margaret with a pie-shaped styrofoam doggie bag on her lap. She was actually too big for this car. She was a fair bit bigger than he was. Backing out, he twisted around to look and their shoulders pressed, his shoulder and a twenty-year-old young woman's, and he thought of Bonaduce touching her. Had Bonaduce touched her? Of course he had.

"Can we, like, stop at a store?"

"Sure. Of course." The gas station where they'd just eaten had had a store. He tried not to sound impatient. "Do you want to go back?"

"No I mean a sort of big one. One that might sell dice."

"Dice."

"He likes Yahtzee, and I could only find four at home."

"Sure. Okay. A dice store."

It's not like we're like in a giant hurry, Margaret. With his mitt he scraped frost off the inside of the windshield. Hard to imagine anyone surviving this kind of cold. Apparently Bob's old car had kept running till the gas ran out, sometime in the night. The tailpipe was in snow and enough carbon monoxide had floated in to do some damage, Margaret wasn't sure which kind or how much. You couldn't help but think brain damage.

"Were you on the phone with him yourself?"

"No. Like, he wasn't quite there yet."

"He wasn't ... quite there?"

"He wasn't able to. Wasn't up to it."

"Right."

Oscar tried to picture how it was going to be, seeing him. What he'd look like, what he'd do. He reviewed the MS symptoms Margaret had listed for him. Curious, the last one, the euphoria, at end stage. Euphoria, perhaps mind shielding itself from its dying body. Clever, the alternative being horror and agony. Euphoria was curious also because at the beginning there was apparently much depression. Margaret claimed Bonaduce had been here in Fredericton depressed for months and no one had known it. Oscar certainly hadn't. The man had seemed happy enough.

"I wonder if he's talking now?"

Margaret shrugged, staring straight ahead. As though to suggest, why would talking matter?

Oscar's gloved hands shifted on the steering wheel. The way Bob smiled, looked at you. In his first anger he'd decided Bob Bonaduce had befriended him only as a way to get to Leah. But he knew now that wasn't the case. He'd always known it wasn't. One look at the man and you could see he wasn't like that.

He supposed he was driving to Woodstock because maybe something about him and Bob Bonaduce had survived, something that had nothing to do with Leah.

§

MARGARET.

Woodstock was tiny, and the mall wasn't far from the hospital. On her way from the Shoppers over to the Zellers, she had to double back past the car, where Oscar sat reading the paper. She waved as she crossed in front, but he didn't see her. Maybe it was just his mood. Robert had called him a good guy, but the man was almost a parody of uptight. He'd actually gotten out and fed the parking meter so that he could sit there in the space. When she'd bought him the gift of the newspaper, he'd thanked her, but slowly, like he was worried she might want something in return.

How hard could it be to buy dice in Woodstock? That Robert would want to play was certain, though whether he could play was not, so maybe this was foolishness. She could roll for both of them, he'd like owning one of her arms as his dice slave, he'd like that joke.

Don't worry about Oscar, let the fellow wait. And yet she'd liked Leah, she'd liked the wife. "The wife." Leah had sounded concerned, decent. Apologetic. "If I had only known he was sick ..." "Why did he feel he had to ...?" "I wouldn't have been so ..." Leah felt more like Robert's friend than Oscar did.

Oscar's nervousness at seeing Robert. He who Robert called the best buddy he had here. What kind of friend was that? She pictured Oscar reading his *Globe* in the car, severe little lawyer with the croaking deep voice. Did he stand up in court and accuse people? She had in her pocket Robert's little essay, which at first she wanted to read to Oscar but then decided he wouldn't care, so screw him, great friend. She found it in her laptop and printed it out to bring, on the chance Robert hadn't left it behind on purpose, his painful little thing about Mahatma Gandhi and Bob Dylan and whether they also knew how to skate. Buddha and the jeep, Robert as usual being funny and sad at impossibly the same time. But to suggest he wasn't good at anything. A professional hockey player! And who played an instrument like that, and sang like a tough angel. Though she knew what Robert meant. And that he was talking for her, too.

She groaned at the image of him not being able to roll dice. She walked, angry, wiping away a tear. Between Oscar and Toby, and the hockey team kicking him off, no wonder Robert was fleeing back to the States.

She'd almost cried seeing the bathroom. At first she was angry when he didn't arrive for the apartment-hunting, fuming while she paced, but that soon changed to worry. Robert wouldn't simply forget. She taxied home and saw his clothes gone, the dreamcatcher taken from the window. And new bathroom drywall put up, a clumsy but thorough job that brought tears to her eyes. No letter, not surprising. Robert wouldn't be one for goodbyes.

Here. Chess, Scrabble, cheap little plastic travel games. Eureka, dice. They were small, four of them in a package. They looked weighty though, well made. Good dice. It was absurd to think of some dice being more lucky than any others, but these did. She bounced them in her hand and found herself wondering if Robert was religious.

Only four to the pack. She plucked a second. If Robert was religious it was in a non-conceptual way, like her. Lately when she wondered whether she was still religious or not, the image of a spade pushing into soft fragrant earth came to mind, a memory from the dig in Hawaii. The good smell of God in that earth, wet, dark, as much rot as growth. Robert would agree. On his deathbed if you asked him if he wanted a priest or a really good sandwich, there's no doubt he'd go for the sandwich. Or a bowl of steaming soft ravioli with three kinds of cheese. Drizzle of spiced olive oil. Shit, she hadn't meant *deathbed*, not literally, not aside from the joke.

She realized she hadn't eaten in far too long. She didn't want Oscar's pie. She could go back to the sub place she'd passed. Was Robert feeling religious now? If he was, she wouldn't try to discourage it. She had some books he might like, ecumenical forays from hard dogma, which old friends had given to her, hoping to keep her with them in spirit, intelligent books that had almost worked their way on her but no. In any case her only plan for Robert, her only strategy, was to try to make him feel good. That was the bare religion she followed now: seeing your way to anything good, in spite of the facts.

If it looked and felt right, even if only to make him feel good she'd offer him the second bedroom in the place she'd just—

The man who grabbed her arm wasn't big, but his fingers dug in and you could feel his anger in them. She had just gone through the glass doors and had stood looking around for the car.

"Come with me, please." He was leading her back into the store.

She had walked out with the two packs of dice. They were so small and cost so little and she'd forgotten them with Robert waiting for her a few blocks away in a hospital bed. She didn't know what to say, how to begin. You couldn't explain things to people. She resisted the man's pull, turned around and waved and yelled *"Help!"* to Oscar's car. Oscar was looking at her, rolling down the window. She laughed while shouting *"Sorry."*

§

It doesn't take a lot of body to drive. One eye worked, one arm was pretty good. He sat back and tried to relax. As long as he didn't have to brake for a moose, the left heel pressing dumbly down on the gas was all the foot he would be needing. Around Woodstock, with the border a half-hour away, he began to practise clearly saying "Utica, New York" and "visiting relatives." This he changed to "on business," which came out less floppy. After you passed the breathalyser, what would a cop do when he discovered a slurring man hadn't had a beer?

He was freezing, and even in the depths of his leather coat he couldn't get warm. He pushed at the heater controls incessantly, maybe that was why he went into the spin. Or maybe it was the search for music. Each time he lost another station to static he wedged his knee up under the wheel to free his hand for the dial. Whatever caused the spin, when he woke in the ditch classical music was on, and he would spend the rest of the night with the CBC.

He'd lost consciousness but came to remembering the feel of the black ice, the sick angling-off, the vertigo, the windshield framing all the wrong things, the car pointing backwards, neither steering wheel nor brakes touching the slide one bit. Big helpless hunk of fast metal loose in the night. Had he actually thought, "If only the tires were skates," or was he just thinking it now?

The car was on its side. The bump on his head showed him how the driver's side window had been broken. Not much blood. His good shoulder was wrenched from its socket. The seat belt held him in position still. He could not feel his legs.

The windshield was in place but fissured along a thousand lines, a Jack Frost pattern, opaque. The passenger window, his lone view out, pointed straight up. Through it he could see shadowy tree branches and, beyond them, stars.

It took a while to understand that the car was still running. Old slant-six just idling away. Then his hand was on the key, thinking *explosion*. Then thinking *freezing to death* if he turned it off. If it hadn't caught fire yet maybe it wouldn't. He could smell no gas. If he turned it off, would it turn back on when it got cold? He took his hand off the key. He had maybe a quarter-tank, at most. He'd been waiting to fill up more cheaply over the border.

He did turn off the radio. He quieted his breathing, and listened. He'd left the road on ice, so no skid marks pointing the way. He couldn't remember hitting any trees. Had he ploughed a visible path? Not a lot of people would be making the journey, at midnight, into northern Maine. Maybe some drunks from Woodstock going to Houlton for the strippers. He imagined an oldtimer hockey team, a string of three or four rowdy cars, we'd all be lucky if they noticed the road, let alone the ditch beside it.

It was maybe half an hour before he heard a car and it was faint. It sounded like he was well off the highway, and maybe down an embankment. If that was a truck he was hearing, he was even further away. In the branches overhead there was no hint of headlights as it passed, its noise fading into the fucking quiet of the idling car. His eye moved to the steering wheel, the rubber panel you pushed to honk at a car in front of you, to honk at a passing car as you lay freezing in a ditch. He couldn't even remember what his horn sounded like, some wire rusting through ten years ago.

He began renewed attempts to get himself out of his belt. Even if he succeeded in this, with no decent arms or legs what were the chances of him climbing up, pushing open that door against gravity, hauling himself out?

He knuckled the radio back on, it was a classical piece he knew, a famous Christmas one, something from the *Nutcracker*? He was halfway into seeing sugarplum fairies, into making the best of this bad time, when the smell kicked him in the nose.

He had shit himself. There was no mistaking it. It hadn't happened during the skid, it hadn't happened during the crash, it hadn't happened when he'd been out cold. It had just happened now. It was still happening, the acrid stench building. His body emptying itself, muscles he couldn't feel.

Only one thing in the car was moving. He could see it, lit by the newly risen moon. The defrost fan was blowing on it, tickling it — the old good-luck charm air freshener. The cardboard tree shape was doing a little dance.

When the car died, the sound of its absence was awful, God it really was awful, and partly for this reason he groaned and groaned to fill it.

He didn't know if he'd been asleep. Terror and panic, if it went on and on, was a sort of huge sleep, so wild and full it was like bad, bad, dreaming. You could control it or not control it like you could or couldn't a nightmare. If you can see your own panic, who is it panicking? You can get bored with panic. Exhausted with it in any case. Too tired to be afraid. Too tired to be or do anything. Except die, the one thing that takes no effort at all.

His brain could still babble to itself like an idiot. Monkeymind, in and out of sleep, chattering, even making lists, too stupid to know it should be nothing but afraid. He found his brain wondering if it should buy a Christmas present for Fournier's girlfriend or not, and what was her name again? He watched his brain fall into a dark, wet crater with Kip, defusing a bomb, over and over. He woke once in the middle of seeing himself writing in Marg's computer, he was writing something that he may have in fact written or maybe was composing only now, about all the guys and their superstitions. The famous ones you saw on TV, Patrick Roy jumping over the blue line on his way off, step on a crack break your mother's. That pitcher who throws an inning then races to the dugout and brushes his teeth at the water cooler, not caring who sees, superstition bigger than shame. The good zone you seek is delicate and there's nothing of it to hold on to, which is why guys have their little thing, they have to be first out or last out of the dressing room, hoping some other guy won't push in, being on the same charm. Shamrock, Buddha, girlfriend's bandana, lucky rock. Trinket in the pocket a trick to keep luck close to your body. Eat a salad, spaghetti, a peach, exactly four hours before the whistle. Have sex don't have sex, drive a car take a taxi. In the d-room some interesting ones, most of them camouflaged in the getting-ready hubbub. A guy whose job grants him daily laundered underwear dons a stinking undershirt that's nothing but stringy rags, more dead skin and dirt than fibre, last washed in 1986. A guy slaps his face hard, twice, or it's his skates laced up then taken off then laced up again, and he'll be late on the ice rather than interrupt this. Number 12 whacks the goalie's pads twelve times. In the road-restaurant at the pre-game meal no one's surprised to see a teammate freak out over his baked potato when he's told, Sorry, we're out of chives. Bonaduce reflecting a moment, then typing that it's like you're with a bunch of fishermen all dangling lures to entice the big luck trout. You've been doing your thing for so long you no longer see it. Your left skate is always first. You can't not start with the left. Sometimes you catch yourself, and ask what would happen if I just went ahead and put on my stupid right skate? You don't even risk it. It feels like doom. You don't want to play around with this stuff. You're typing in her laptop that you understand nothing about luck, meaning you know nothing about anything.

Except that you're so tired you're on the other side of everything you've known. You're cold and living off something vital, draining it. You want advice, you want magic, you want your luck back, any luck you've ever had, especially now that terror has arisen, terror that isn't crazy and has brought you through the crust of dreams into clear time, terror that claws this present moment as though it were the inside of a coffin.

. . .

They were apparently real. Or as real as sight was real. They were lit up from within and impossible, because he knew that it was night and that real life was sideways in a car.

Maybe his screams had brought them, maybe he had screamed, and screamed himself backwards into dreams. They were lit up and sometimes alone, sometimes together, appearing out of nowhere and through no effort on his part that he knew of.

At first he thought they were here to help him get out of the car, thought they had real bodies and could help. He could hear them as they approached, one by one, he could hear them and he probably yelled, *Who's here! Who's here!* and then here they were, right in the car but not looking at him, not helping at all, knowing he was there and even his situation but doing nothing. Guys he hadn't thought of in years. His grandmother. An aunt whose name he couldn't for the life of him. Jan Dionne, Gail Smith, Whetter. Toby. Fournier. They all came, each in their time, or perhaps all at once, none of them looking at him. Here was Leah, and here was Jason with her, but they were just faces in the line of teachers, friends and teammates, and they ignored him in no way more special.

He woke out of his own gibberish into a melting roomscape, into fragments that began and ended in dream-swirl. Once, the content of wakefulness was nothing more than the prodding weight of a headache. Another time it was knowing that he was finally warm. If he opened his eyes, seeing with only the one, what he saw was good because it was less frantic than his dreams.

Waking meant a different kind of seeing. The sun hard through the orange curtains was best, the light making the fabric more orange than orange, you could taste it, it quenched the hunger for all the sights he had ever been denied.

Sometimes vision leapfrogged a dark tangled hump and landed him in sudden clarity, where he understood not only the mechanics of seeing, but also the profound friendship between the seer and the seen. The radiator under the curtain was white, unless curtain went brighter orange and radiator turned grey. The change took place as much in his eye as it did outside of it. The single eye made this a simpler certainty, though these understandings, and clarity itself, may have been drug-induced. In any case the lucid times were but pinholes in the swirl, respites from endless slogging through mud.

Drugs were a dam, and pain a swelling reservoir behind it, deep and vast and ready to drown him if the dam gave way. Sometimes pain did push through a crack and overcome him with such ease it was terrifying. Body's terror. Quick nod to the nurse's offer of morphine. Christine wouldn't look at him, she would administer the IV injection with sober efficiency and an air of withholding. Marie though, Marie was with him eye to eye, and she would joke how some guys just wanted to keep partying.

Drugs could do anything. They could make you content with diapers and stupidity. Oh yes the unbearable lightness of peeing, whenever and wherever. Drugs could roll you over and sponge your fouled nether zone and your dead unit, so dead it ignored all nursely attention. Drugs would not allow the tiniest bit of shame to stick.

He woke, one eye staring up at the little TV set, hanging from its mechanical arm. In one of his home towns he'd watched such a thing from a dentist chair. Waking up this way irritated him — without his consent they'd turned it on and plugged him in — plastic earphone was jammed in his right ear — them assuming he preferred the jokes of *Frasier* to the less-staged ones unfolding out the window, or in his body, which was maybe or maybe not coming back to him, a finger or a foot too long hidden from sense but now uncurling, unwrapping itself like a gift. Who knows, though — perhaps he had consented to the TV. Perhaps *Frasier*, these jokes, perhaps distraction was part of the cure. The most irritating thing about this TV was that the noise was so close, wedged into his headbone in fact, while the action it was supposedly connected to hovered up there near the ceiling. In the tinny earphone the acting sounded like barking. Punctuating each joke, the canned laughter was so loud it was only static. It sounded exactly like surf. Each time the distant Frasier pulled a face, in your head the surf roared.

He woke to Marg and Oscar at the foot of the bed, whispering about whether or not to leave.

He smiled, but didn't know if it showed.

They were quiet and nervous at first, afraid of looking at him. He managed to meet Marg's eye and they held it for a second, and when she understood he was okay she loosened up and could laugh a little. Oscar, poor Oscar, had to begin with a speech about Leah wanting him to say how sorry she was and such, and that she would visit soon. Infected by Oscar's formal tone, Marg added that Fournier was also on his way, and that he had a cheque for him, from his old hockey-team owner, and that it was a lot of money.

It was good to see his friends. Though odd to see these two together. Two worlds. And Fournier coming, a third. Leah would make it four. It would be too much. All the smiling.

Silence fell as they sussed he wasn't too good at speaking. Marg elbowed Oscar and said that, well, the important news here was that she'd just been arrested for shoplifting.

"I was so out of it I totally forgot the thing about *paying* for things." She dropped two rattling Baggies onto his chest. "These'll be ready when you are."

"Bones," he said, in a voice of inventory. Though it sounded more like "bo's."

"Yeah, and here" — Marg dug into her book bag — "Toby brings you this. We should probably hide it." She placed a bottle of home-made wine on his side table.

"Less see." He tilted his head at it. Marg understood, and spun the bottle by the neck so he could read the label. It read, "Gift Horse '98."

"I brought something too," said Oscar, again taking his cue from Marg. He rifled through a Zellers' bag.

Bonaduce tried for "Merry Christmas" but said, "May Chriss," which they didn't hear over Oscar's rustling.

"He decides to like, 'do some shopping' while I'm being interrogated." Marg snapped her gum.

"I realized," Oscar said, bringing out a new walkman, encased in its package, "that here you were, stuck up here in nowhere with no music. Leah had these two in her car. She stole them from me, I stole them back." He took two cassettes from his coat pocket and put them on his side table, then began tugging at the walkman's vacuum-formed packaging.

Bonaduce made his head fall to the side. He read Oscar's printing. One tape was "Van Morrison," the other "Early Bowie."

"Suck here, wih, briss."

"Sorry? What?"

"Stuck, here, wih, *Brits*."

"Bob, when I come back up I'll bring—" Oscar visibly stilled his panic by taking a breath. He looked up at Bonaduce, meeting his eye for the first time. He smiled ironically. "Next time, I'll bring you your damn Everly Brothers or whatever it is you like."

"Than's, Ah'car."

Bonaduce managed what might be a smile too, and a little waving finger of demand. Bring me something pure. Roy Orbison. Gene Pitney. Something that doesn't make your thoughts for you.

"Well, so where'd they, like, put your stuff?" Marg suddenly getting all stern with an idea. "Your tapes. Your guitar."

He shook his head and raised his brow just enough for her to see.

Marg walked off on her mission. Right, indeed, where was the car, where was his stuff. He remembered getting hauled up, out of the passenger door, the pain of this, the pain forcing him beyond relief into bad clarity, it was almost like leaping right out of his damn body into the bitter night. But, yes, he'd seen the strewn back seat. Leaving town he'd pretty much just thrown it all in, but now it looked liked someone had hit the blender switch. When they lifted him out of his own mess he'd been embarrassed by his smell, but then also by the brown skeleton of a Christmas tree bungeed to the roof.

"Bob?"

Oscar hovered nearer and hunched in, his deep voice hushed to a conspiratorial croak. He was going to get serious now, which was fine.

"Bob?"

Bonaduce lifted his eyebrows for him. You don't want to talk too much.

"Leah, she wanted me to tell you—"

"No. Ah'car? *Oss*-car."

"Yes? What?"

"Sorry."

He tried to show with his eyes that people, friends, don't do to each other what I did to you. You just don't.

"It's — it's not your fault. You had — you two had unfinished business."

Right. So we did. But that brand of business is never finished.

"Leah said, she wanted me to say, about the fight you two had, that Jason, well hell man, Jason *is* yours. Is your son." Oscar shook his head, smiling at the lunacy he hadn't witnessed. "And that she's sorry. She was pretty angry, I guess."

Bonaduce had known, of course. How could he have ever not known? Just look at the boy's body.

"No he'sh not." He tried to smile wisely. Oscar didn't know what to make of this.

"And, and also that, Leah said to say also that Jason wasn't paid to go to see Bob Dylan with you."

Bonaduce smiled. His muscles felt it to be a grin.

"In fact, he loved it, he loved the concert, he raved about it, and he loved going with you, I'm not just—"

"Ah'sar? Does' mahher."

"Sorry? Does ...?"

"Does*n't*. Matter."

He tried to show with his eye all he'd learned trapped in his car. How phantoms had arisen before his face, and how, when they dissolved, he was free of them and had always been free of them, for they were just phantoms all along, and isn't it funny how you have to keep learning what you already know. He tried to show with his face, too, that what mattered here was not Jason but you, Oscar, *you*, because it is you leaning over the bed, blinking, tender. Just like you don't matter when it's Marie sitting here on her stool, skipping the grey peas for the decent dessert, attuned to him, knowing when he's geared up ready for another spoonful, whereas doing the same duty Christine's mind would be elsewhere and so in fact she wasn't here at all. What matters is this light streaming glory through the orange curtain, lighting up half your face, Oscar, dramatic, noble blood-colour, the rest of your face in shadow, it's—

"Ah'sar, you ..."

"What? Bob?"

"You look *grea'*."

Poor Oscar, on the verge now. Sometimes you really shouldn't say anything.

He may have dozed because the light was different and Marg was clomping back in, and Oscar seemed to have moved his chair further back. Marg put a sack of his cassette tapes on his bedside table, beside Oscar's two. She stood over him, shaking her head.

"You broke your guitar."

*Twank*. He remembered, yes. The sound. First the spinning. Tumbling. Then hitting a final something, the ground probably, with a pow and a *twank* of a snapping string.

He nodded for her. He'd heard its death song.

Oscar was grateful to go through the tapes and organize them for him while Marg disappeared into the little bathroom.

He cocked his head to the sound of the water running, its rush interrupted by something moving under it, being washed. Marg was hugely entertaining. Now paper towels ripped from the dispenser. Sounds of Marg drying, dabbing, then periods of no noise, of some kind of care.

She used the stool to hang the wet dreamcatcher, fastening its cord to the curtain rod, tying it tightly and well, setting up house, betraying that she had talked to someone and had learned he wouldn't be leaving this room for a while.

She clambered down, saw he had been watching her and smiled, pointing back to the dreamcatcher. She sighed, looked around, sat happily on the foot of his bed. When she realized she was sitting an inch from his feet, from his fresh wounds, she gasped, leaped up.

"Sorry! Sorry! Did I—?"

"Did' feel a thing. S'okay." He paused. "Si' a'ywhere on me y' wan'."

No one laughed at what was a decent joke. They were more numb than he was. He laughed at this, laughed again, then coughed, and started coughing, he hated the coughing because at the base of the deepest ones you could taste exhaust, and the taste filled his head with the memory and the fact of poison.

He tried to sleep. Fournier coming with lots of money. Pack his bags with money, buy a new car, drive Marg to Maui, she could show him Maui. This he would love, because so would she, wild about me. Lie on the hot sand, he was wearing a big huge wacky bathing suit, cover his delicate condition, his diapered nether bulk. He'd listen to the surf. The canned laughter, the

Maui trucks. Marg is soothing his burned face, her vials of morphine lined up in the sand. He's still thinking of Leah. Frasier's funny little brother is everywhere. Marg content pointing out parrots flitting tree to tree, God aren't they big, perched shoulder-to-shoulder in trees black against the sand.

"Robert? Did— What? 'Parrots'?"

He could hear himself laughing.

But poor Marg was crying, he'd made her cry, she was grabbing her face, trying to stop.

"Mar'? 'S okay. Cry."

"I'm not." She smiled, her face wet, her body lurching with sobs.

He could feel his laugh. He could also feel his tears, not on the side of his face but when they landed in his ear.

"Mar'? Me either."

## ACKNOWLEDGEMENTS

For their insight, heart, and humour, I'd like to thank
Rita Donovan, Dede Gaston, Carolyn Swayze,
Beverley Endersby, and Jan Geddes. All lapses in form,
coherence, taste, and good sense — remain mine.